Devil May Care

Devil May Care

Patricia Eimer

Entangled Publishing, LLC
2614 South Timberline Road
Suite 109
Fort Collins, CO 80525
Visit our website at www.entangledpublishing.com.

Edited by Libby Murphy
Cover design by Libby Murphy

Ebook ISBN 978-1-62061-088-6
Print ISBN 978-1-62061-087-9

Manufactured in the United States of America

First Edition February 2013

To Ben

For being my soul mate

Every moment of every day

Is better because you're in it

Chapter One

"I can't believe I'm getting married in two weeks." My best friend Lisa dropped her head into her hands, her caramel colored ponytail fanning out over the table. "Two weeks and nothing is ready. Tolliver hasn't even helped me move the last of my stuff from your apartment to the one we got together."

"It'll be fine. Besides there's no rush on moving your stuff out. You're only moving downstairs and it's not like you can't just come over to get things as you need them." I tried to make my voice soothing as I reached across the table at the mall's food court and patted her hand. "As far as the wedding goes, I promise we'll make it work. What do you need me to help with?"

She looked up at me with big brown eyes fringed with sooty black lashes. "Can you put your foot up your brother's ass for me? In the past month he has done nothing. Not one thing. After he proposed it was like he threw his hands up and walked away from the whole deal. Now I'm molting from the stress."

"You're molting? How bad?" I tugged at one of my blond curls, which had escaped its clip, and gave her a sympathetic smile.

She lifted her head and gave me a frustrated look. "I have patches of naked, leathery wings. It's so gross. *I* wouldn't sleep with me with wings like this. Not even out of pity. It's so bad I don't want to even talk about it. It's like my wings have had a botched Brazilian."

I shook my head. Poor Lisa. All she'd wanted the night she met my brother was an Amaretto Sour. She hadn't asked to become a succubus.

Then again, I probably should have told her I was the daughter of the Devil before I let her move in three years ago. That would have solved a lot of problems in the long run, but at the time all I wanted was a roommate who wouldn't let her boyfriend rummage through our fridge in his birthday suit. Stupid me. Now the naked guy complaining about the lack of orange juice in the fridge was my half-brother Tolliver, otherwise known as the Archdemon of Gluttony.

"After the past month I'd be surprised if you weren't molting. Besides, it's nothing to be embarrassed about. We all molt when we're stressed. When it happened to me at thirteen, Hope told me that it was natural and then convinced me to pluck out all my feathers. Six months of naked wings. Even now I wish Dad would have let me kick her ass." I squeezed her hand and tried to send comforting vibes between us.

"So it's not just me?"

It would be easy to lie and tell her I was molting so we could commiserate. After all, it had been a stressful couple of weeks—between my older sister Hope and her soon-to-be-ex-husband's arrival, my parents' decision to move to Pittsburgh, and the stalker I'd faced last month, I *should* be molting. Because, after all that other stuff, some guy blowing up your boyfriend's car would've been the feather that broke the archangel's back. But I wasn't. The thing is, nothing surprises me where my family is concerned. When they're around I just expect chaos to kick off and panic to reign.

I shook my head at her and tried to give her my most sympathetic smile. "No, but I'm not the one marrying Tolliver in two weeks. That's enough to make any girl molt."

"He's not that bad," Harold, my ghostly former-boss-turned-personal-poltergeist, said. I turned to where his self-important voice had faded in like a stereo coming into tune—only his disembodied head was hanging out right over my shoulder. He hovered for a bit and gave us both a naughty grin. "He's just trying to get ahead. Get it? A. *Head*?"

"Yeah, we got it." I gave him my best bitchy-but-amused face. "That doesn't mean we particularly wanted it. You're supposed to be out messing with Dr. Cupertino and Dr. Thompson's golf game. Remember? Bought your tee time off the golf pro? You wanted revenge?"

"Eh, they're both so lousy that nothing I could do would have made them worse. I can't believe they let them out of medical school with their sub-par golf games. The Ivy League is losing sight of their priorities. Going soft, I tell you."

"Harold." Lisa shook her head and I could tell she was trying not to laugh. "How can you be so mean?"

"I'm just telling the truth. But let's not talk about those two. Let's talk about you and my boy Tolliver. Getting excited?"

"Nervous." She picked at her teriyaki chicken.

"Why?" Harold fully materialized and snagged one of my fries. I narrowed my eyes at the ghost and snagged it back before anyone noticed a fry floating in mid air with nothing attached to it. One of these days I was going to get Harold to understand that he was no longer visible to non-Celestial beings—which meant no more playing with physical objects and freaking out the humans. Unless he wanted someone to go all Ghostbusters on his ass.

"Because." Lisa speared a piece of her chicken and pointed it at Harold. "We're getting married in two weeks. If he doesn't start helping soon we'll be forced to hold the wedding in the Notre Dame replica your mother is using for her wedding next Saturday. Or even worse, if I don't have a church to take my mother to soon she's going to insist on using our family's church and that would be *really* bad. Once your groom has exploded in a giant ball of hellfire and brimstone you can't really come back from that. It's memorable, but not in a good way."

I munched on another fry and shook my head. "You seem to forget you're a demon, too. Step in an active church and boom. Bride flambé. With a side accompaniment of barbequed wedding party."

"I know." Lisa turned to look at the squalling two-year-old seated in a high chair at the table next to ours and raised her eyebrows. The little girl stared back, eyes wide, and immediately fell silent. Smart kid. "At least the Alpha has been flexible. I've been able to hold my mother off but I know that's not going to last. So I'm hoping Tolliver will decide to pitch in this week and help while I get everything finalized, but I'm not holding my breath."

"You're upset about that? Tolliver not pitching in, I mean." Harold tugged at the collar of his ugly ass green golf shirt and then wiped his palms against the legs of his khaki pants.

"Of course I'm upset." Lights flickered as Lisa's eyes flashed red, and the whistle of static emitted from the overhead stereo speakers. "It's our wedding and he doesn't even care."

"Uh." Harold looked over at me and pretended to cough.

"Actually…"

"What did you do?" My bitchy-but-amused face dropped the *amused* part and went straight to *bitchy*.

"I well, you see…" Harold ran his fingers through what was left of his gray fringe.

The lights above me flickered again and the low rumble of thunder sounded outside as the stereo speakers gave a loud *pop* and then died completely. "What. Did. You. Do?"

"I was only trying to help," Harold muttered. Ghostly sweat beaded on his forehead. "I am a bit of an expert when it comes to weddings. I've been through four of them."

"Harold." Lisa set her fork down. Her aura turned black, power crackled around her, and the lights around the food court hummed ominously, like they were about to explode. "What did you do?"

"I told him to stay out of your way," the ghost mumbled. "I didn't tell him to avoid you, though. I told him, 'You are one step down from her purse on her wedding day and don't get it in your head that it's not *her* wedding day.' That's all. I didn't say *not* to help."

Lisa slammed her hands on the table and leaned over so they were nose to nose. "You told him not to give me his opinion? To just shut up and say yes no matter what I did?"

"That's exactly what I told him." Harold nodded. "Matt didn't think it was a good idea but I told them both to trust me because I've been through this wedding stuff before. *Four times*, remember?"

"Matt didn't go along with your idea?" I asked.

"Angel Boy said he needed to be honest with you and meet you halfway. Told Tolliver that it was his wedding, too, and he needed to do at least half the work. I always thought the boy was a bit loco, but personally, I think that right there proved the Angale are even more insane than we thought."

Lisa tapped her long, ballerina pink fingernails on the table and the brimstone rolled off of her in waves. "In the name of all that is evil and wicked, you should be ashamed of yourself. You're a doctor and my fiancé is a centuries-old archdemon. Between the two of you, you didn't have the few measly IQ points necessary to figure out I needed help?"

"No?" Harold's voice squeaked and his image wavered. "I'm sorry? I'm just a dumb guy? I don't know any better?"

"I want to trade boyfriends." Lisa leaned back in her seat. "I want Matt, crazy Angale family and all. I don't even care that they're a bunch of nutty bigamists who want to rule all the earthbound realms. Apparently they've raised the only intelligent supernatural male in existence."

I laughed and shook my head before stealing her eggroll. I understood her frustration with my brother, but the whole kissing cousins fetish was an angel thing. Demons preferred to go with the old standby—leather and bondage—instead. It worked so much better with our image.

"Tolliver isn't that bad," Harold said. "He just got some bad advice. You should have expected that, though. He was listening to me."

"He should have listened to Matt." Lisa snagged the other half of her eggroll out of my hand before I could finish it. "And people wonder why I'm molting so much."

"We'll go by LUSH after lunch and pick up a few bath bombs and some bubble bath. They might help fluff things up a bit." I hoped it might help calm her down. The last thing she needed to do was get more stressed out.

Lisa sighed before wiggling her fingers at the nearby toddler to tickle her toes and put a happy grin on the little monster's face. "My credit cards cry every time I open my wallet. Our honeymoon to Fiji is entirely on plastic right now. Tolliver swore to me he was going to handle it, but we had to pay the travel agent and he wasn't there to pick up the bill. Now every time I mention it he's got somewhere he has to be."

"I'll take care of it." I bit the inside of my cheek and tried not to growl in frustration at the thought of my brother skimping on his wedding. He had an unlimited bank account thanks to Dad, and she was busting her ass working as a post-surgery nurse at a pediatric hospital to pay for things? That was going to change as soon as my brother and I sat down and had ourselves a little heart to heart. Or baseball bat to knee caps if he got too stubborn about it. "Harold will go tell Tolliver he's made a mistake and light a fire under my brother's ass. You and I are going over to LUSH and I'm buying you an early wedding gift. When we get home you'll give me your credit card and I'll talk to Dad. He'll take care of it."

"I don't want your dad paying my bills," Lisa said. "I'm a grown woman with a college degree and a job."

"Who said anything about paying them?" I laughed and decided to handle things until I could force my brother to come clean to his future bride about his financial affairs. Tolliver probably hadn't even told her that Dad gave him an allowance. "Devil, remember? He'll simply make them go away. You charge on the card and they approve it but no bills ever come your way. No muss no fuss."

"But won't the credit card company notice? They're losing money."

"Never noticed before." I put my chin in my upturned palm and smiled at her. "Besides, I don't particularly think those bastards are hurting in the checkbook, do you?"

"Probably not." She smirked. "But what does Matt say about that? He's usually on the straight and narrow, what with the whole nephilim thing."

"Yeah, the children of angels are a bit stubborn," I muttered.

Harold nudged my shoulder. "The Devil's children aren't exactly the most flexible people around, either."

"Tell me about it." Lisa chuckled then rolled her eyes, her mood obviously starting to pick up a bit. "I must be out of my mind. I'm roommates with the Devil's youngest daughter and marrying his only son. I need my head examined."

"Not my specialty, sweetheart." Harold floated over to give her a quick hug-like pass through her body that made her shiver. "Brains always bored me."

"Yeah, well, they aren't your defining attribute, either," I said. "Get out of here and go tell my brother what a moron you are."

"Is that an order, Demon Girl?"

"Consider it a very strong request. Otherwise I might have to try my hand at banishing roaming souls to the Grey Lands."

Harold blanched at the mention of Purgatory and his spectral appearance wavered. I reached for my soda and shook it, hoping some of the ice had melted into watery soda-like goodness. Before I could be too disappointed to find my cup empty he'd dissolved, leaving the place in front of me empty, but ten degrees colder than the rest of the room.

"You are so lucky to have Matt." Lisa pointed at me with the last bit of her eggroll half. "When you two get married you won't have any of these problems."

"Whoa." My eyes widened and my chest tightened. Thankfully I had a bag to breathe in if need be. "Who said anything about me and Matt getting married?"

What in the combined names of the Alpha and the Omega was she smoking? Just because everyone else was suffering from wedding fever didn't mean I was in the market for a big white dress any time soon. Or ever, for that matter. I had almost done that once and it hadn't turned out well. There was no way I'd ever put myself in that position again if I could help it.

"You *are* planning on marrying Matt one day, aren't you?" Lisa asked, her jaw hanging open, food forgotten. "You're perfect together. You're soul mates. Everyone knows it."

I swallowed, panic coursing through me at the very thought of getting married. My stomach rolled and every light in the food court dimmed. "That doesn't mean I've got to handcuff myself to him for all eternity."

"Faith, you don't mean that! You and Matt are perfect together. You're going to risk screwing that up?"

"I'm not screwing anything up. I just don't think I need some sort of ceremony tying me down. It's not like a piece of paper matters when you're going to live until the end of time. Well, given that you manage to keep your physical form from being mortally wounded and crazy nephilims don't try to suck out your soul to steal your powers."

"I can't believe you." Lisa gaped at me and the toddler from the next table started to sniffle, obviously feeling the change in Lisa's mood. "This is about Dan, isn't it?"

"Dan?" I tried to keep the defensive note out of my voice. "Who said anything about Dan? I didn't mention Dan."

"You didn't have to. I can tell by looking at you that he's

who you're thinking about. You're going to refuse to marry Matt because of what happened? How is that fair to him? He's not going to dump you because of who you are."

"Dan didn't dump me because of who I was…or at least not intentionally. My guess is that he didn't plan on having a complete mental breakdown the week before our wedding. Then again, he wasn't expecting the in-laws from Hell, either. "

"Faith." Lisa sighed and I got the definite feeling she thought I was being stupid. Or pathetic. Possibly both. "Matt isn't Dan. He's not going to freak out and run because of your family. He loves you. No matter how evil your family is."

"I know he does. But the thing is, I loved Dan, you know? He was it. Prince Charming come to life. We had everything all worked out. We were building a life together. Plans for a house, adopting a couple of kids. The whole nine yards."

"Adopting kids?"

"I told him I couldn't have any." I looked down at my hands, guilt flooding through me at the lie I'd told him so long ago. "You think I wanted to risk bringing another demon child into the world? I'd have never kept my real identity a secret."

"I thought you said he was the guy for you? If you have to lie about who you are…"

"We all have to lie about who, and what, we are. I notice your mom isn't knitting you sweaters that have holes in the back for your wings and no one has once mentioned how we'll manage your veil around the horns."

"That's different."

"Is it? Either way, I loved him, and when he fell apart like he did I wanted to just curl up and die. It was like there was nothing left in my life that mattered. If I could have found a way to end it…"

"So start over with someone who won't lose his mind when your wings and tail come out. Matt is that guy."

I ran my fingers through my hair. Why the hell was I having this fight with her, too? Any idiot—including me—could see I was hurting Matt by being closed off about these sorts of things. And hurting him made me feel like crap but didn't change my stance on matrimony in the slightest. "He's also the guy who understands how I feel."

"Are you sure about that?"

"Can we just drop it please?" I was sick of trying to get people to see my side of things. I knew Matt wanted some sort of commitment from me—and I wanted to give it to him—but the whole idea made me lightheaded.

We were very careful to not use the L word with each other. Not because he wasn't cool with saying things like "Love" and "Feelings," but I'd had a full-fledged anxiety attack when he mentioned either word during the romantic, candlelit dinner we'd had together last week. Love was too close to Commitment. Which was way too close to Marriage. And that brought up kids and all sorts of other things I wasn't ready to deal with. Ever. Not that Lisa would get that.

"We might get to that point one day but for the near future I'm leaving the white dresses to you and Mom. They always make my complexion go sort of sallow looking anyway. Now, let's go get you some bubble bath and see if we can't save your feathers. I can't have my best friend molting on her wedding night."

Chapter Two

I walked into my apartment carrying a bag full of groceries and found myself staring at a nephilim lying on my couch. He was perusing the sports section, with classical music playing and a full table setting for two spread out on my coffee table. That was weird. Not the nephilim—he was pretty common around here since we started seeing each other naked, but usually he didn't bring Beethoven and flatware.

"Well, hello." I moved into the kitchen and put my groceries on the counter. "What's up?"

"My client's court date was pushed back at the last minute, so I decided to leave at lunch." Matt turned the page and whistled like he was surprised by the scores from last night's game.

I shoved the bag of perishable stuff into the fridge without bothering to unpack it. I know, I know, not the best way to stay neat and tidy but, given that I had a gorgeous nephilim in my living room who obviously had something romantic hidden underneath his halo, I was pretty sure putting away the grapes properly could wait. "So you came here?"

"I wanted to surprise you and have a nice picnic lunch together on your floor, but, alas, I found my lady love missing." He flipped the paper down. He was wearing his glasses, but I noticed that his usually neat "work" hair was already sticking up in inky black spikes.

He wasn't a big, bulky guy, but his early morning five-mile runs and the three-day-a-week gym habit kept his body in stunning condition. I sucked in my tummy and made a silent oath to cut back on my morning cheese Danish routine. If you're going to date a man who was built like a Greek god, sacrifices had to be made. Even, occasionally, when it came to pastry. "I had errands to run, groceries to buy. That doesn't explain why you're here and not at your place. So?"

"So?" He set the paper aside and gave me a mischievous grin.

"Why are you here?"

"I was waiting for you. So we could get naked." He swung his legs off the couch, standing in one smooth movement. "That was the romantic part. I had planned a naked picnic on your floor."

"But…" I moved backward, like I was making for the front door. "What if Lisa had popped in?"

"Who do you think came up with the idea?" He inched forward, stalking me like an animal. "She said I should be waiting for you wearing nothing but a big red bow. The thing is I thought that the whole waiting naked thing might look desperate."

"A bit." I swallowed and nodded as my back hit the door. For a being of love and light, he had one hell of a predatory instinct. I was torn between running like there were missionaries after my tail and surrendering so we could get on to the ravaging-his-victim part.

"It wouldn't be much of a stretch." He loomed over me, both

hands coming up to pin my shoulders.

"What wouldn't be much of a stretch?" My gaze flickered between his lips and his brilliant green eyes. In the name of all Evil he was gorgeous. And crazy enough that he wanted to keep coming around me and my particular brand of chaos. His eagerness to date me—and see me naked—could have been low self-esteem on his part but I didn't care. One hot, immortal lawyer who liked to surprise me with naked picnics? Yes, please.

"Calling myself desperate?" He nuzzled my neck. His nose traced along my jaw while his hand dropped to grab my leg and wrap it around his waist. "I haven't managed to get you alone since our little vacation last month."

He was right. After saving the world last month we'd only had a week away together at my father's private island in the South Pacific and ever since we'd been living with nonstop interruptions. First it was my mother and Lisa constantly showing up to discuss their weddings. Then Hope kept coming down to badger me into doing evil for her now that she was powerless. When that didn't work she was constantly down here banging on the door because of broken appliances.

Once my family was handled, I'd gotten stuck with a ton of overtime at work. A week later Matt had been put on a case that required eighty-hour weeks. The most quality time we got anymore was a quick kiss in the hall and an anti-climactic grope over breakfast.

"It feels like someone, or something, is trying to keep us apart." He pressed himself against me from shoulder to knee, brushing his hips against mine and trailing hot, open-mouthed kisses down the length of my neck.

I moaned and tangled my hands in his hair, pulling him closer.

I had no idea what he was yammering about, but he was a pretty smart guy. Whatever he thought I'd go along with, as long as he kept up with the kissing.

"I think your father is trying to play the Overprotective Daddy role again."

"My father isn't that petty." I gasped when he wrapped his arms around my waist and picked me up. I wrapped my legs around his waist and bent my neck to the side so I could nibble on his ear.

He sat on the couch and I shifted so that I was straddling him, while I used my tongue to find the spot behind his ear that always made him shiver.

"He's the Devil." Matt tugged my shirt up and over my head before I could protest. "He *is* that petty."

He did have a point. The guy who'd taken my virginity still flinched every time someone said dear old Dad's name. Or when he saw deep fried foods. Yep. All the interruptions had Dad's name written all over it.

I found the spot I was looking for with my tongue and his entire body shuddered. He grabbed my hips and shifted us so that I was on my back with him looming over me. His blue eyes glittered possessively and he raised his right eyebrow at me, daring me to argue. Like I was stupid enough to pick a fight *now?* Not likely.

"Okay, he's that petty." I rolled my eyes and kicked off my ballet flats. He fumbled with the button of my jeans, and once freed, he pushed them down my hips.

I suspected my father had help, but his brother, the Alpha, had a strictly hands-off policy when it came to the Earthly Realms. He had some sort of idea that humans were an experiment meant to be kept in a bubble and allowed to mess with each other, evolving until they reached whatever stage it was that He and Dad found themselves born into. Yeah, talk about depressing. The Omnipotent Good, the Alpha, the Beginning of All Things, was merely an overgrown twelve-year-old with an ant farm. A big, complicated ant farm. But at least He stayed the hell out of our love lives.

Meanwhile His younger brother, the Omnipotent Evil, the Omega, the Blackness, the Death of All Light—whatever you wanted to call Dad—he definitely wasn't hands-off. In fact, he was the original helicopter parent. Which meant he had no problems stooping to petty tricks to ruin my love life.

"Well," I said, kicking my jeans off, "he's not here now."

"No." Matt licked his lips and desire pooled in the pit of my stomach. He leaned back to look at me, his broad hands dropping down to caress my shoulders, across my breasts, stopping at my waist. "And thank God for that."

I laughed and arched my back when he trailed one finger up the side of my neck and stroked my cheek. I bit my lower lip, and love and affection and all those emotions that I knew I couldn't deal with started bubbling up inside me. Instead of getting into that right now, I decided to get him back on track to making me one very happy little creature of unspeakable evilness. "Let's leave my uncle out of this. And why are you still dressed? Get naked already."

"Yes, ma'am." He tugged off his shirt while I fumbled with the button on his pants. With two pairs of eager hands we managed to get him out of his clothes before most women would manage to say, "Thank you, God."

At least if they took the time to get a gander at Matt's abs. Because, I've got to say, if I didn't have an inside track on the whole Heavenly Order thing, that man's six-pack would be all the proof I needed that there was a God who'd earned one hell of a Hallelujah when He created the man on top of me.

He dropped the last of his clothes onto the floor in a neat pile and grabbed my hand, lacing our fingers together before bringing them to his mouth and kissing my fingertips. Black power and emotion flowed through me. Birds outside began to screech. A cat across the alley howled like it was in heat. I fought against the urge to stretch my power and let a little general chaos out into the world. Too bad I hadn't had my new couch fireproofed yet.

"You're pretty good at stripping off your clothes while horizontal and straddling a girl. Anything you need to tell me about? Women in your past I might have to hunt down and kill?"

"Less talking now." He lowered himself so that we were pressed against each other at all the major important parts, and brushed his lips against mine once before letting his mouth dip lower. He worked his way down my neck, between my breasts, moving south with every seductive kiss.

"So what *should* I be doing?" He nibbled along my belly button and I sucked in my breath. This guy should come with a warning. I'd think he'd been getting tips from the incubi, but last I'd heard, none of them knew the belly button trick. Or they didn't use it if they did. I shifted, trying to keep my wings folded up so they didn't kink my back, but I let my tail slide free since it didn't get in the way. My horns itched and, rather than fight to keep them under control, I let them uncurl.

It wasn't like Matt was going to be surprised to find himself making love to a demon. In fact, he seemed to enjoy it last time. If all that screaming had been any indication. Or had that been me?

"Much more moaning and begging." He kissed his way from

my belly button toward my right hip while his fingers teased the inside of my thigh, his own white wings unfurling with an audible *snap*. "And I'm definitely going to want to hear my name in there a few times. I want to see if you can set the couch on fire."

"You're never going to let that go, are—" I moaned and he looked up at me with a playful grin before kissing back toward my center. Some things weren't worth fighting over. Besides, what were a few scorch marks? Especially when your lover was a nephilim who believed that old saying about "any foreplay worth doing was worth doing thoroughly."

The world grew tighter and blacker around me. Hellfire prickled at my skin, and I fought the urge to scream. He kissed the length of my right leg, stopping to lick the sensitive skin behind my knee.

"Matt."

He nipped at the tender spot there, where muscle met nerve, and I grabbed the arm of the couch to keep myself from grabbing his hair and pulling him back up to me.

"What?" he asked, his tone mimicking mine. He looked up at me with glittering eyes and his lips curled in amusement.

I tightened my grip on the couch and wiggled slightly, trying to entice him upward with a decent view of cleavage so that I wouldn't have to beg. The cocky bastard had become entirely too sure of himself after he'd gotten me to beg. If he weren't so damn hot it would be infuriating.

"You know what." I licked my lower lip and gave him my best come-hither stare.

"Say it." He kissed the sensitive skin of my inner thigh. "Say it, and I'll do whatever you want."

I huffed dramatically and stuck my tongue out at him so he

would know that there weren't any hard feelings. "Fine, you're the world's best lover."

"And?" he asked, tickling my side.

I giggled. "I've missed you."

"And?" He slid upward so his mouth was barely a fraction of an inch from the apex of my thighs.

I tried to wiggle closer. He tightened his grip on my legs, holding me in place. "And, I sort of adore you, okay?"

"I sort of adore you, too, you stubborn, wicked, demon temptress."

"Ah, hell, now you're just flattering me to get out of trouble." He kissed my hip and started up the length of my body and I couldn't hold back the moan I knew he wanted to hear.

He nuzzled my breast with his nose. "Is it working?"

"Yep." I wrapped my arms around his neck and pulled him close.

"Good. Because I have a whole list of things to do to you this afternoon, all sorts of ways to show you just how much I've missed you."

"Matt."

"Yeah?"

"Shut up already. We can talk about our feelings later. Right now can we skip to the moaning and screaming each other's names thing that you suggested earlier?"

His eyes widened when I pressed my hips upward against him. "Yep," he said, nodding vigorously.

"I thought you'd see things my way." I sighed when his body slid into mine and the entire world fell away, leaving me with nothing but the angelic being in my arms and a body that felt too full of pleasure. We shifted together on the couch, moving in sync with each other, and everything seemed to speed up as all my nerves fired together at once. My climax washed over me, leaving me gasping for air as the nephilim above me dropped his forehead down to lean against mine.

"If sex were an Olympic sport," he groaned. "You would be a gold medalist."

"Only if I were competing in the pairs events. I'm pretty sure I'd be lousy in solo competition."

"The only pair you will be working in involves me." Matt reached down to tickle my side and I tried to squirm away from him, laughing.

"The only pair I *want* to be in—"

A sharp rap on the door sounded and we both froze.

If this was the Jehovah's Witnesses coming to spread the good news I was going to eat one of them.

"Whatever you're selling we're not interested," Matt yelled and gave me a wicked smile. "We don't care how much it will simplify our lives or revolutionize our home."

He let his hands skate up the length of my sides, tickling as he went. "Now where were we?"

Whoever it was knocked again, and I brought my hands up to cover my eyes, fighting the urge to scream. "Who does a demon have to kill to get off multiple times with a hot nephilim in this realm?"

"Damn it," he growled and pushed himself up. He grabbed his pants off the living room floor and jerked them on as I sat up and reached for my own clothes. Matt quickly scooped up my clothes and tossed them onto the far end of my couch. Then he grabbed the blanket I kept on the back of my couch and handed it to me with a raised eyebrow. "If it's a salesman I'm going to beat them to death with my wings. Then we'll go back to what we were doing."

"Kill him quickly, then." I wrapped the blanket around me like a towel and burrowed into the couch so I could watch the potential carnage without Matt's victim getting an eyeful of naked demon at the same time. "I'm already starting to get cold."

"Somebody better be dying on the other side of this door, because if they aren't when I open it, they will be by the time I close it." He flung the door open and froze. "Brenda?"

I bolted upright, completely forgetting about my lack of outfit. *Brenda?* As in the *Ex-Girlfriend-Wannabe* Brenda? What was she doing here? How the hell had she found him? Found *us*, for that matter? I mean hello? It's not like my address is listed in the *Supernatural Being's Guide to Pittsburgh*. Damn it, if Mom had gotten me listed so people could find me to RSVP for her wedding shower I was going to throw away all her spell components.

"I know I shouldn't come here," a sweet, feminine voice said. "But I didn't know what to do. I don't have anywhere else to go."

"What about your brother?" Matt ran both his hands through his hair and tugged on the ends. He had carefully angled himself so that his body was blocking the doorway, and while I was grateful that Brenda couldn't see in, I'd be lying if I said I didn't want him to move a smidge to the right so I could check out my former competition live and in the religious fanatic flesh.

"Tony took one look at me and freaked out. Something about how he wasn't ready to deal with Mom and Aunt Val. Last I saw him he was muttering to himself and rocking back and forth on the couch like he'd lost his mind."

"Oh, damn it. Come in."

"But..."

"Come on, get in here before someone sees you." His arm

shot out, and he pulled her into the room like she was some sort of naughty kid who couldn't keep up with their parent in the grocery store.

I took the time to give her a once over, starting with the Fifties saddle shoes, past the overly thin knees, to her navy blue skirt and her baby pink twinset. If it weren't for the big hazel eyes and the shiny blond hair hanging down to her waist I'd completely dismiss her. Then again, I knew for a fact that a pair of big eyes and blond hair could get you past a lot of fashion sins. Not nearly as many as big breasts and a killer ass could, but that was beside the point.

She froze at the sight of me, her eyes wide. She pulled her arm away from Matt's grasp and I could tell that she was trying her hardest not to gasp and bolt. Not like she'd get very far with Matt standing behind her, blocking her escape, but that healthy survival instinct was there, nevertheless.

"I didn't know you had guests over." She swallowed and I could see sweat beading out over her forehead.

"He doesn't." I gave her a tight smile, bringing my arms up to cover my breasts inside their blanket cocoon. "I live here."

"You moved a woman in with you?" she asked, her voice faltering. She tugged at her skirt and glanced at me again, then shuffled her feet and crossed her arms. I wasn't sure if she was hugging herself to keep from panicking, or if she was trying the old makeshift cleavage routine. I sort of hoped it was the panic—the push-up bra arms never worked.

"No," I said slowly. "Nobody moved me in anywhere. This is my place."

"Your place?" Her voice had gone high-pitched and sort of squeaky as she moved into the living room and sat down.

"Matt lives across the hall." I stood and moved over to the

love seat to grab my clothes, trying to figure out the best way to slip them on without exposing more of myself than necessary. I didn't want to leave the two of them alone together but at the same time I was pretty sure this was one of those situations where a shirt might be helpful in diffusing the tension. "I'm Faith."

"Faith?" She swallowed and glanced toward the door again. Damn this was awkward. Talk about a time to be underdressed.

"If you'll excuse me for a second?" I jerked my thumb toward the hall and gave her a quick smile, trying for a sort of nonverbal *these things happen* attitude. Before anyone could say anything else I hurried out of the room and down the hall toward my bedroom, silently cursing my inability to have clothes on at the worst of all possible times.

I closed the door of my bedroom and leaned back against it, trying to get my bearings. Matt had told me that their *relationship* had been all in his mother's head and that Brenda didn't want him any more than he wanted her, but who said he had the whole story? Girls lie about being okay with the *just friends* bit all the time. That doesn't mean we're ever okay with it.

Either way, when it came to dealing with your lover's exes it was always best to follow my sister Hope's Number One Rule of Demonhood: keep your rivals close enough to bludgeon to death and make sure your girlfriends were on speed dial to help get rid of the body. Lucky me, my best friend was still my roommate for a few more days.

I slipped on my clothes as quickly as possible and ran shaky fingers through my hair, trying to make it look like less of a rat's nest. Why was it that I could never have good bedhead after sex? No, I had "recently attacked by a ravaging badger" hair. Oh well, my hair was going to have to wait; they'd been out there alone together long enough.

I hurried into the living room, trying to act put together and unconcerned, while still feeling *back off, bitch* at the same time. "Okay." I stuck my hand out toward Brenda. "Let's try this again. I'm Faith Bettincourt. Matt's landlord, neighbor, and more demonic half."

"You're a demon?"

"Um, yeah." I didn't want to ignore the obviously demonic elephant in the middle of the room so I let my horns curl up slightly.

"Oh my goodness." She fondled the silver crucifix hanging from her neck. Amateur. Next she was going to get out the holy water.

"Those don't bother me." I motioned to her necklace. "I won't burst into flames or anything at the sight of it."

"Oh." She swallowed. "That's good. I think. I'd always heard that demons cower at the sight of the true God and that's why you would never wear religious symbols. The touch of a holy object causes you unendurable suffering."

"Nope, sorry."

"Well." Matt looked between the two of us. "If we're done with the formalities, can I ask the obvious question?"

"What exactly is in tofu that makes it so spongy?" I smiled at him and hoped it would break the tension.

But he ignored me and turned to face the other woman. "Brenda, how in the name of Heaven and Hell combined did you find me?"

Chapter Three

"I didn't come looking for you if that's what you're worried about." She looked…*guilty* was the best word I could think of to use. Not *I'm Hiding Something From You* guilty. More like *I'm Embarrassed and Did Something Stupid* guilty. I knew that guilty pretty well. I lived it on an almost day-to-day basis.

Which meant she was probably telling the truth. I can admit that I wanted her to be lying so that I could turn her into a ruffle covered throw pillow and donate her to a nursing home for fat old ladies to sit on, but she wasn't. She was an honest to Alpha refugee from the Angale so I had to muzzle the crazy girlfriend part of my brain that was advocating kicking my lover's sort-of-ex to the curb to be eaten by lesser demons and be nice. She was alone and scared and I couldn't let her almost-past with Matt keep me from helping her. Besides, I sort of had to respect her for walking her ass out of an angelic army's version of Crazy Town.

"Brenda." Matt sat beside me, running a hand through his hair. Before he could say anything else I nudged him in the ribs and narrowed my eyes at him in warning. Whatever it was she'd done to land herself on his—*my*—doorstep, she didn't need him giving her grief about it now. He gave me an annoyed look and I raised an eyebrow at him in a silent signal to lighten up already. He shook his head and tried to plaster a smile on his face. It didn't help. "What happened?"

"It's not fair." Brenda pointed at him, her eyes glowing a brilliant gold that was almost identical to Matt's when he was channeling angelic power. "You just left. You and Tony both did. Then Levi. You decide that the life we live isn't enough and you took off, leaving the rest of us behind to deal with…things."

"By 'things' you mean Matt's mom?" I hoped to make him realize he wasn't the only one the lunatic tormented. I had some experience with bullies—I'd grown up with Hope and Tolliver for older siblings—and if Brenda had bolted to get free of Matt's mom I could sympathize. No matter how much the jealous bitchy part of me said otherwise.

"Not just her." Brenda twisted her fingers together in her lap. "Everyone at home kept staring at me and pointing. Whispering behind my back. Talking about how I wasn't able to keep you. No one let me forget that I wasn't enough to make you happy."

"So you're here and it's my fault?" Matt frowned first at Brenda and then at me, his shoulders tense.

"You and Tony—neither one of you even thought that I might hate it there as much as you did!" Brenda pointed at him. "You didn't care that when you left it would be a scandal and I'd be the one who was blamed."

"Brenda, I thought we'd discussed this." Matt reached for her hand. "It wasn't you, it was me."

"Well, why shouldn't it be me?" She jerked out of his grasp. "Why should it only be the men who get to flee your mother's wrath? Who says I can't make my own decisions? I'll be punished the same for my crimes. Your mother will assign me to hard labor like she would any man. So, if I'm going to take the same punishment, why is it okay for you to risk yourself for a better life but I can't?"

Oh shit. Apparently, Miss Arranged-Marriage had decided to buck the gender roles that the Angale had developed and gone rogue. Even with her unfortunate sweater set and headband combination, I had to admire her take-charge attitude.

"So you ran off?" Matt asked, his voice sharp and his eyes blazing. "Then you went straight to Tony?"

"Where else was I supposed to go?" She threw her hands in the air and I could smell the waves of anger coming off of her like super sugary taffy with just a hint of cold syrup. Not the healthiest anger I'd ever smelled but considering her upbringing I wasn't surprised to find that her anger had a nice dose of emotional repression mixed in. "What would you have me do? I had nothing but the clothes on my back and some money I managed to snatch from the church office before I ran. I couldn't survive alone."

"When you take off you're supposed to stay low for at least six months. Contact no one. Didn't Tony tell you that before you hatched this harebrained scheme?" Matt leaned forward so they were almost nose to nose.

I slapped his arm lightly. The girl was alone, scared, and had most likely gotten her older brother caught up in something bigger than all of us. The Angale were not the type to handle dissention within the ranks by their foot soldiers with any semblance of grace. They were hardcore, in their own angelic army sort of way, and they didn't tolerate opposing viewpoints. They also had access to explosives and were willing to use them. Matt's brother Levi had gone on a car-bombing spree last month that had destroyed Matt's car and, more importantly, my Dad's Lamborghini.

"I didn't tell Tony what I was doing. I saw a chance and I ran for it. The wall between our realm and the mortal world surrounding us was thin. No one was around. So I snatched what cash I could and ran. No one even noticed." The cold calculation in her eyes still gleamed, even as she tried her best to look weak and girly for him.

"What did you do next?" I asked.

"I ran all the way to Biloxi and found a bus station. I knew Tony was here in Pittsburgh because of the little clues he dropped when he called to talk to me and Mom. So I bought a ticket to here and then I spent all but twenty bucks on bus tickets for other people, just to throw your mother and the rest of her soldiers off my scent if they come looking for me."

I frowned. For someone who had run on the spur of the moment she had thought her plan out pretty well. She was never going to be James Bond stealthy or anything, but she wasn't doing badly for someone who was supposed to be thinking on the fly. "What did you do with the other tickets?"

"I gave them away to the homeless people at the bus depot. They were all so grateful and it did my heart such good to show them simple Christian charity." She touched her crucifix again and gave me a smug smile.

"I'm sure everyone else was bowled over by your generosity as well." I tried not to think what it would have been like to ride next to some homeless guy and his stench all the way to Detroit. Or even worse, L.A.

"So you showed up here, and let me guess…" Matt rested his elbows on his knees, dropping his head into his hands and shaking it in disbelief. "You didn't call your brother from a payphone. Did you?"

"Why would I do that? It was much simpler to open myself up to the Celestial Powers—"

"You told them exactly where you were." Matt abruptly stood, looming over her like one very pissed off parental unit. I knew that look—I'd been on the receiving end of it for a good portion of my adolescence. "You put yourself and your brother in danger. You've put me and Faith in danger, along with her family."

"Her family?" Brenda looked at me, her eyes filled with curiosity. "How have I endangered the denizens of Hell? Unless you have a portal here the Angale can't access the Kingdom of Darkness."

"Her sister and brother both live in this building. Her parents—well, it doesn't matter where her parents live—but it's closer than the Grey Lands. You've brought the Angale down on all of us and put them at risk. You have to go." Matt turned so that he almost completely blocked me from sight.

"Matt." I tapped his hip, motioning for him to quit hiding me behind his back like a pilfered cupcake until he stepped aside. "You're over-exaggerating."

"I am not. She only came here to tell us because her brother is missing and she needs a place to stay." His eyes were filled with anger and more than a little fear. "She's put us at risk. You're at risk."

"Tony isn't missing." Brenda slumped back in her seat. "He's on the run. For all I know it could be panic on his part. No one from the Angale has contacted us. But when he saw me at the door last night he flipped out. I need someone to help me. To take care of me. I had no choice but to come here."

"What did Tony do when he saw you at the door? I mean besides panic." Matt sat beside me, wrapping an arm around my shoulder.

"He invited me in and let me sleep in his room, but when I woke up this morning he was gone. He left a note on the kitchen table that said he'd paid the rent for the month but he wasn't coming back."

Her brother sounded like a gem. I tried not to roll my eyes.

"Sounds like he overreacted," I said. "Like some other male Angale we all know."

"He was playing it safe." Matt scowled at me. "If my mother knows where Brenda is she'll come after us. She'll run all of us to ground. There will be nowhere to run, nowhere to escape to once she's here."

"But she can't find you here, you said so yourself. No one thinks a nephilim is crazy enough to live in a building infested with demons. It would be suicidal. We're one big black power signature that masks all your little efforts at goodness and light. A demonic smog cover."

"No offense, but if one barely legal second-tier nephilim can find me this quickly then we're all exposed," he said. "And you're not really smog…more like a light haze of air pollution."

I gave him a smile and tried to ignore the way my tummy rumbled at his praise. Now was really not the time.

"I didn't track you from your power. I got your address off Tony's computer monitor." Brenda shrugged. "It was on a Post-It note about where to forward your mail. It had your name, address, phone number, and email on it. Then I got on the Internet and looked up the bus schedule. You're only five stops apart on the same bus line. I might have grown up in a compound filled with nephilim, but even an idiot can manage that."

"A Post-It note?" Matt rubbed his eyes before pinching the bridge of his nose. "Am I the only person here who takes our security seriously?"

"Oh quit being so melodramatic." I nudged him with my shoulder. "She just told you that she can't find you by tracing your powers. That means, if you're both here then no one will notice her, either. Think about it. Dad's already caused four meteorological incidents and they've only been living in Pittsburgh two weeks. The trick is for everyone to sit tight until we can find somewhere else for Brenda to start over."

"Excuse me?" Brenda asked, her voice high pitched and reedy. "What do you mean somewhere else?"

Matt shook his head, red patches creeping up his neck toward his face. "You're out of your mind if you think she's staying here. She's going straight back to the bus station. I don't care where she goes after that."

Obviously he was still in the mood to be dramatic about this.

"Come on, Matt!" I said.

Brenda had made a mistake. It happened. The last thing she needed was him riding her ass about it while working on his Best Actor in a Melodrama nomination. I mean really, what good was this doing?

"No." He grabbed my arm and pulled me up. Giving Brenda a pointed look, he hauled me into the main bathroom and slammed the door. "It is not safe for her to be here. Not safe for us. Not safe for the mortals who live near us. This is a bad idea."

"She's a young woman who's lost on her own. You told me yourself that people from the compound don't know how to live in the real world. That's why only you and her brother have managed to stay rogue in the history of like...forever. We can't turn her away."

"We can't let her stay."

"Why not?"

"She will lead my mother, and my mother's army, straight to us. They will come straight here. No stops. No consulting a map. She will find Brenda and there will be nowhere to run, nowhere to hide. No escape."

"So you're saying your mom is like Lisa at a shoe sale looking for the last pair of size-nine stilettos?"

"Way more dangerous than a shoe sale." Matt grabbed my shoulders and looked me in the eye, as if that would make me see things his way.

"You weren't with Lisa last year at the Black Friday sales."

"Faith!"

"Brenda has to stay in our building. She can sleep on your couch." I gave him my best "it's going to be fine" smile. Even though I would much rather send her upstairs to bunk with Hope. And I would if it weren't for the fact I didn't trust my sister to not recruit her to the *Doing Hope's Evil Bidding to Skirt the Alpha's Ban on Hope-Related Mischief* cause.

"Faith, she was the girl I was contracted to marry. You really want her on my couch?"

"I trust you to do the right thing." I wrapped my arms around his waist and did my best to swat away the image he'd just put in my mind of the two of them. I was trying to sound like a good, supportive girlfriend, even if he was making that hard for me right now. "You told me yourself that she means nothing to you, so I have no reason to worry."

He kissed the top of my head. "It's much more fun when your

partner has a dark and twisted imagination. That doesn't change the fact that I don't want to let my ex-girlfriend sleep on my couch. For all we know she could decide to have her wicked way with me one night when I least expect it."

Crap. He was being a loving, supportive guy. He was an angelic being, and evil anywhere but the bedroom made him uncomfortable, so I did my best to minimize my bad deeds. Now I was stuck playing the supportive sweetheart to his ex. Sure she was nice, but that didn't mean I would be opposed to turning her into an ugly lamp while we tried to find a way to deal with the chaos she might have unleashed.

"Oh please." I tried to sound completely okay with the situation. I could be a sweet girl when I wanted to be. The problem was it gave me indigestion. "She's a tiny thing. A strong wind would knock her over. You could protect yourself from her roving hands if she decided to make a play for you. Besides, can two nephilim have a wicked way with each other? Or is it a good, holy, and entirely church-sanctioned procreation?"

"I really don't want to contemplate what sex with Brenda would be like, thanks." He shuddered and then lifted me to sit on the vanity, standing between my knees. "She's not my type. But even if she was I don't want you to worry that something's going on that's not."

"I really doubt she's going to make a play for you. Not to hurt your ego or anything but I think she's got more important things than your ass on her mind."

"I don't know." Matt wrapped his arms around my waist and rested his head against mine. "She's always been persistent. If she were a normal girl we'd call it stalking."

"But she's not normal. None of us are. Besides, she smelled

like she was telling the truth. I mean, it's always hard to tell the first time you meet someone…" I waited for him to confirm that she'd smelled truthful to him as well.

"I don't know." He dropped his head down to rest on my shoulder. "Nephilim don't smell emotions like you do. If you say she smells like she's telling the truth, I'll trust you."

"So that means she didn't come here to stalk you. She came here because she's alone and desperate. Think about how hard it was for you the first time you set foot in the outside world—and you had been preparing to run. She did it on the spur of the moment. Cut her some slack, huh?"

"All right." He nuzzled his head against my neck and I combed my fingers through his hair, trying to comfort him. "But I still don't like the idea of it just being the two of us alone in that apartment together."

Good point. "Fine. She can sleep at your apartment and you can stay here until we find a place for her. We can manage some kind of temporary sleepover thing for a few days."

"She has to be gone by your parents' wedding this weekend. There are too many dangers related to having her here with a large group of demons. It would be too much of a temptation for my mother not to attack if she has the chance."

"I know another demon in Philadelphia who can put Brenda up. She works with battered and abused women for a living. If anyone can help her acclimate to life outside the compound it would be Deidre. Lisa and I can drive her there on Thursday and be back before Mom and Dad's rehearsal. Is that soon enough?"

"It's going to have to be. Now let's go tell her the news."

"But I don't want to go to some other city where I don't have anyone to take care of me," Brenda said five minutes later, after

I'd explained my plan—which I'd thought was entirely logical—to her. "I can't live in a shelter. That's where *fallen women* go. What would people say if I was in one of those places?"

"They'd say you needed somewhere to go until you could get back on your feet and find a place of your own," Matt argued. "But we can worry about what people will say on Thursday when you get to Philadelphia. For right now, let's get your stuff moved into my place and try to get you settled."

"But if I'm staying with you why do I have to leave Thursday and go to a shelter?" Brenda persisted. "You know I can't survive on my own."

"Brenda, I can't take care of you like you want, and you're not *with me*," Matt said gently. "You're staying in my apartment, alone, until Thursday. I'm staying with Faith. My girlfriend."

"Oh." Her voice came out flat. "I see. So by staying here I'm putting you out of a bed and forcing you to live in sin with a demoness?"

"Well if you want to get technical about—" I stopped myself. "But it's not like we mind or anything."

"I mind." Brenda gave me a tight smile. "I don't want to inconvenience Matt any more than I already have by showing up here. So I'll stay here with Faith and Matt can keep his apartment until we figure out exactly what I'm going to do. Alone. Unloved. Vulnerable to the evils of this world."

"That would be…" I swallowed and looked first at Matt and then at the tiny woman standing between us. "Great. I mean really, *really* swell."

Brenda sighed and gave me a stare that I'm sure was meant to be one of long suffering patience. "Good. So what room is mine?"

"Well, this is it." I opened my arms to encompass the living room. "I only have a two-bedroom apartment."

"So why can't I stay in the guest room?"

"That's my roommate's. She and my brother are moving into the apartment right beneath this one, but the room is still hers until she gets her stuff out."

"Oh." Brenda's eyes were questioning, and she bit her lower lip. "Where will I be sleeping, then?"

I patted the sofa. "It folds out into a bed."

"Wonderful." Her smile faltered. Obviously, whatever she'd been expecting when she showed up here today wasn't what had happened.

Sounded a lot like my life.

"Don't worry," I said. "It's only for a few days. Then we'll take you to Deidre's and you'll have your own room."

"A few days." Her eyes welled up with tears and her shoulders trembled. Being independent in the real world was probably a lot scarier than she'd expected. Not that I blamed her. Who doesn't deal with a little bit of shock the first time they're completely on their own and the shit hits the fan?

The last thing the girl needed right now, after getting metaphorically gut punched by the guy she'd been expecting to help her, was for the same guy to watch her break down. Talk about adding insult to injury. I took pity on Brenda. If she was going to break down, the least I could do was arrange for her to have some privacy to lose her shit in peace.

"Hey, Matt," I said. "Don't you need to get back to work?"

"Huh?"

I raised my eyebrows before looking blatantly at Brenda. His eyes followed mine and he nodded, catching the hint I was lobbing at him like a bowling ball. "Oh right, work. Are you sure you can handle it here without me?"

"No problem." Following him to the front door, I reached down to snag his shirt and then wrapped my arms around his waist before giving Matt a quick kiss. He brushed his lips against mine and then stepped away, his hands lingering for just a second. After he left I turned to face my new guest.

Evil save me, I wanted to hate her just because she was my boyfriend's needy ex. But there was this stupid, little voice in the back of my head that kept telling me that I needed to be nice to someone who was definitely less fortunate than I was right now. I thought it might be my conscience, and cursed my mother for the crappy altruistic genes she'd passed onto me. Couldn't she have come up with something more useful? Like another three inches of height or some sort of recessive superpower?

"So I'm going to go"—I pointed at the hallway toward my bedroom—"organize my socks or something. Make yourself at home."

"Thank you for letting me stay here, Faith." Brenda sat on the couch and wrapped her arms around her waist. "I know this is hard for everyone but I hope you understand that I didn't have a choice."

"Yeah well, families will do that to you." I tried to sound noncommittal.

"I had to come for Matt's sake," Brenda persisted, her eyes glowing golden. "He needed me here. He's my fiancé. He's living in denial right now and eventually he'll come back to me. When he does, he'll need me to help him pick up the pieces that you've left his life in, and help him to find his way back to the path of the right."

I took a deep breath and tried not to snap at her. She was just like most of my patients in the Pediatric Intensive Care. She was hurt. She was scared. She was lashing out. I wasn't going to let her get to me. I was going to be the bigger woman until Thursday. No matter how much it killed me.

"Either way…" I motioned toward the couch. "Make yourself at home."

Chapter Four

"You let your boyfriend's former girlfriend move in with you?" A few hours later Harold's voice echoed around the staff changing rooms at the hospital while I put my purse in my work locker. I should have known he'd have an opinion on the whole affair. I peered into the cover of the romance novel sitting at the top shelf of the locker and found that my pet ghost had superimposed himself onto the male model's face. Even with all those muscles he still wasn't a hunk.

"You thought this was a good idea why?" I stared at the cover of *The Virgin Pirate's Ravisher* and tried not to gag as Harold—now sporting a flowing blond mullet—somehow managed to move the book in a way that it made the cover model Harold's pecs dance.

"Because she needed a place to go, and I didn't want Matt stressing out any more than he already was about the whole thing. If she's staying with me I can keep an eye on her."

"It's a bad idea. Trust me. I've been there, done that. No man with any brains lets two women who've seen him naked anywhere near each other. It's like asking to be tasered in the testicles, only more emasculating."

"He didn't ask me to let her stay and for the record I don't think she's ever seen him naked." I grabbed the book and shook it before tossing it into my locker hard enough to bounce off the back, and slammed the door shut.

"Then who did? Let her stay, I mean, not see Matt naked. I don't want to know about anyone else getting an eyeful of naked nephilim." Harold floated out of the metal door and stood in front of me, six inches above the ground. Now dressed in his golf clothes and a white lab coat instead of an open-to-the-navel white shirt and tight black pirate pants, he crossed his arms and pretended to tap one of his toes on the empty air beneath him.

"I invited her to stay with me. He didn't like the idea, but it seemed like the only way keep the peace." I pulled my name badge out of my pocket and headed to the time clock.

"You should have listened to Matt."

"That's what I said." Malachi, the dread demon who was supposed to be my personal bodyguard, popped out of the time clock like a demented jack-in-the-box. He was a three-foot-tall vision of the grim reaper—without the scythe—and the hood of his cowl was pushed back to show off the newest artwork tattooed on his bare skull. Personally, I'd have expected a Demon Lord to go with something a bit more dangerous looking than a group of butterflies, but what did I know? Maybe he was trying to get in touch with his softer side?

"Demonesses never listen. Especially Faith," Malachi continued. I quit focusing on his uber-feminine tats and instead glared at the tip of where his nose should have been. "No, they always have a better way of doing things. Then it blows up in their faces and someone has to fix it for them. This will all lead to tears and then you and I, my ghostly friend, will have to save the day."

"Enough, you two," I said. "It was either let Brenda stay until we could arrange to put her in a shelter, or throw her out onto the street. Then what would she have done? You haven't seen this girl. No survival skills. She'd have died on her own before lunch was over. So get off my back already."

"Sure, no problem," a familiar voice said.

My stomach immediately twisted into one solid lump and plummeted to my toes. Oh damn it. It couldn't be *him*. Not today of all days. I spun around and my knees weakened. This was so typical. Of course Dan was here. Because I needed this one last thing to take my day to new and inspired levels of shit. And an ex-fiancé with a fragile hold on reality—thanks to a Celestial intervention to wipe out his memories of me and our life together—was exactly the level of crap I had been reduced to.

Dan looked exactly the same as the last morning I'd seen him in Chicago. He still had the neatly trimmed blond hair, cornflower blue eyes, broad shoulders, and dimples that could cause a saint to sin. He was even wearing the same shirt he'd worn on our last day together.

I tried not to grimace. He'd been sitting in the kitchen at our townhouse, eating Cheerios and commenting on the font I'd chosen for our wedding invitations. For a brief, spectacularly normal moment, I'd believed we could have a future. Of course the big old hand of Fate had intervened, in the form of my father, and shattered Dan's mind into tiny fragments before we could get our happily ever after.

Not that he'd remember any of that after the Alpha's version of a mindwipe last month. Nope, masochist that I was I'd let the

Alpha tinker with his memories while saving mine. Which put me at a bit of a disadvantage right now since I could remember *what should have never been* and he couldn't.

"I was just talking to myself." I tried not to stare at him while I regained my composure. Like all the other mortals he couldn't see Harold or Malachi, which was good on the *Not Scaring Regular People on the Street When Creatures Out of Horror Stories Appear* plan, but lousy when someone catches you having an argument with the time clock.

He was clearly trying not to laugh. "I can see that. It seemed pretty intense. Anything I can help with? Would you like me to call some of the staff to help you out? It's a big hospital. I'm sure patients get lost all the time. Although you do seem to be a bit old for a pediatrics patient."

"I work here." What a great way to make a first impression—okay, a second first impression—on the man I'd once loved. With shaking fingers, I lifted up the pink lanyard from around my neck and flashed him my badge. "Faith Bettincourt."

"Dan Cheswick, software engineer for MEDTECH Technologies. I'm doing some upgrades and running the staff training for the new medical supply system." He stepped forward, sticking his hand out for me to shake.

"Don't touch him!" Malachi floated between the two of us, his arms up to stop me. "Claim it's a contamination hazard or something."

"What the hell is your problem?" Harold asked. "I mean sure he's an engineer, but besides that, he doesn't seem like too bad of a guy."

"This is *Dan*," Malachi said. "*The* Dan."

"You mean human ex-fiancé Dan?" Harold tilted his head

and scrutinized Dan. “The guy who’s complete mental break led to Faith’s dry spell and her lack of trust in Angel Boy?”

“One and the same.” Malachi nodded grimly and pulled the cowl of his robe lower, to cover his face.

I narrowed my eyes at him. He had been a vocal opponent of my dating Dan in the first place and his disapproval had turned into an unspoken *I told you so* when the relationship had so spectacularly fell apart.

“Oh shit,” Harold said. “Mal’s right, Faith. Don’t touch him. Back away from the mortal and run for your life.”

I sliced my hand through the middle of Mal’s liver, making him shudder at the intrusion, and shook Dan’s hand instead. The last thing I needed right now was to trigger a memory of me that might cause the Alpha’s mind wipe to fail. We couldn’t risk it. So Ghost Boy and his sidekick, the Three Foot Demon Wonder, were just going to have to deal.

“Nice to meet you, Dan.” *Smart, Faith.* I dropped my hand and stuck my hands in the pockets of my scrub top. This was…surreal. And that was saying something coming from me.

“So you said you were here to do MEDTECH software updates?” I tried to sound nonchalant and polite. It wouldn’t do for me to run away but I needed to find a way to be basically unmemorable at the same time. And asking about the updates would be boringly common. Normal curiosity. But not asking? That might send up a red flag. Especially considering how much trouble the last MEDTECH system failure had caused.

A few months ago, we had a systems failure that lead to missing morphine in the pediatric ICU. Which led to my filing a report with Harold, who’d still been alive at that point. That report had led Lisa upstairs to Harold’s office, where she used my former boss for a quick—and very unhealthy—succubus snack. Which led to Harold dying and the whole *Haunting Me at Work* thing he had going on now.

Now, it appeared that MEDTECH had sent the man I was supposed to have married to fix the problem. Great. To think, usually my Tuesday midnight shifts were slow. What could I expect when I got upstairs? A dozen patients with projectile vomiting?

"Why are you talking to him?" Mal floated closer to him, peering into his face. "Don't you think you might trigger a memory? Cause another mental break?"

"His eyes aren't dilated," Harold said, floating closer. "Respirations are normal. Color seems fine. I hate to burst your bubble, Mal, but he doesn't exhibit any signs of mental distress."

"So," Dan said. "I'll just leave you and the time clock to your argument and get going."

"Right." I nodded and quickly swiped my badge at the time clock, trying to keep my hands from shaking. I started out of the otherwise empty locker room and into the hall. "I have to go on shift. But I'm sure I'll see you around at some point. Or one of your assistants. Whichever."

"What floor are you on?" Dan asked. Damn it. Normally the locker room was packed before shift and I could have fobbed him off on someone else. But I'd come in twenty minutes earlier than usual today and the normal change of shift crowd wasn't here yet. Which meant I was now stuck talking to my Chatty Cathy ex-fiancée who couldn't remember having ever met me in the first place.

"Fifth." I opened the door to the locker room and then looked back at him. "Pediatric ICU. Why?"

"Really?" He gave me a bright smile.

"Yeah. Why?" I tried to keep my voice from sounding too wary. It wouldn't be good for Dan to think I specifically didn't want to talk to him. That would make me stick out. Instead I needed to persuade him that I was a total bore. An absolute nonentity on the personality scale so that he forgot I existed.

"That's the very first group I want to scan. That's where the MEDTECH problem started so that's where I'm going to open up shop. Trace the problem from the source if I can."

"Great." My voice wavered. "Come on. Let me show you upstairs so you can get started."

"Thanks." Dan followed me out into the hallway, oblivious to the fact that Malachi was hovering over his shoulder. Dan had never been very spiritually sensitive so he'd never noticed Malachi before, but I was still worried. Before the Alpha had wiped his memory, he'd seen my father morph into his large, black demon manifestation and rain hellfire down on one of my mom's short-term boyfriends, and he couldn't ignore the creatures hidden in the corners of his eyes. He'd earned five years in an inpatient facility for that and if it wasn't for the Alpha's intervention last month he'd still be there, claiming that the monsters under the bed were not only real but very, very pissed off.

We reached the elevator and I hit the button, intent on ignoring my paranormal companions while taking part in perfectly normal, mind numbing, social chitchat. "So, Dan, is this your first time to Pittsburgh?"

"Yeah." Dan, completely oblivious of our eavesdroppers, rocked back and forth on his heels. "I don't normally handle the service calls or any of the sales work. I work in the research division but they sent me out because this is my system."

"Well, yay for him." Malachi floated between us and flipped

the engineer standing next to me a bony middle finger. "It failed. They should be firing him and not sending him out to make more mistakes."

"Why does it matter who designed the system?" I asked, ignoring Mal completely.

"I know that system inside and out. If someone cracked it I'm the best person to figure out who was behind it. I'm going to tear into the system, find out what failed, and then find out who caused it to fail. Sure, someone else could probably do it but I can do it faster, more effectively, and if there's some sort of new bug in there that we haven't seen before I'm your best chance of fixing it on the fly."

Yep, still the same Dan. Still intense and passionate about his work. Still determined to be the very best. Still cocky as hell when it came to how he did his job. And the way his eyes flashed when he was fired up still made me quiver.

I was desperately trying to ignore that, though. Even if he did make me weak in the knees it wasn't like anything would come of it. I had Matt and, even if Matt wasn't in the picture, Dan had his sanity—and his life—back. No amount of knee jelly could make me steal that from him again.

"Quit looking at him and trying to figure out what might have been," Malachi ordered. "Remember Angel Boy? Dark hair, big white wings? Lives next door? Will not go crazy from having dinner with your parents?"

"If you'll excuse me for a second," I said to Dan, and pointed down the hallway. "The main desk is right there, but I need to use the bathroom before I start my shift."

He gave me a quick nod. "I'll just go let the charge nurse and the attending on duty know I'm here."

I hurried into the women's room next to the elevators before he could say anything else.

Harold floated over the bathroom stalls and came to rest on the diaper changing station. "Coast is clear. Now spill it."

"Will you two just shut up already?" I turned to look at myself in the mirror and ran my fingers through my hair, trying to make it look presentable. "I can't even think with you two around."

"You need to find a way to minimize your contact with him," Malachi warned. "Spending time with Dan will turn out bad. For everyone's sake, stay away from the human. He's mentally fragile. Discovering our existence a second time could cause him to break beyond even the Alpha's repair."

"I'm not going to have anything to do with him outside of work. There's no reason for me to go out of my way to see him." I took a deep breath and puffed out my cheeks before letting it out in one great big huff.

"Good," Harold said. "Just pretend he doesn't exist. Everything will be fine. Soon the temptation will be gone, and you can go back to your relationship with Matt with a clear conscience."

"My conscience is fine. There's nothing going on with Dan. There's no temptation to fight. I'm just some nurse as far as he's concerned."

"Keep it that way," Malachi said.

"I will. I'll go let Andrea know I'm here early to help out before my shift, then I'll sit down with Dan and give him the rundown on what happened with the drug thing. After I've done that I'll go on about my day like none of this ever happened."

"Don't sit down with him." My dread demon floated over to block the door. "Tell him you have no idea what happened and you don't think you can be of any help. Then ask to be reassigned to another floor until he's gone. Avoid him like a plague of acne. Or wing rot."

"I'm not being reassigned to another floor."

"They're too short staffed on nurses with Faith's ability up here to let her transfer anyway. The only place she could go is into a surgical rotation, and most of the surgeons are terrified of her so that's a no-go." Harold sat on one of the sinks and crossed his arms. "So we need a plan to get him off the hall instead of her."

"Wait. Why are the surgeons terrified of me?" I'd never screwed up with a patient before, especially in surgery.

"They think you're overly protective of your patients after the whole *Threatening to Castrate Bob Duttweiler* thing last year," Harold said.

"He had it coming. I mean what sort of asshole complains about missing his tee time because of a two-year-old girl's cardiac surgery complications? Especially after she's already dead? Losing his balls is the least of what that asshole deserves."

"Yes, it is." Harold uncrossed his arms. "That's why I had his right to practice at this hospital revoked the first time I got the chance. It's also the reason I screwed his wife—and his girlfriend. We won't even talk about the threesome I managed to finagle out of it when the two of them found out about each other."

"Harold." I shook my head and tried to fake disapproval. Harold had always been a bit of a skirt chaser. Okay, more than a bit. But he'd been an amazing pediatrician and, given the number of "corrected" entries I'd seen on some of my patients' charts lately he wasn't letting a little thing like death slow him down.

"So maybe the threesome was to pour salt in the wounds." He shrugged. "That doesn't change the fact that Mal is right. You can't go back out there and start up again with your ex. I know a thing or two about how men and women relate. Post-failed relationship hookups never work out. Plus it will destroy what you've got going with Matt."

"I'm not hooking up with Dan." I walked over to the bathroom door and pulled it open. I stepped into the hall, looking around to see if anyone was watching. When had work gotten so complicated? "I'm only going to explain what happened with the MEDTECH system and after that I'll forget he even exists. Proper procedure and nothing more."

"I still don't like this idea," Malachi said, sounding gloomy.

I ignored him and swiped my badge against the ICU security system. "You don't have to like it." I gritted my teeth and waited for the door locks to click. When they did, I walked into the PICU, glaring at my demonic companion. "But I still don't have a choice. It's protocol."

I ran straight into Dan as he came out the door at the same time I was going in.

"Hi," he said. "I was just coming to wait for you in the reception area. Is everything okay?"

"Everything's fine. Why? Do you need something?"

"Yeah, the charge nurse on duty, Alice—"

"Andrea," I corrected.

"Right. Andrea. She said since you weren't scheduled yet and they have things under control, we're clear to go somewhere off the ward to discuss the security breach. She suggested the staff cafeteria."

"Just like our first date," I said under my breath.

"What?" Dan asked, his eyes wide.

"I can't watch this." Mal floated closer to Harold. "Come on, Dr. Death, if she's not going to listen to us I know we can be of more use somewhere else."

My demonic bodyguard and my ghostly friend disappeared, both of them glaring at me. Which was all for the better in my opinion. There was no way I'd be able to keep my cool and deal with their bickering at the same time. "I said that sounds great. Coffee is great. But maybe we should do my handprint scan first? Since we're already here?"

"Sure." He motioned toward the medication room. "Step into my lair, fair maiden. Don't worry, I'll only bite if you ask me to."

Yeah, that was the problem. Once upon a time I'd asked him to but only one of us remembered what had happened next.

Chapter Five

"Your lair, huh?" I tried to keep my gaze focused forward and not at him. He still smelled the same—coffee mixed with hot buttered popcorn. I never figured out where that second part came in but it had always clung to him. "I thought it was *my* lair. After all, I am the oncoming charge nurse."

"That may be." He pulled out a badge and waved it in front of my face, showing that he had temporary access. "But for the next few days your medication room is my new office. So that means it's temporarily my lair. You've been evicted."

"Yeah well, that means you've got suppository duty. Since it's your lair they're your dirty job."

"Maybe we'll have to work out a lair sharing plan. But first, what can you tell me about the MEDTECH system failure last month?" Dan swiped his badge and the door to the medication room popped open.

"Not much." I still stood in the open doorway while he made his way into the room. The MEDTECH system failure was the one thing I couldn't figure out. We'd always suspected the security breach had been part of the scheme Matt's younger half-brother, Levi, and my former brother-in-law, Boris, had cooked up to steal my father's and the Alpha's powers and then rule the world. Like most megalomaniacs they hadn't thought it all the way through, though, and they were now locked in a pocket of Purgatory, forced to think about what they did.

In the chaos that followed I'd forgotten about the MEDTECH breach and Levi had never bothered to explain how stealing morphine was related to world domination. I guess he could have planned to drug me and steal my powers, but it seemed a bit more subtle than you would expect from a guy who used car bombs at a local restaurant to draw the Devil into his trap.

Dan sat on the metal stool next to the counter and ran his finger over the touchpad of his computer. He used two fingers to type his password and then turned to look at me.

"So walk me through the MEDTECH failure." He brought a complicated looking program up on the screen. A small black box beeped once and the top lit up, turning blue.

"What do you want to know? That thing looks sort of spooky, by the way. You're sure it's not going to fry me or something?" That would be bad. The *Not Dying After Taking a Hit of Electricity* thing always made people a bit nervous around you. Given present company it might also be enough to re-break his brain.

"MEDTECH wouldn't let me use anything that could increase their legal liability. Besides, why would I want to make a doomsday machine to attack nurses? Politicians maybe, but nurses?"

"Well you know what they say: people are strange."

He raised an eyebrow before standing and gesturing for me to walk through an open doorway and farther into the chilly white medication room. I tried not to gag on the scent of bleach and antiseptic that filled the air. It never mattered what time of day I came in here, the place always sort of reminded me of Hell's version of a chemistry lab—for souls who thought Purgatory was returning to high school every single day for the rest of eternity.

"So what happened? With the MEDTECH system, I mean." Dan placed his hand on my back and guided me to the table where we normally mixed medications, which he was now using as a desk.

I tried to subtly remove myself from his arm, but this new version of Dan was a bit more touchy-feely than his former incarnation had been. Or had he been groping nurses our entire relationship and I didn't realize it? "When I left, the MEDTECH system worked. When I came back on shift the next night it didn't."

Dan picked my hand up, caressing it lightly before he reached for an alcohol wipe. Jolts of electricity shot up my arm. Usually touching a human was like sticking your tongue against a battery. Dan? He was like sticking a metal file in an active light socket.

I felt myself blush when he dragged the wipe over the back of my hand, and trailed his fingers along my wrist. He put my hand on the top of the box and it warmed beneath my touch. He'd definitely acquired a cheeky side since the memory wipe.

He hit another button and it scanned my hand. "So you have no idea what happened to the security system?"

The machine finished scanning my hand and I bit my lower lip, trying to ignore the way he was making my heart pound. "Not a thing."

He picked my hand up and set it back on the counter before pulling over a second stool for me to sit on. He grabbed a notebook and a pen then looked up at me with a quirked eyebrow. "So tell me what you do know."

"When I left everything was working fine. When I came into

work the next day the medication room's locking system still worked, but the cabinet was acting funny." I sat beside him, facing toward the door, and leaned my back against the table. The lights above me flickered and the cool locker, where we kept narcotics that needed to be refrigerated, clanked. That wasn't good. I pulled my stool farther away.

"Funny how?" Dan turned so we were facing the same direction and slouched backward, mimicking my pose.

"Bernice swiped her badge and it didn't beep. That's when we noticed the locker was open. Not all the way, but just a crack, like someone had been in a hurry and hadn't closed it all the way."

He leaned closer and I closed my eyes, trying to remember all the reasons I couldn't stand the smell of hot buttered popcorn. I drew a blank and focused on thinking about Matt's face instead. I was a good girlfriend. Even if I was a demon.

I opened my eyes and noticed he was closer than was strictly professional. Time to focus on the professional. Otherwise I was going to have to turn Dan into a frog and send him to a sorority so I could get that tiny part of my heart lingering on could-have-beens to focus on the here and now instead. Let the sorority tramps try to kiss him back to his more princely form, because in the end, no matter how much he flirted and made my heart pound, Dan wasn't the guy for me. I cared about Matt, crazy family and all.

Groaning internally, I pulled away from him and the lights dimmed.

Nothing strange, I reminded myself. *You are a normal woman and nothing weird is going to happen around you tonight. Calm down, already.*

"Keep going," Dan said. "So you found the medicine cabinet unlocked. What happened next?"

I scooted backward on my stool, trying to put as much space between us as possible, but on a normal night the medication room was a tight fit. With all his equipment stashed in here there was nowhere else to go.

"We found the morphine missing and reported it. The hospital opened an investigation and now you're here. Last I heard the police didn't have any leads on who did it, but you'll have to ask someone in admin for more details. I'm just a nurse."

"But you have some ideas as to who it might have been?"

I shook my head. "Not a clue."

I put my hands behind my back and wiggled my fingers. *We're finished here*, I thought, and projected the idea toward him. He didn't even blink. It had to be the mind wipe the Alpha had done, making him resistant to my psychic messages. Damn it. "It could have been anyone, and the theft occurred on someone else's shift. Back then I worked days. I didn't switch to nights until two weeks ago. After Bernice requested her transfer."

"It must have been a tough transition," Dan suggested. "I've never been one to stay up until the wee hours of the morning. My ex-girlfriend…" He stopped and looked at his hands, his face serious.

My heart was pounding and my stomach rolled like imps were inside of it throwing a party. "Your ex-girlfriend…?"

It shouldn't matter to me. When I'd asked the Alpha to strip me from Dan's memories I knew that meant he was going to date other women. That didn't change the fact that small, irrational parts of my brain were considering ways to make this ex-girlfriend of his feel pain. Lots of pain. Then turn her into a fruit fly—the one transformation even Jesus couldn't reverse because of a fly's tiny life span.

"She used to say I kept grandpa hours," Dan murmured. "Looking back, our incompatible sleep schedules probably should have been one of those big glaring signs that we shouldn't be together. Here all I wanted to do was have a romantic dinner and a movie, and she didn't think a night was complete unless we'd closed every bar in south Chicago."

"Oh." I should have felt bad for him. His ex-girlfriend was right—he did keep grandpa hours—but I'd always found it endearing when he tried so hard to be a traditional romantic. Okay, so he was more likely to take a girl out for burgers and a sci-fi movie. But still, he always tried.

"Anyway, enough 'woe is me.'" Dan stood. He brushed past me and opened the door. "That's the last thing you want to hear about the guy who's here to fix your security system. So anything else you think I should know about the MEDTECH breach? Anything that maybe didn't seem related at the time but was just odd now that you think about it?"

"Not a thing." I shook my head and tried to hold back my sigh of relief that we were almost done with the questions. Now I could go about finding the most effective way of avoiding the man.

"Well, thanks." Dan smiled. "If you think of anything else…"

"I'll let you know. But Hospital Admin is probably right about it being some sort of weird power glitch. Like when your power goes out and the alarm clock doesn't ring. That sort of thing."

"Somehow I doubt it." Dan grimaced and then turned back to his equipment.

Taking advantage of his dismissal, I left the medication room, closing the door behind me. Right now all I could hope was that he wasn't nearly as good of a programmer as I remembered. Otherwise he was very quickly going to figure out that there were things going on in this hospital that normal mortals might classify as *strange*. Or worse.

"Hey, Faith?" Dan called out before I could latch the door behind me and make my escape.

"Yeah?" I turned around and pushed the door open a crack so that I could see him.

"If you come up with any ideas about what happened, maybe we could discuss it over dinner?" Dan's eyes widened like he was surprised he'd actually managed to ask me out.

My jaw sagged and I stared at him, dumbfounded. The first time we'd started dating I had to ask him, because he'd been so shy around me. It had taken months of *accidentally* bumping into each other, and pouring an almost full bottle of tequila down his throat for him to work up the nerve to ask me out for coffee. Now he was just suggesting dinner like it was no big thing?

I suspected the Alpha had done more than wipe out Dan's memories of me. He'd changed his whole personality. Which could be a good thing since that meant he was no longer *My Dan*. He was just some guy who looked like the man I once loved.

"I don't think that's such a good idea." I wiped my sweaty palms on my hot pink scrub pants. "I've got a boyfriend. A serious boyfriend."

I didn't bother waiting for him to answer. I flew down the hall as if a score of the Heavenly Host had appeared with the intent of converting me by force. Or even worse, the Girl Scouts on a cookie selling expedition.

I passed the nurses' station and made my way to the stairwell, threw the door open, and hurried inside. I sprinted down three flights of stairs and stopped on the landing above the cafeteria. I bent over, breathing heavily, and put my hands on my knees. The last thing I needed was anyone else to see me going right around the bend and into a mental breakdown.

• • •

"You've got to tell Matt," Harold said. The cool breeze of him shimmered into existence behind me when I clocked out after my shift the next morning. Instead of answering, I scrawled my name on the signup sheet to do training on the new MEDTECH system Thursday morning at nine. That would give me time to get a cup of coffee after my shift ended and maybe grab some breakfast. Hopefully it would only last an hour or two so Brenda and I could be on the road to Philly before lunch.

"Tell Matt what?" Lisa asked. She swiped her own badge and followed me to our lockers, which were side by side in the bowels of the hospital.

"She had a run-in with Dan." Malachi floated next to my shoulder with the hood of his black cowl pulled low, doing his best impersonation of a cartoon grim reaper.

"Dan? Dan who?" Lisa asked.

"*Dan-the-Formerly-Mentally-Incapacitated*," Malachi said.

I pulled my locker open and let it swing through where his body would be if he inhabited a physical space. The metal door banged against the locker next to mine and bounced back toward me, smacking me in the shoulder. I winced at the sting of metal against flesh, then emptied out the pockets of my pink kitten-covered scrub top, throwing various odds and ends into the locker.

"Dan's here?" Lisa asked, her voice flat. "In Pittsburgh?"

"Well, she didn't fly to Chicago mid-shift, did she?" Harold asked from his place in front of the door to the women's showers. If my mind wouldn't have been other places, I might have scolded him, but I knew it would do no good. Harold had been a pervert in life, and death hadn't changed his personality in the slightest.

"I don't want to talk about it." I slammed my locker shut. "I want to get out of here and go home."

"But I don't understand. What is Dan doing here?" Lisa shoved a couple of pairs of surgical gloves and a few pens into her locker. "Oh shit, he's the MEDTECH consultant they sent? I thought he was strictly an R&D guy?"

"Again, I don't want to talk about it." I grabbed her hands. I'd driven into work earlier, but right now I wanted to get home lightning-quick so I could start making plans to get rid of my unwanted houseguest. Glancing around to make sure we were alone, I let a tear in the fabric of reality open with its unpleasant, burnt plastic-like smell, and ushered her and the rest of my paranormal entourage through it. Once we'd all stepped into my living room, the hole shrank to the size of a pinprick and disappeared with a *pop*.

"You have to tell Matt about this," Malachi said before I'd even caught my breath. "He deserves to know."

"I deserve to know what?"

I looked up to see him sitting at my kitchen island, drinking coffee. Brenda was at the stove fixing a plate of food. She scampered over to put the plate in front of him, making sure to lean over enough that, if he were interested, he would be able to see a less-than-modest amount of cleavage. Accidentally, of course.

I narrowed my eyes at the two of them and sauntered over to the stool next to his. I bent down to give him a long, slow kiss to mark my territory for the deluded little angel waiting on him like he was some sort of king.

"Nothing," I said. There was no way in Hell I was telling Matt about my ex-fiancé showing up with Little Miss Wonderful soaking it all in to use against me. "Not a thing."

Chapter Six

I leaned into him, so that our shoulders were pressed together. He wrapped his arm around my waist and grabbed the far side of my stool, dragging me closer to him and nuzzling his nose into the side of my neck.

Brenda stared at us, her eyes filled with hurt and jealousy. When she caught my eye she spun back around to the stove. I was pretty sure if she stirred that pot any harder food was going to start flying, and not in that cool high school food fight or weird sex sort of way. Lisa stood by the coffee pot, watching the silent exchange with a look of amusement on her face.

"Are you eating breakfast here?" I asked Matt. It sounded dull, but given our conflicting work schedules—with me working nights and him working normal people hours—breakfast was actually some of our best quality time together.

"You weren't here when I got back from my run, but Brenda invited me over and said I should wait." He kissed my cheek once before letting me go and grabbing his fork. "She'd made breakfast, and it smelled so amazing I couldn't resist."

"That was nice of her. I really appreciate that, Brenda. Let me and Lisa fix ourselves some plates and then we can have breakfast together."

"Oh, there isn't any left." Brenda gave me a tight smile.

"Excuse me?" Lisa said, putting two coffee cups on the counter next to the pot.

"Well, it would have been rude to feed Matt any old thing since he has such a long day ahead of him, making sure justice is served." Brenda beamed at him, fluttering her lashes. "Now he's had a good, healthy breakfast to start the day."

"He's in labor law," Lisa said. "It's not like he's facing down hardened drug dealers and putting away serial killers. You could have saved us some breakfast. Since some of us *were* busy saving lives last night."

"Well if you'd bring a doctor home with you next time I'll make sure that he's got plenty to eat." Brenda gave her a bitchy smile and even Matt tensed. "But Matt practices law and that's an important job. It affects the lives of other people, and to do it properly he needs a good breakfast."

I looked over at the four eggs and what had to be a half a pound of bacon heaped on his plate. Forget about serving justice—he was going to need a nap if he ate all that.

What did this twerp think she was getting away with, anyway? Just because she was sleeping on my couch for the next few days didn't mean she was going to take my boyfriend to Philadelphia with her as a door prize. Besides, if she dissed my nursing career one more time we were going to be making that trip to Philly with her strapped to the roof of my Civic in a dog carrier.

"I can fix you something else if you'd like? Some oatmeal, perhaps? Or maybe a low-calorie fruit smoothie? I know how it is when you've packed on a few extra pounds and are trying to watch your waistline." Brenda batted her eyelashes at me like some sort of demented housewife.

I froze, the piece of bacon I'd snagged from Matt's plate halfway to my open mouth.

You could have heard an angel fall in the sudden silence. My face flaming, I swallowed, stunned. I'll admit—I'm not a tall, slender goddess like my sister and Lisa, but I wasn't obese. Hell, I wasn't even chubby.

"Faith is perfect." Matt coughed and draped his arm over my shoulder.

"She doesn't need to count calories," Lisa added, her voice a low growl. Her body was enveloped in a brilliant blue-black corona of hellfire. "Her weight is fine."

"I didn't mean to suggest there was anything wrong with the way Faith looked." Brenda's voice tapered off, and she looked around, shifting her feet back and forth.

Lisa's horns curled upward. "Of course there isn't, Pollyanna."

"Lisa..." My tail slipped down the length of my leg and my wings itched.

It wouldn't do any good for Lisa to pick a fight with Brenda. In a few days we would drop Brenda off at Deidre's and then she'd be someone else's problem. But if she and Lisa were fighting, it would lead to nothing more than a tense ride there between the two of them and awkwardness between me and Matt. He might not want her here, but I knew that if she left on bad terms he'd feel guilty. That's just the type of guy he was. "I'm sure Brenda didn't mean anything by it. Let it go."

"I wasn't trying to hurt Faith's feelings." Brenda's voice faltered. "I thought all women who lived in the big city were super obsessed with things like watching their weight and shoe shopping."

"Sure you weren't," Lisa said, hellfire still enveloping her. She turned back to the now full coffeepot to pour us both a cup. She opened the freezer and pulled out two chocolate-filled frozen pastries and dropped them onto a pair of plates before slathering them in chocolate peanut butter and pointing her index finger at them, giving them a quick zap.

She handed me a plate and sat on the remaining stool, making sure Brenda was going to have to stand through breakfast. My spirits perked up. I sighed at the beautiful culinary triumph sitting in front of us. Leave it to Lisa to warm my favorite breakfast.

I ate half of mine and then fed Matt a bite. I sniffed—yep, Brenda had gone out and bought turkey bacon for him. I knew there wasn't any of that stuff in my kitchen. I didn't even have regular bacon. That stuff took way too much time to cook when I could zap a frozen confection of yummy doughy goodness instead.

I finished my pastry and Matt grabbed my left hand and kissed the tips of each finger before leaning in to kiss the tip of my nose. I picked up my coffee cup and smiled when the heady smell of Kona Select reached my nose. Lisa had brewed my emergency stash. Talk about a wonderful roommate. My half-brother seriously didn't deserve to marry someone this good.

"Hey, Lisa?"

"Yeah?"

"Have I ever told you you're my hero?"

"Am I everything you wish you could be?"

"But she doesn't need you to fly higher than an eagle," Matt cut in, killing our Bette Midler sing-a-long. "My girl has got a set of wings for that part."

"You're killing the love, Matt." I pulled my hand away from his and punched him lightly in the shoulder before turning to give Brenda my sweetest smile.

She narrowed her eyes at me, and if she'd have been a cartoon, smoke would have poured out of her ears.

"What? You have wings. They're awesome. I'm just stating the obvious." Matt shrugged. He pushed his plate full of healthy breakfast away.

"And mine are still molting," Lisa grumbled. "I tried to say something about it to Tolliver yesterday evening, but I don't think he was listening."

"Yeah." Matt gave her a weak, *what are you going to do*? smile. "Guys just molt. It's like shaving. Or nose hair. You accept it and go on."

"Yuck." I wrinkled my nose at him before turning back to Lisa. "Try that bubble bath we got and if that doesn't work we'll get you some olive oil. That stuff always works, but you have to eat two tablespoons like cough medicine and it's nasty to drink straight."

"Or, you could just let your feathers replenish themselves," Brenda said. "Wings are meant to be tools to spread the message of love and deliverance to others. It's vain to worry about their appearance beyond their usage as a tool."

"No." Lisa shook her head. "I'm marrying the Crown Prince of Hell in twelve days, and I'm not going to be molting when it happens. Besides, my wings are one of my best features. Call me vain, but a girl's got to work her best attributes where she can."

"Well." Brenda swallowed. She brought her right hand up to gnaw on her thumbnail. "I think I'm going to go. Matt said that if I didn't use my powers at all, and stayed within a five-mile radius, then no one should notice my presence. I just have to be discreet."

"Very discreet," he warned her, gold sparks of power crackling along the lengths of his arms. "An absolute wall flower."

"No one will even see me. I'll just fade right into the background. Besides, I'll be less than three blocks from the library where Faith's sister is working as a volunteer so she should mask me without any problems."

"Of course." I nodded, eager for her to go so that I could get some quality time with Matt before he left for work. "What did you have planned for the day?"

"I was going to visit the Art Museum and then the Natural History Museum," Brenda said. "After that I thought I'd spend some time at the Carnegie Library to catch up on my reading. Then maybe I can find Hope and she'll show me around the city?"

"Sounds like a blast." I suppressed a giggle at the idea of Hope and Brenda sightseeing together like a couple tourists. "We're shorthanded on the PICU again so I'm working a double shift. If I'm not here when you get back just have Matt let you in."

"Right." Brenda hurried toward the door. "I'm sorry about bringing up your weight problem, Faith. I didn't think it was something you'd be too sensitive about."

I clenched my fist and fought against the very real urge to shoot a bolt of hellfire at her. Not only would it be bad manners, and potentially start a war with the Angale, hellfire stains were a bitch to get out of the carpet.

"I don't like her," Lisa ground out once Brenda was gone. "And when I say that I don't like her I mean that I'm a feather width away from outright hatred."

"She's not normally this bad," Matt said. "I think she's just edgy because she's in a new situation and she doesn't know how to act. I'll say something to her tonight."

"Don't worry about it. If being called fat is the worst thing that ever happens to me, then immortality is going to get dreary pretty damn quick." I shook my head and glanced over to see the poodle across the alley staring at me through the window over my sink. The little monster looked frazzled and that meant I was going to have to talk to Malachi about laying off his torment of the mutt. Fritzi was much too fragile for grim reaper peek-a-boo.

"You're letting Brenda walk all over you," Lisa huffed. "Matt, tell her she's letting that girl walk all over her."

"You're letting Brenda walk all over you." Matt picked his coffee cup up and took a drink.

"I'm not. But I don't want things to be any more awkward than they need to be." I tried to push down the growing sense of dread in my stomach that told me the two of them were right and she was walking all over me. Even if she was, it was only for a few more days and then we'd never have to deal with her again.

"Things won't be awkward." Matt grimaced. "Well, anymore awkward than having her staying on your couch is, anyway, but I appreciate how much you're trying to help out with this whole mess. It means a lot to me."

Lisa pretended to stick her finger down her throat. "Look, you two love birds, I'm going to go take a hot bath and then I'm supposed to meet up with Tolliver to finalize the décor for our wedding. We're between a replica of the Sistine Chapel and the Hagia Sophia. That means you have thirty minutes before I'm going to be walking back into this living room so I can phase into Hell."

I shot Lisa saucy grin. "So should we be done by then or just out of the living room?"

She pushed herself up off her stool, leaving her dishes stacked on the countertop with mine. "If he's done in thirty minutes I'd demand a do-over if I were you."

She left the kitchen, her shoulders drooping and grayish black feathers peeking out from the bottom of her scrub top. Two feathers fluttered onto the floor. I grimaced. If she was molting this bad already she'd be sporting nothing but leathery, featherless wings by her wedding.

I turned to Matt. "So?"

"So?" His gaze trialed down to the V-neck of my scrub top. He licked his lower lip and my breath caught in my throat.

"Want to try for a repeat of yesterday? Without inconvenient interruptions by Celestial beings this time?" I lifted my leg over his hip and scooted to sit in his lap. "You, me, couch?"

"I wish I could." Matt gave me a brief kiss, his eyes full of regret. He dropped his head back and groaned. "But it's already eight, and I've got to leave if I'm going to get to work on time."

I decided to take the incubus by the tail and tell him about Dan. I was going to be honest and assure him that there was nothing for him to worry about. Dan and I were the past and the past wasn't going to come back and kick us in the wings if I had a say about it. We were going to be open and honest with each other, no matter how icky it made me feel. "What if I opened a phase portal for you? Because I think we need to discuss some stuff and I really think we should maybe do it now."

"Can we do it later?" Matt sighed. "I really do need to get to work and I can't take the chance of someone noticing that my car isn't in the lot again. The last time I barely managed to get Fitzsimmons in Accounting to let go of it without zapping him. I don't want to risk it."

"Fine." I pressed closer, lifting my face to his for another kiss.

"But we really do need to talk later. Not like a 'let's see other people' talk or 'surprise we're pregnant' or anything but this is still sort of important. Okay?"

"As long as it's not the 'it's not you it's me' talk I'll defer to your judgment," Matt said. "But if you want to talk about whatever it is before I go then that's what we'll do and I'll figure out some way to explain my sudden appearance at work."

"Agghhh!" Lisa's scream echoed through the apartment.

I pulled away from Matt and looked down the hallway. He twisted around and I hopped off his lap, torn between finding out what the heck happened to my roommate and trying to persuade my boyfriend that his career would not be harmed by coming in late just one day.

"Never mind." Matt quirked an eyebrow at me and stood. "It sounds like your attention might be needed elsewhere."

"Spoilsport," I muttered.

"Have a good day." Matt gave my cheek another kiss before releasing me and making his way to the door.

"You too," I said.

"I'm going to kill her!" Lisa screamed, storming into the living room, covered in a white towel. "I'm going to murder her, then I'm going to have you bring her back to life, and after that I'm going to kill her again."

"I'm not actually so good at the whole resurrection thing." I wrinkled my nose. "I mean I can do it, but it never quite turns out the way it's supposed to. Maybe you could ask Jesus to do it as your wedding present? Otherwise he's going to go with one of the old standbys and you don't need another blender."

"I don't care how messy it is. In fact, I want it to be messy. Because I'm going to tie her down and pluck out every one of her feathers one by one. Then I'm going to get her luggage and burn every one of those awful twinsets while she lays there and pleads for mercy."

"Okay, a bit harsh." I knew I wasn't going to like what was coming next. But I had to know. "What did Brenda do now? Besides call me fat?"

"Oh, this transcends the fat comment," Lisa seethed. Her eyes were blood red and hellfire crackled around her. The power flickered and thunder rumbled in the distance. "This is in a whole different league."

"What did she do? She's not even here."

"Go look in the bathroom."

Humoring her, I headed toward the bathroom and pushed open the door. My heart sank. The place was spotless. It sparkled. But worse than that, Brenda had organized Lisa's stuff. No wonder Lisa was pissed. Who wouldn't be if someone came into your bathroom and rearranged all of your personal junk? There's nothing worse than not knowing where someone stashed your birth control.

My stomach sank to my toes. "She reorganized it."

"That's not the worst part," Lisa said. "Look at the trashcan."

Look at the trashcan? What could she have done to the trashcan? I looked over at the white plastic bin and noticed the bright yellow bag peeking out the top. Oh, no she did not. Please, sweet Alpha, tell me she didn't. I sniffed and curled my nose up at the subtle, sickly sweet stench coming from the bathtub.

"She used all of it," Lisa said, her eyes flashing and her tail whipping back and forth. "Every single bit of the stuff we bought from LUSH yesterday. All at once. Look at the tub. It's got a blue ring around it."

"I'll replace it all." I knew how particular Lisa was about her baths.

Lisa's ritual was breakfast and a bubble bath before she found my brother. No matter what was going on she needed that. Before she walked into that bathroom, try as she might, she was Lisa DeMarcos, Post Surgery Nurse. Once she'd soaked for a bit she became Lisa DeMarcos, Demon of General Unhelpfulness and Future Consort to the Crown Prince of Hell. Messing with her bath stuff was like starting a war. And Brenda had no idea what a pissed off demoness ready to throw down could do. Even one who was as weak as Lisa.

Lisa cracked her knuckles. "She used it like it was no big deal. I'm going to kill her and then I'm going to eat her."

"Please don't. Things are touchy enough with Matt already because I pushed him to let her stay. If you eat her I don't know what will happen, but I'm sure the words *I told you so* will be used at least once."

"Fine," Lisa huffed. "I'll wait. But once we've dropped her off at Deidre's, she's fair game. I may not go after her right away, but I promise you this: one day, when she least expects it, Brenda and I are going to have a long discussion about not touching other people's things. And she may not come out of it whole."

Chapter Seven

I walked into the hospital that night for my shift and glanced down the corridors, trying to avoid the software engineer who worked oddly late hours. I breathed a sigh of relief when I didn't see him. Maybe now that he'd done the palm scans he'd stay on the day shift?

I didn't know what I wanted to happen more—to find out Dan had figured out our problem and solved it, or to find out he hadn't. I knew what I *should* want to happen and that was for him to find the security breach ASAP and then get the hell out of my hospital and my life. The only problem was the stupid, nostalgic part of my brain that wanted to see him again, to hear him tell one of the corny jokes I'd always loved, and to basically just know that he was okay and I hadn't broken him in some secret, indefinable way that even the Alpha wasn't able to fix. But some part of me couldn't help wanting to get the chance to see him one last time and say good-bye. Just this once.

"Faith!" Sally, our evening shift human resources director, called.

I tried not to groan at being caught in the hospital gossip-spider's web. "Hi, Sally."

"Faith, I'm so glad I found you." The plump redhead stood in front of me in a kelly green dress that made her look like a Christmas tree with her hands on her hips. I knew for a fact Sally once had a man tell her she looked like a "bonnie Irish lass" when she wore green because of her red hair, and she was going to keep working that compliment until her dying day. "Come on. I need to talk to you *alone*." She pulled me into the locker room and hurriedly closed the door behind her, locking it.

"What's up?" I asked.

"Dr. Turnbow was visited by a police officer today. *About Harold*." Sally's mouth was set in a grim line, but she smelled like bubble gum ice cream, which was her personal *Eau de Ecstatic*. Gossip was her lifeblood and a police visit to the head of the hospital was like Christmas, her birthday, and a magic diet that lets you eat donuts but look like a supermodel, all rolled into one.

"About Harold?" I hurried past her toward my locker so she couldn't look me in the eyes.

I spun the dial of the padlock on my locker around a few times to make it look like I was using the combination, then gave it a brief, subtle zap so it actually would open. Alpha forbid, I'd never actually used the lock. I probably wouldn't be able to remember the code if I tried.

"Well, you know the whole subject has been rather touchy. Harold's officially on an indefinite leave from the hospital but the truth is, no one knows what happened to him."

"He disappeared, didn't he?" I hoped I sounded innocent. Harold had done anything but disappear. Which was my biggest problem. I clocked in for my shift and tried to formulate a way to get out of here without looking suspicious. "Didn't he just leave one night and never come back?"

"We were all speculating that he was running away from something, most likely his alimony debts. When he first went missing Dr. Turnbow called the police but they couldn't find anything. They said his house didn't appear to be broken into, and his office looked like he'd just stepped out for a cup of coffee and never came back. Which I thought was suspicious, because what sort of man just walks out and never comes back? The police put out a missing persons alert but he's a grown man, and according to the State of Pennsylvania he can just disappear and there's nothing they can do about it. I think that's the wrong way to do things, but who listens to me?"

"Look Sally, interesting as this is..." I grabbed the various things I always kept in my scrub pockets—an emergency stash of gloves, pens, finger puppets, and a couple of dime store toys to bribe my patients—before I slammed the locker shut.

"They found Harold in the North Allegheny Waste Disposal Facility." She stepped between me and the exit so I couldn't escape from her announcement. "In a container of biological waste that came from our hospital."

"What?" I never expected them to actually find his body. I always thought it would have decomposed and no one would have been the wiser. Isn't that what happens in those mob movies?

"Someone killed Harold and stuffed his body into one of our Dumpsters," Sally repeated. "And the last night he was on duty was the night *after* the MEDTECH break-in."

This wasn't good. We did not want the police to link these things together. Hell, we didn't want them to even investigate what happened to Harold, but now that he had been found it seemed pretty likely they would. I just hoped it wouldn't somehow trace back to me or, even worse, to Lisa. I could lie to save my own ass, but she was so lousy under pressure, she'd crack and confess to killing him before they ever asked her a question.

"Do you think they're related?" I crossed my arms over my chest and shoved my hands into my armpits to hide the way they were trembling.

"I don't know. The police seem to think Harold may have been mixed up in a scheme to steal drugs from the hospital and sell them on the street. But whoever he was stealing the drugs for may have killed Harold to keep him quiet."

"No way." I shook my head, feeling honor bound to protect my phantom friend. "Harold would have never taken drugs that were meant for the children in this hospital. Never."

"But…" Sally shifted her weight from one foot to another.

Harold was a good doctor and he'd never, not in a million years, steal medicine from this place. Rogers was his life and there was no way I was going to let them destroy his reputation by suggesting he was involved. Yes, he was an ass-grabbing breast-ogler who still couldn't be certain my eyes were green without checking them first, but he was a good doctor.

"He wouldn't have done it," I insisted and pointed my finger at her. "If Harold's death and the MEDTECH security breach are in any way related, Harold must have discovered who stole our morphine, and when he confronted them about it they killed him."

That would give her something else to think about. Who said Harold couldn't be the hero? He'd like that. Going out in one last great blaze of glory. Even if it wasn't true. Plus it would give us a convenient scapegoat for Harold's untimely death.

"I know you don't want to think ill of the dead—" Sally

stepped out of my reach, holding her hands up in front of her.

"Harold wouldn't have done that." I was done with this conversation. I spun on my heel and stormed away. "I don't care what Administration thinks. Until I see a video of Dr. Winslow stuffing that morphine into his lab coat and walking out of this hospital with it I refuse to believe he would steal from these kids."

"Well, I have to admire your loyalty." Sally followed me to the time clock. "But since you brought him up, have you met with the young man MEDTECH sent over? Talk about gorgeous. I mean I know you've got your own piece of seriously yummy man at home but this guy could give your boyfriend a run for his money."

"Dan? I met with him yesterday. We walked through what happened during our security breach but that was about it. I didn't notice if he was attractive or not, like you said, I've already got my share of handsome at home."

"How could you not?" Sally leaned against the wall beside the clock while I swiped my badge. "I mean sure you've already ordered off the menu but who doesn't at least compare the steak to the lobster in a restaurant? I mean seriously, Faith, on a scale of one to ten—the MEDTECH engineer is a solid twelve. Even better he seems like he's such a sweetheart. He's the total package—handsome, sweet, and very polite."

"Sure. He seemed nice enough but I'm still really not interested."

Dan was a nice, polite guy. His mother, who used to adore me before the whole *Faith never existed at any point of reality in Chicago for you or any of your friends and family* thing that the Alpha did to Dan, had drilled it into his head from the time he was young. He also knew the best times to lay it on thick in order to get what he wanted. Not in a sick, manipulating sort of way, but somehow he always managed to persuade people to do things according to his plans and then make the same people think it had been all their idea. Sally was definitely vain enough to eat that type of flattery up with a spoon and ask for seconds.

"Well," she sighed. "I'm glad you two got along, even if you have suddenly become blinded by love. I hope that you won't have any problem working together."

"Why would we? But I really need to go, Sally. I'm supposed to be on the floor in—" I pretended to look down at my watch. "Less than five minutes. So if you'll excuse me?" I didn't wait for her to answer before I unlocked the door and headed out of the room toward the elevators. If I was lucky I'd have time to find Harold before I was due on my floor.

"Hey, kiddo." The ghost of the moment's voice was soft in my ear and his translucent form shimmered into visibility next to me while I walked to the elevator. I jabbed the elevator button as hard as I could then glanced over and gave him a weak smile. Today he was in a black, three-piece suit with his hair neatly combed. He looked like he was going to a funeral.

"Hey Harold." I bit my lower lip. "What's with the monkey suit? You're normally much more golf pro casual."

"Yeah well…" he trailed off. "I guess you heard the news?"

The elevator in front of us dinged and a group of visitors and patients stepped out. I entered the empty elevator alone. When the doors closed I hit the button for my floor and gave him a weak smile, all the fight going out of me at the look of misery on his face. If this was bad for me and Lisa I couldn't imagine how he felt. "I heard they found your body."

"Yeah," Harold said, his voice wavering. He sniffled. "Do you know I went to visit all four of my former wives and only Harriet seemed upset? I knew I should have stuck with her instead of being a bastard and chasing women. She was too good for me."

"I'm sorry." I patted the air where his hands should have been and hoped the sentiment counted for something. It wasn't like there were too many ways you could physically comfort a depressed ghost.

"I married her my senior year of college on a whim," Harold continued. "I was finishing up at Penn State and had gotten my admission letter to Yale Medical. I was so happy that I thought I was going to burst. There we were in this little diner near campus and I got down on one knee and did it. Just blurted everything out. Told her I loved her and couldn't imagine living without her. I didn't even have a ring."

"It doesn't sound like she minded." I tried to nudge his shoulder, sending out as much positive energy as I could muster. Which, given the whole demon thing I had going on, wasn't much. "She did marry you without it."

"I had to use my class ring from Penn. It was so big it only fit on her thumb and even then it just hung there. Ten months later there was Annie. Beautiful as her mother but a little loudmouth like me from the moment she was born. I cried like a baby when they finally let me hold her." He sniffled again and waves of misery poured off of him. The elevator was five degrees colder than normal and the walls had become damp. I'd heard it was possible for ghosts to manifest strong emotions into physical rcactions but Harold had gotten upset enough to make the walls of an elevator cry. Like the ghostly equivalent of *stepping-onto-a-ledge-and-ending-it-all* bad.

"Is there anything I can do?" Even though Harold was annoying I'd gotten used to him, and the idea of him giving it all up to walk into the light bothered me more than it should have.

"What?" Harold laughed, humorlessly. "Are you going to drop by their houses and tell them you received messages from the other side? That I'm happy? That I love them both?"

I swallowed. The last thing I wanted to do was go pretend to be a psychic and lie to Harold's family. I'd do it, if it made him feel better, but I wouldn't like it. "If you want."

"Let them grieve on their own. People aren't meant to get messages from the other side. It never gives someone peace. They just suffer longer."

"Are you sure?" I tried to give him my most encouraging smile. The elevator stopped and I turned back around so people wouldn't think I was talking to thin air.

"Yeah." Harold floated out of the elevator beside me, his outfit changing from the dark suit to his normal khakis and polo shirt with a lab coat and stethoscope over the top of it. "You could go to my funeral, though."

"Of course," I muttered, trying to keep my voice low. "I wouldn't make you go to that by yourself."

"And you and Lisa could spring for some nice flowers," Harold continued. "Since the two of you are responsible for my death. Not that I have any grudges or anything, but a big spray of flowers would be nice. Or you could give a healthy donation to a charity in my name."

"Fine," I whispered before swiping my badge at the PICU security door. "Anything else?"

"Then go visit my other three ex-wives and tell them you're a psychic who has been in communication with my spirit. Tell them I'm happy and deeply satisfied to know that none of those greedy, conniving bitches are going to get a dime of my money. And, that if any of them even thinks about harassing Harriet or my baby girl I'll haunt their asses for all eternity."

"Deal." I pulled the door open, stepping into my second home and getting sucked into the whirlwind of a busy nursing unit.

Six hours later I slumped down in my chair at the nurses' station and took the bottle of Mountain Dew that Tonya, one of my floor nurses on the night shift, handed me. "Nectar of the Gods."

"You're telling me." She sat in the chair beside me. She used her feet to wheel herself over to where our patient charts were kept.

"Hand me Dickerson, Matthews, and Xavier?" I took a long drink of my soda and stuck my hand out for the charts. "I need to get their admissions paperwork finished. Oh crap, and hand me Petrovsky. I've got to fill out the paperwork on her code."

"How do you think that one's going to play out?" Tonya asked, and both of us frowned. Nicole Petrovsky was a six-year-old who'd suffered head trauma in a car accident the day before. She'd been responding favorably since admission and, when I flipped open her paperwork, the first piece of paper in her chart was the transfer form to move her out of PICU the next morning. That was before the massive seizure she'd had during dinner that had caused her to stop breathing.

"I don't know. After we get the charts done, I'll call Lisa and see if they've heard anything. She can at least give us a temporary update."

"Is now a bad time?" a sweet, masculine voice asked.

I shivered at the sound. My toes curled and my tail itched. I looked up to see Dan leaning over the nurses' station, his elbows resting on the counter.

"Is it ever a good time here?" Tonya smiled at him.

"Is there something you need, Mr. Cheswick?" I opened one of the charts in front of me and tried to focus on it, instead of the gorgeous man looming over my counter.

"I wanted to apologize for yesterday." He looked first at me, and then at Tanya. "I was out of line and unprofessional. I'm sorry."

"It's fine." I glanced up at him briefly before returning my attention to the chart. Or I tried to. I wasn't even sure which patient's information I was looking at.

"I'm going to go do rounds," Tonya announced suddenly. She stood and scurried around the desk, then into one of the nearby rooms. One I happened to know was empty. The coward. See if I helped on her next case of explosive diarrhea.

"I wanted to say I was sorry, and I hope I didn't upset you." Dan said.

I closed the chart. "You didn't upset me." I fought the urge to lean closer to him. "It was nice. Flattering, actually."

"Was it?" He moved closer, and I wrapped my ankles around the chair legs to keep still. The last thing I was going to do was move any closer to him. Avoiding temptation was not one of my stronger virtues, especially when someone else was waving a road map full of bad right underneath my nose.

"Yeah, I mean, if I didn't have a boyfriend I would have said yes without a second thought." Dan had always been a nice guy and even this cheekier version of him still seemed to have a sweet side. I didn't want to hurt his feelings by completely blowing him off, but at the same time there was no chance of us being together. Even if Matt weren't in the picture there was the fact that I was a demon and Dan was mentally fragile. Add Matt into the mix? Well, even if I was just a normal girl and Dan was some regular guy, there still couldn't be anything between us because what I'd had with Dan on our best day wasn't nearly as sweet as the worst moments I'd shared with Matt.

"And since you do have a boyfriend?" he whispered. "Have you given it a second thought?"

What girl wouldn't think about what could have been when she found herself face to face with an ex? But thinking and doing it were two different things. I had loved Dan once upon a time, but that was the past, and I wasn't willing to ruin the here and now. No matter how sweet it could have been.

"Yes." In spite of myself I leaned closer to him. There was barely an inch between us and I could smell his warm, woodsy natural scent.

"So what do you think about dinner?"

"I think—" My cell phone beeped and I grabbed it out of my pocket, glancing at the text message on my screen.

Can we do lunch tomorrow? My dad is in town to see your dad and wants to meet you. He might have some ideas on the Brenda situation.

"I think it would be a bad idea." I sat back down in my chair, trying to put as much distance as possible between me and temptation. "Sorry."

"Give it a third think."

"I don't need to. I have a boyfriend who I care deeply for. Dinner is out of the question." I closed the chart in front of me and picked up my phone. Deidre and I had been playing phone tag since Brenda had shown up, but maybe if I called now I could get her on the phone and we could work something out. Then I could impress Matt's dad with how organized and efficient a demoness I was. "Now, if you'll excuse me, I need to make a call."

Chapter Eight

"So…" I tugged at the hem of my most modest little black dress. The neckline buttoned at the base of my throat, the sleeves hung past my elbows, and the hemline was at least two inches below the knee. I looked like a Mennonite. Not that there's anything wrong with the Amish. I'm just not one of them. And I'm pretty sure they wouldn't welcome me with open arms. Then again, if I were a religious group, I'd stay the hell away from me, too. "How do I look?"

"Sort of like a very hot-but-scared nun." Matt grabbed my hand and kissed the back of it. "What's with the dress?"

"I want to make a good impression on your dad." I laced my fingers through his while my other hand patted at the tight knot I'd wrapped my hair into at the nape of my neck.

"It'll be fine." Matt took both of my hands in his, pulling them down between us, and then wrapped his arms around me. "Dad is willing to at least give our relationship a chance. Which is sort of surprising, but he mentioned that the Alpha said we looked good together during Dad's last performance review and he may be trying to avoid pissing off his boss. But either way he promised to be nice and keep an open mind. So if we can just get him focused on how he needs to take responsibility for Brenda and either get her to go back home or find a new place for her to live then we should be okay."

"Right. The problem in front of him. Hopefully, if he can't persuade her to go home, he'll at least agree to the plan that we have. Deidre said she's got a room set aside for Brenda; all we have to do is bring her up and drop her off. Whenever's convenient for you. Or as soon as possible. Whichever comes first."

"Just a few more days." Matt squeezed me tighter. "I promise she'll be gone by the end of the week. Okay?"

"Sure." I smiled and tried to pretend having Brenda as a houseguest wasn't a complete nuisance. This morning I'd come home to find out she'd thrown out all of my emergency junk food—including the Rolos—and replaced them with "healthy, low-calorie alternatives."

I got it. She thought I was fat. I thought she was annoying and had bad fashion sense. That didn't mean I was going to put her dry clean only twinsets in the dryer and turn it on high just because I could. Then again, if she messed with my junk food one more time…

"Thanks." Matt opened the front door for me and I snagged my purse before he ushered me out into the hall. "And hey, since we're early, if you want to we could talk about whatever that thing was you brought up yesterday. The important thing?"

"Oh." I did my best breezy and nonchalant voice as I brushed past him into the hall. The last thing I was going to do was bring up Dan *now*. "Turns out it was no big deal. Forget I even mentioned it."

"Are you sure?" Matt asked.

"Oh yeah." I smiled at him reassuringly. "It was nothing. Just work related bitching. You know how it is."

"Hello." Brenda was standing on the landing at the bottom of my stairs, glaring at us, when we turned toward her. She gave me a once over and her eyes lingered on Matt's hand, which was still holding mine.

"Hey," Matt said. The agitation came off of him in waves and I could feel his shoulders tense. I knew she'd gone out of her way to drive him crazy last night—or be *helpful* as she called it—but I hadn't realized how on edge she had him until seeing them together just now.

"Big plans today?" I cut in. "Since you've already cleaned my apartment from top to bottom and completely reorganized Matt's, I'm sure you're dying to get some fresh air."

"Oh I didn't mind cleaning in the slightest. Someone needs to take care of Matt. All that clutter couldn't have been good for his mental well-being." She widened her eyes at him and did the crazy eyelash batting thing again.

"My mental health is perfectly fine, Brenda." Sparks of golden power snapped around Matt as he tried to reign in his temper. "Now if you'll excuse us, Faith and I are going to be late for lunch with Dad unless we hurry."

"But Matt." She put her hands on her hips and smiled. "You told me we were having a family lunch."

"Yes, a family lunch. Emphasis on the word *family*," Matt said, obviously not even trying to be civil. He walked down the stairs, pulling me along behind him, and brushed past her. My inner demon smiled at the hostility between them. Whatever Matt's mom had been thinking, trying to set them up, obviously it hadn't been a love match. These two could barely stand to be in the same hallway together.

"Besides," Matt continued. "I wouldn't think that you'd want to go to lunch with Dad. You know that there's a very good chance that he could send you right back home to the compound."

"But he won't." Brenda's eyes had gone a brilliant gold color in her fury and her own power crackled around her. "When he sees the mess you've made of your life by shacking up with such a shameless, wanton hussy—"

"Hey!" I took a step forward and Matt's hand instantly tightened on mine, pulling me behind him. "Who are you calling a hussy, you Doris Day wannabe?"

"Bassano will be grateful when he sees how I've risked my own soul to come here and save yours, Matt. You'll see. Once your father understands the situation he'll make you return home and deal with your responsibilities."

"Yeah," Matt said. "Because Dad is the guy most likely to be nominated 'Mr. Responsible.' He's not going to force me back to Biloxi. There's no profit in it for him and Dad is all about the profit."

"Either way..." Brenda started and I could see that she was trying to keep her temper in check even though the smell of burnt cookies was almost rolling off of her like cheap cologne did off of a novice incubus.

"Is there any reason that you three are clogging up the entryway with your conference of lame or is it just to ruin my day?" My older sister Hope glided down the stairs in a pair of super high, navy blue wedges and a white sundress so short that if she moved just so, men on the street would be seeing more of the demonic unpromised land than they'd ever bargained for.

Matt turned to glare at her and I could see that Brenda was scowling as well.

"Brenda is insisting on going with us to meet Bassano," I explained while the two nephilim turned their glares on each other. "Matt doesn't think it's a good idea."

Matt shook his head. "I know it's not a good idea. Brenda is not going."

"Oh yes I am." She stamped her foot and the faint traces of power crackling around her arms grew stronger.

"No you're—"

"Oh, why don't both of you shut up?" Hope asked, completely ignoring the pissed off nephilim. She pulled a compact out of her purse and flipped it open, checking her makeup. "I have a hair appointment and you're in my way. Now someone tell me what in the name of Lucifer's hooves you two are fighting about."

"We're having lunch with Matt's dad," I said, narrowing my eyes at her. Hope had lost her psychic abilities as part of the fallout from that whole *Stalker Who Tried to Steal My Powers With the Help of Her Ex-Husband* thing last month, but we still knew each other pretty well. If ever there was a time my sister could do me a solid and butt out, it would be right now. Or so help me I would not be going upstairs to fix her dishwasher the next time it flooded her kitchen.

"And I'm going," Brenda said.

"Fine." Matt narrowed his eyes at her. "Then I'll argue for him to make you go home to Biloxi where you can't inconvenience the rest of us."

"I wouldn't have to be a burden if you'd just accept that it's your responsibility to take care of me. But instead you want to send me to a house of ill-repute to be sneered at and abused."

"Whoa." Hope looked up from her mirror and closed it with a *snap*. "You're telling me that you're taking my sister to lunch with your father? The angelic equivalent of the world's dirtiest old man? *And* that *Touched by An Angel* Barbie here wants to go along because she's thinking about becoming a hooker? And people complain about the daytime soaps getting canceled. Who needs them when I've got this crap going on outside my door?"

"Faith and I are not trying to send you to a brothel, Brenda." My boyfriend rubbed his free hand over his face, ignoring my sister. "We're trying to send you to a place that can help you get on your feet and start making a life for yourself. But if you absolutely can't stand the idea and you feel like you have to talk to Dad about it, I won't stop you. It's your life and in the end it's your decision to make. I'm sick of fighting with you about this. So have it your way."

Instead of saying anything I tugged Matt toward the door and slipped on my sunglasses, my sister and Brenda following. I looked back and saw that Hope had whipped out her cell phone and her thumbs were flying over the keys.

"What restaurant are we going to?" she asked when we reached the tiny parking lot behind our building.

"The Church Brewworks," Matt said. "Why? I thought you had an appointment to get to?"

She brushed past Brenda like she wasn't even there and patted him on the cheek. I knew that look. Hope was almost glowing at the thought of engineering a family fight without having to personally do evil.

"Dad's been meaning to try the Church Brewworks out for a while and he hasn't had the chance. Besides, he and Matt get along ever so well. And your dad? Well we *all* know what he's like." Hope smiled and started toward my car as if she were a queen and we were nothing more than her servants.

"You consort with the Devil?" Brenda asked Matt, her eyes wide with disbelief.

"On occasion," Matt muttered. The back of his neck was turning red. He was either embarrassed at being caught by another member of the Angale in what she would consider a flagrant act of heresy, or he was about to lose his temper. I wasn't sure which one would be worse.

"I think Hope and I should take my car, all things considered." I gave Matt a tight smile. I didn't want to leave him alone with Brenda any more than I had to, but at the same time I knew putting her and my sister in the backseat of Matt's car together would most likely lead to murder. And I was not dressed for dumping a nephilim's corpse somewhere today. Not in these heels.

"Are you sure?" Matt asked. "I don't want you to feel like you have to be in a different car."

"It's better for everyone if we don't have to explain to your dad how my sister killed one of his subjects." I leaned in to give him a kiss and retrieved my car keys from my purse. "Besides, we were supposed to meet Mom and Lisa later for dress fittings, so now we can go straight from the restaurant."

"Okay." He gave my hand a reassuring squeeze.

"Well are we going or aren't we?" Brenda stomped over to Matt's car, pulled open the passenger side door, climbed in, and slammed the door behind her.

"Good luck." I smiled at Matt and then hurried over to my car. If we had to do this we might as well get it over with. Maybe Bassano would decide to take Brenda back to Biloxi and make her stay there. Then she'd be out of my hair tonight instead of tomorrow. And save me thirty-two dollars on the toll roads.

Hope slid into my passenger seat and put her sunglasses on, but tilted them down so she could look me in the eye. "What are you thinking leaving your man alone with that psycho church girl? She's going to make a play for him."

"She's doesn't need me out of the car to do that." I shook my head. "She's shameless when it comes to Matt."

"So you're giving her more of an opportunity to work her game?"

"Yes." I smiled at her. "And while she's playing games I'm showing Matt that I'm above her pettiness. I trust him and if it comes down to it I have no problems protecting what's mine. Besides, if we're in the same car as Brenda we can't plot about how to take her down and get her ass express shipped back to Mississippi. Can we?"

"I thought you said you trusted him?"

"I do. But that doesn't mean I have problems getting rid of some of the baggage from his past. Especially if it's getting in the way of my present." I bit my lower lip and tried not to think about my own baggage and how it was currently lurking around the hospital, possibly thinking about asking me out again.

"You should have tossed her out the minute she showed up," Malachi said through the car stereo's speakers. "Harold warned you it was going to turn out this way when you let her sleep on your couch, and if I were you I would have listened to him. But that's just me. Which, speaking of me? Am I invited to this little shindig?"

"It's for the entire family." Hope turned the volume up on the stereo and gave me a wicked smile. "No matter how crazy they might decide to be."

"Oh, splendid." Malachi chuckled darkly. "I have the perfect outfit."

Chapter Nine

Oh. My. God.

My parents were mid-grope against Dad's new car when I pulled up beside them in the parking lot of the restaurant. The Devil had gotten past second base in a public parking lot of a former church. That was so wrong. Hope snorted and I shook my head in disgust. Not just at the groping, though. I'd thought his old black Lamborghini Diablo had been desperate overcompensation on his part. But he'd replaced it with a fire engine red Porsche Cayenne. Hello? Could you say insecure guy having a midlife crisis? Well an immortal life crisis, anyway.

"Discretion is something they can't grasp, is it?" I threw the car into *park* and looked at my older sister, sighing.

"Nope." Hope unhooked her seatbelt and popped her door open. She slid out of the car and hurried off toward our parents before I had the engine shut off. She smacked my father across the back of the head and grabbed him by the earlobe, pulling his face close to hers for a brief conference.

Matt pulled his black sedan into the other side of the parking lot and came over, clearly frazzled, with Brenda trailing after. I narrowed my eyes at Brenda, making them flash red. Let her be afraid. Up until now I'd been nice. But I'd hit the limits of my patience with her. She was from Bassano's little community, that meant she was his problem now.

I met Matt at the front of my dad's car and stood on my tiptoes to kiss his cheek. "How did it go?"

"Can your parents adopt me?" he whispered back. "Please? She spent the entire ride here nagging about how I need to leave you and marry her. She even suggested we move back to Biloxi so we could be closer to our mothers. To make it even worse, she's already started thinking about decorating. She wants to do our living room in shades of pink and mint green. With flowers."

"I'm sure it will be a lovely home." I struggled to keep the black power that wanted to erupt along my arms in check and did my best to make a joke out of it. Brenda was delusional and I wasn't going to let her see that she was getting to me. Even though she was making me seriously homicidal. "I bet she can even find you a recliner and the cat to snuggle with while she gets your pipe and slippers each night."

"Not funny." My do-gooder, angelic half frowned at me. "I'm traumatized here and you're making jokes."

"Matt." My father opened his arms wide and wrapped them around both of us in one large bear hug. "It's good to see you, son. How's my favorite defender of the little guy doing?"

"Couldn't be better." My boyfriend wheezed, the air knocked out of him by my father's punishing grip. Caught between two men who were both over six feet tall, my toes scraped the ground and my ankles were going numb. "But your daughter is starting to turn purple."

"Crap, sorry." Dad dropped both of us and ran one tanned, well-muscled hand through his black hair, his emerald green eyes twinkling. "I keep forgetting my own strength. This form is very deceptive."

"Yeah," I croaked, leaning over to catch my breath. "Sure it is. Go introduce yourself to my super special houseguest Brenda. Hug her good and tight for me."

"Right," Dad said, patting me on the back before turning to Brenda. I felt Matt's large hand on one shoulder and my mother's smaller one on my other shoulder, and both of them helped me to stand. Mom turned my face toward hers and pushed it first to one side and then to the other, checking my makeup.

"You look gorgeous," she assured me. Her blond corkscrew curls were tousled and her cherry red lipstick was smeared. I spotted a bright red blotch on her neck and tried not to roll my eyes. I couldn't believe my father had given my mother a hickey. Wait a second. I ran my finger along the mark and it smeared. Lipstick transfer. Ugh. That was almost as gross.

"You're dressed a bit more conservative than normal, but it's still lovely. Your brother and Lisa said they'll be here but they're running a bit late. They've got some wedding errands to do. So don't worry, all of us are here for you today." She smoothed her hands over her own flowing black peasant skirt and the gold bangles on her wrist tinkled. Between the bracelets, the poufy white blouse, and with the flaming red scarf she had wrapped around her waist, she looked like a cross between a hippie and one of those carnival fortunetellers. She pulled me into a hug and pressed her cheek against mine.

"Are you feeling okay?" I whispered. Sure, Mom was always sort of *hands-on* with her whole pseudo-Wicca stuff, but she was rarely supportive.

"I feel fine," she said. "You relax and enjoy lunch. Hope texted your father and I about that nasty little angel who's infested your apartment with all of her positive energy. If she tries anything today your father said I could trap her inside of a pentagram of dark crystals and use her power as an additional boost to my spell work. I might even relocate her into Purgatory so I can try some of the more complicated spells I've been working on."

"You're going to hex someone into Purgatory?" I pulled away to look at my mother. "I thought you didn't believe in all of that?"

"Well a girl is allowed to change her mind." Mom sniffed. "And only a stupid woman doesn't learn from her mistakes when they're shoved right in front of her nose. It's rather hard to deny the existence of Heaven and Hell when your new vacation home is sitting on a lake of fire, with naked, sunbathing imps lounging nearby."

"You have a point there." I glanced at Matt, giving him a brief smile. Apparently Mom had decided to be a bit more open minded to the whole *the father of your children is the devil* thing. We'd probably never get her to give up the whole Wicca-Earth Mother bit, but if she quit considering me an abomination against nature, I'd go with it. Hell, I'd even chant if that made her happy.

A ball of blue-black, flaming phase portal flared to life in a shadowed corner of the parking lot, and a leggy redhead in a black leather miniskirt and turquoise blouse appeared. To make it worse, her arms were wrapped around an angel, well into middle age. The angel sported a sagging belly and a light brown mullet coupled with a receding hairline, and he had his hands on her too-perky-to-be-natural ass.

My shoulders slumped and I tried not to groan. Even if I hadn't seen a picture of him on Matt's computer I would have known the guy with a handful of demon ass was Matt's dad, Bassano. All I could do was wonder how in the names of Chaos and Evil had someone that icky fathered the so-hot-he-made-my-bed-smoke angel standing next to me?

"Aw man." I got a better look at the demoness and realized it was my dread demon in drag.

"What? Who?" Mom turned to stare at the vixen sauntering toward us. "Mal? Sweet Goddess of All Things, you look amazing. I mean, you seriously have the ass of an eighteen-year-old. A really hot eighteen-year-old. Not that I'd look or anything but, I just, well wow."

"Your Majesties." Mal bowed, flourishing her hands dramatically in front of her and ignoring my mother's rather clumsy compliment. "You both look lovely. Engagement agrees with you splendidly, my future queen. And may I say I'm anxiously awaiting my role as head of security for your impending nuptials? It will be the second greatest honor of my service, only after being trusted with the care of your darling child."

"Bassano." Dad stuck his hand out, ignoring Mal's obvious ass kissing techniques. "It's wonderful of you to join us."

"I wouldn't have dreamed of missing it." The angel shook Dad's hand without flinching but his eyes stayed focused on Mal and his now pretty much infamous backside. "I'd heard my son had aligned himself to your daughter. I wasn't sure which one it was, though."

Dad wrapped his arm around my shoulders, hauling me forward and against his side. "Bassano, this is my youngest child, Faith. Faith, this is Bassano, a member of your uncle's cherubic choir."

"Enchanted." Bassano turned his eyes back to me and Dad before he leaned forward to kiss my hand, sniffing the inside of my wrist as he brushed his lips across my knuckles.

"Dad." Matt snatched my hand away and stepped in front of me, shielding me from his father's gaze. "Please quit trying to hump my girlfriend's leg. We have a surprise guest joining us. I'm sure you remember Brenda?"

Bassano's attention turned to Brenda, and gave the nephilim a cold stare. "Why am I not surprised to see you here?"

"I-I-I don't know what you mean," she stuttered and took two steps backward, her eyes fixed on the ground, while her shoulders hunched forward protectively. "Aren't you happy to see one of your followers?"

The waves of fear rolled off of her like caramel corn left out too long after Halloween. Something wasn't right, and suddenly Bassano's meeting with Dad seemed a lot more ominous than a quick lunch and a chat about how to behave now that their kids were dating.

"I'm sure you know exactly what I mean since you're so close to the immortal hag I've unfortunately aligned myself with for all eternity. But you, obviously, know what I've come here to warn Louis and his family about. Don't you?"

"I have no idea what you're talking about." She cowered even more. She was almost in a standing version of the fetal position, trembling in fear, and the smell of stale candy was so thick that everyone was clearing their throats. Even Mom shifted uncomfortably, and she normally didn't notice those sorts of subtle emotional shifts since she was still mortal. "I came to talk to you today about finding a place for myself outside of the compound."

"Liar." Bassano glared at her. "We both know better."

Hope stepped in front of Brenda, sheltering her from Bassano's wrath. "Then why don't we go inside and you can explain it to the rest of us? Right now your little intimidation scene is keeping me from a cold beer and, if I have to put up with angels, beer is going to be necessary."

What the Hell? I knew she couldn't do evil but that didn't mean she had to go all momma bear protecting her cub where Brenda was concerned, either. Last I checked my sister didn't even like Brenda.

"What are you up to?" I grabbed her hand and pulled her toward the restaurant, letting the others trail behind us. "Are you trying to cause trouble?"

She pointed to herself. "Can't do evil, remember?"

"Okay, so what gives?"

"Nothing makes me hungrier than a bully." She opened the restaurant's outer door and stepped inside the cool interior of the former vestibule. "And if I can't torture him for days and eat his soul to teach him how it feels to get picked on by someone stronger than you, then it doesn't seem fair to let him get away with it, either."

She nudged my shoulder with hers and pushed open the inner doors, grimacing at the carving of the Crucifixion above it. My father had stepped through the doorway sideways, avoiding the touch of any of the religious carvings, keeping his eyes fixed forward.

A jolt of hellfire raced along my fingertips and I took a deep breath, trying to control my instincts. The brewery was a decommissioned church, without an altar or any of the blessings to protect the grounds from demonkind, but the memories of both still tingled around us. The collective faith of the people who'd built the building acted like a catalyst in the air, forcibly preventing our entrance. Heat radiated from the carvings and I inched away from them, knowing that if my skin even brushed across one of them I would be severely burned.

"Do they bother you?" Brenda asked, a sharp edge to her voice.

"Does what bother me?" I stepped through the door sideways, my back almost resting against the far doorjamb.

"The carvings made depicting the glory of our Faith?" Brenda straightened her shoulders and I could see her mentally rebuilding herself after the dressing down she'd taken from Bassano. As much as she annoyed me, I had to give the nephilim in front of me props—she was a lot tougher than she looked.

"I'm not real fond of the Crucifixion, but it's not like you can blame me. Who wants to look at pictures of their only cousin being tortured?" I tried to sound flippant but I could hear the tension in my voice. If this place didn't have the best pierogies and beer in town I wouldn't set foot inside. But when it came right down to it, my stomach always prevailed over my common sense. Not that I'd tell her that.

"It's a sign of the glory and the power of the Heavenly Order. It is a marker to show us that we are on the right path to destroying your kind and bringing a new age of wonder and righteousness to Man, ruling them with the authority of the right." Brenda glanced back to make sure that Bassano wasn't paying attention to us and then let her eyes glow, doing her best to taunt me. Which would have been sort of pathetic if she didn't already have me completely on edge.

Hope sucked in a breath behind me, and my skin started to crackle. I tended to leave people to their beliefs and I never—

ever—got into a religious debate because, come on, the ways of the Celestial world aren't exactly a mystery to me. But the Crucifixion was something we were all a little sensitive about. Especially J. He didn't talk about it and we didn't ask. No one mentions the fact that he disappears on Ash Wednesday and shows up looking worse for wear on the Monday after Easter. If anyone's got the right to some mental health time he might be top of the list.

It was also the one sore spot in our family when it came to the holidays. To be fair, the Alpha hadn't ever intended for J to spend time in this plane. Before J became fascinated with mortals, we didn't mix. Well, *they* didn't mix. I hadn't even been alive yet. And I wouldn't have ever been a thought in anyone's lust-fueled brain if the no mixing policy had stayed in effect. That's not the point, though. The point is, J got intrigued, convinced Tolliver to get involved, and the two of them came to Earth, got into a bit of trouble, and that's where the family fight started. Because the Alpha is always hands-off, with our love lives and everything else. Including living symbols of mortal faith on a hilltop near Golgotha.

I glowered at Brenda and narrowed my eyes. "You think that carving is a depiction of a good thing? Something that should be celebrated? How about we get your brother Tony here and let you guys have a real live, breathing, screaming symbol to follow for a while instead? You'll only have about three days to get your rebellion going, but who knows? He could hold out longer. What do you say? Want to turn *your* big brother into a living symbol of your faith?"

Her face went white and her eyes widened as she stepped away from me. "I think…"

"Go away," Hope snapped, her sympathy for the other woman gone in an instant. Instead of waiting for Brenda to answer her, she stepped around me, slamming her shoulder against Brenda's so hard the other woman stumbled across the vestibule. She stalked up to where Matt was talking to the host and tapped him on the shoulder. "Have you gotten us a table or not? Some of us have places to be after this."

"They're getting a couple of the bigger tables put together now." Matt looked at me and raised his eyebrows. Apparently the sensitive-caring-woman's rights crusader was gone and my bitchy big sister was back. I'd have sighed in relief, but even though she couldn't do evil she still scared the imps out of me.

"I've got them set up," a young man in black said, his voice cracking as Hope turned her best satanic glare on him. He grabbed a stack of menus and tried to smile at us; his lips were wavering at the edges, and I could see that his jaw was trembling as he tried not to cry at the sight of the pissed off demoness in front of him. "If you'd all like to follow me I can seat you now."

"Wonderful." Matt came back to stand beside me, and wrapped his arm around my waist. He pulled me to the front of the group and we followed the host down what had once been the main aisle, toward the decommissioned altar, and let him lead us to a large, heavily carved cherry wood table as the smell of incense and food wafted around us.

My father took a spot at the head of the table and Bassano at the foot. Dad motioned for me to sit on his right and my mother took the spot on his left. Matt sat beside me and Hope slid into the chair next to him, shooting Brenda a triumphant grin when she beat the other woman to the spot. Instead of rising to the bait, Brenda walked to the other side of the table and sat beside my mother, across the table from Matt.

"Can I get you anything? Some beers to start with?" The

scrawny host tugged at on the blond hair curling behind his ear and shifted back and forth on his feet like he'd rather be anywhere but here, dealing with us. Not that I blamed him.

"We'll need six Pious Monk beers, pint-sized if you don't mind, and a glass of water." Dad smiled at Matt. "My daughter's boyfriend doesn't like to drink at lunch."

"Actually..." Matt cleared his throat, and the waiter stopped. "I think today might be an exception to the rule. If I could have a beer, too, I'd appreciate it."

"Right," the young man said. "Seven beers. I'll be right back with them and your waitress should be here soon if you have any questions with the menu."

"I would prefer water," Brenda announced. "I don't believe in drinking demonic spirits."

"Neither do I." My father laughed, obviously thinking she was making a joke. "It makes it hard for them to work later."

Bassano rolled his eyes at Brenda. "Loosen up and have a beer already. Have two, in fact. Who knows, maybe we can get you buzzed enough to remove the stick my *immortal beloved* implanted in your ass. Just think how much better you'll feel afterwards."

"Since you brought your darling consort up..." Dad coughed. "You mentioned during our phone call that there was something that you needed to discuss with me?"

"Oh right." Bassano smoothed back his mullet and winked at me before he reached over to wrap an arm around Mal's shoulders, his hand dropping down to give her breast a quick grope. I felt my stomach lurch and tried not to shudder. Was it possible that Matt was adopted? "I was hoping to have a few more beers before we had this discussion—ease into it if I could, but that's not possible, is it?"

"I doubt it." Dad shook his head in annoyance, acting like he was dealing more with a naughty puppy who kept piddling on the rug rather than an ancient member of the Celestial Choir. "So? What did you do now?"

"I haven't done anything." Bassano held his hands up and gave Dad what I thought was supposed to be one of those hapless *I'm-a-dumb-guy-what-can-you-do?* looks, but instead it just looked like he had gas.

"Have you lost control of a civilization again? What's the problem?" Dad sat back and crossed his arms over his chest.

"Problem?" Bassano gave a forced laugh. "No problem. Unless you consider that I know for a fact Matt's mother Valerie has been in contact with a certain young lady sitting at our table."

"What?" Matt bolted upright and gaped first at his father and then at Brenda. "What does he mean, you've been talking to Mom?"

"Honey." I tugged on the back of his shirt, trying to get him to sit down. "You're going to make a scene for the mortals. You don't want that, do you? You know how difficult it is to keep them calm when people's wings come out."

He took a deep breath and sank back into his seat. He grimaced at Brenda, and I could smell furious waves of burnt vanilla and gym socks rolling off of him. "How could you?"

"I didn't know what else to do." Brenda leaned over the table, clutching at his hand and kissing the back of it like he was some long lost prince returned home from the wars. He jerked back and I couldn't help smiling at his revulsion. She might have a thing for my boyfriend, but after this there was no way he was going to want anything to do with her. "I saw the path that you were going down and I just became so frightened. What was I supposed to do? Especially when the demon decided to exert her influence and force me out of your life? I knew she meant to do you harm. I called your mother to protect you."

"Delusional," Bassano sang, his voice cracking on the last syllable.

"Dad. That isn't helping right now." Matt turned back to Brenda. "What we need to do is figure out how you're going to persuade Mother not to come here. Or, if that doesn't work, how long I have until she shows up to ruin my life."

"Good luck," Bassano scoffed. "She knew I was coming today and I hear she bullied my secretary Hester into telling her where we were meeting for lunch. I'm actually surprised that she hasn't arrived yet."

"What?" Matt looked between Brenda and his father before he dropped his head against the seat and banged it lightly against the carving on the chair's high back. "Oh God."

"Was totally out of the loop on this one." Bassano shrugged. "Besides, you think your mother's going to listen to him? They haven't had a civil conversation in *years*."

The front door to the restaurant flew open and crashed as it slammed against the side of the building. Everyone in the place looked up at the sound and a woman, engulfed in a brilliant golden light, stalked toward our table, her fists clenched. One look at the set of her shoulders and I could tell she was Matt's mom. He definitely hadn't learned his pissed off look from Bassano.

"And speaking of the bane of my existence…" Bassano gave his son an apologetic grimace. "She's right on time."

Chapter Ten

"Oh God damn it." Matt slammed his fist against the table hard enough that it shook, then turned to glare at the woman barreling toward us like a freight train. "Fuck. My. Life."

That made two of us.

Apparently I was going to meet both of his parents today. And this, this right here, was why I'd given up the whole marriage concept. There was no way that making my friends and coworkers suffer through the funky chicken dance while I pranced around in a fluffy dress was worth how awkward this meeting was going to be. Not even videotaping the whole thing for prosperity was worth this.

Bassano turned to face the woman and stood, opening his arms toward her. "Valerie, how are you? Still ruling everyone else with an iron fist and making other people long for death rather than being forced to spend more time in your presence?"

Wow, I thought my parents had been vicious during their various separations. Apparently the Devil hadn't cornered the market on bitter and antagonistic divorces.

"I would be better if your son hadn't inherited your love of cheap floozies." The woman put one of her hands on the table so she had her back to us, and was staring down the angel at the end of our table before her gaze flicked over to Mal. "Something I see has obviously not changed. At least he never picked up your love of leather pants. I guess I have that to be grateful for."

"Trust me." Mal sniffed at Valerie in dismissal before she held her right hand out like she was inspecting her manicure. "The last thing I am is cheap. You wouldn't believe how much of your money Bassano has already spent in just the past hour alone to keep me happy."

"I wasn't talking about you," Valerie snapped. "I was talking the devil's youngest brat sucking my son's bank account dry. I couldn't care less about what you decide to do to the fool sitting beside you."

"Hey! Did you just call my daughter a gold digger?" My mother shot out of her seat and lunged across the table. Thinking quick, Dad rose and grabbed her around the waist, lifting her into the air, even though her arms kept swinging in an attempt to get at Valerie.

Valerie turned to look at my mother and crossed her arms. "If the wings fit…" She gave Mom the once over and lifted her upper lip in a sneer. "Obviously it's an inherited trait."

Bassano stood and wrapped his arm around Valerie's shoulder, then clamped his hand over her mouth. "I apologize. I've tried to teach her manners, but what can you do? A child raised by wolves only has so much of a chance at refinement."

Valerie growled, her eyes flashing fire, and Matt dropped his head into his hands, shaking it back and forth. Waves of anger, remorse, and—strangely enough—shame, rolled off of him.

"What was that, dear?" Bassano sat in his chair and pulled her roughly into the free one next to him. "Remember, we're in public. No more craziness or the normal people might start to think it's more than a weird weather phenomenon that blew the door open. As it is we're going to have to think they're stupid enough to believe your Heavenly glow was just a trick of the light."

Her shoulders tensed and I watched as he tightened his grip on her mouth, making her eyes bug slightly.

"Besides," he continued. "You know what happens when you cause problems where the mortals can see it. I have to banish you to the Grey Lands and take another wife to fill your space while you're gone."

Malachi giggled and leaned over to kiss the cherub on the cheek before winking at Valerie. "Oh, Bass, surely that's not necessary. You can always give her to me for a few decades. I can teach her how to behave. Or beat her into submission. Repeatedly."

Valerie's eyes bulged even farther and she struggle slightly against Bassano's hand like she wanted to say something and couldn't.

"What do you say, Val?" Malachi smirked at her. "We could be roomies. Think about all the time the two of us can spend together. Gossiping, painting each other's nails, having pillow fights."

Val's eyes widened even further; she started to really struggle against Bassano's hands, trying anything to get away. Bassano clamped his hand down tighter over her mouth. She let out an undignified yelp.

"We could even, you know…" Mal's voice was flat. "Reminisce. Chat about the good old days."

"You two know each other?" I turned to my dread demon and raised my eyebrows.

"We've met in passing." Malachi narrowed his eyes at Valerie. "Nothing more. Right, Val?"

Matt's mom gulped and I knew there was more to the story than what Malachi was telling me. Immediately I started thinking about the best way to bribe the dread demon into spilling the imps and telling me what had happened.

"Mom?" Matt looked at Valerie, her mouth still covered by Bassano's hand. "How do you know Faith's bodyguard?"

Bassano took his hand off Valerie's mouth and gave her a pointed look. "That is a good question. How do you know the former head of Louis's Legions?"

"Passing acquaintance," Dad cut in. His poker face was in place and I knew there was no way anyone was going to get the gossip from him. I looked over at Hope and she raised her eyebrows before glancing at Malachi. Which was pretty much her way of letting me know that she agreed with my earlier assessment—we were going to have to bribe the dread demon with something good to find out what sort of dirt he had on Matt's mom. Unless… I glanced over at Brenda and saw that she looked as mystified as the rest of us. Damn, so much for torturing it out of her.

"Whatever." Bassano sniffed and turned back to Valerie. "Now you, why are you here?"

"I am trying to fix a problem you refuse to acknowledge. A serious problem. Our son is—"

"Valerie, our son is old enough to live his life and date whomever he sees fit. Or marry whom he sees fit. He doesn't like the girl you've chosen. Give it up and let him marry whoever he wants."

"Yeah, Val." Malachi leaned in close to Bassano so that she was almost nose to nose with his wife as well. "Let him marry

Faith."

"We're not getting married." My heart pounded erratically at the mere mention of the "m" word. "We aren't even living together. I mean he's asked but I didn't think we were ready to take that step yet."

"Matt asked you to move in with him?" Mom asked, her eyes glittering, an excited smile blooming across her face.

The waiter returned with our beers and looked at Valerie, annoyed to be short one beer, but not sure whether he'd miscounted or someone had shown up at our table after he'd already taken our drink order. I, meanwhile, ignored my mother's question, and gave the waiter my order. Once he'd left the table again, I took a sip of my beer and hoped she'd let the conversation drop.

"You asked a demon to move in with you?" Valerie asked, her eyes wide. "What were you thinking?"

"She's a better cook than he is?" Mom shrugged. "I mean I almost starved when she went to college. If it wouldn't have been for TV dinners I'd have been a goner."

"That sex on tap is always better than having to put your pants on and walk across the hall for it?" Mal suggested.

"Matt asked you to move in?" Lisa stopped in front of the table, holding Tolliver's hand, and completely ignoring everyone else. She pushed him into the seat between Valerie and Brenda and then plopped down in his lap.

"Let's get back to the real issue." My stepbrother pushed a lock of long black hair back behind his ear and focused his dark gaze on mine. "Why did you say no? You move in and we could take over the bigger apartment. As it is we're living in a shoebox and you've both got half a floor to yourselves."

"Hey," Hope snapped. "If anyone gets Faith's apartment when

she decides to shack up with Angel Boy, it's me. I'm the one who's stuck living in an attic."

"I am not moving in with a guy just so you two can fight over my apartment," I said. "Besides, Matt and I are trying to take this slow."

"Yeah." Mal cut in. "Besides, I've got dibs on Faith's place. I'm not sharing with the lovebirds after all. It's bad enough I phased in on their last game of naked Marco Polo. I'm not going to be there 24-7 during the honeymoon stage."

Dad slammed his hand on the table and we all turned to look at him, our mouths hanging open. "Enough with the apartment swapping or I'm going to ground all six of you to Purgatory. Including you, Mal."

"Sorry," Hope grumbled.

"Yeah, sorry our sister's so stingy she can't let me have the better apartment," Tolliver added under his breath. Valerie glanced at him, giving him a quick once over and sneering.

At least Matt's mom and I had one thing in common. Apparently we both thought my brother was in need of a good smiting.

"Good. Now, can we please get back to the situation at hand?" Dad asked.

Mom patted his hand, her touch somehow managing to soothe him. My heart warmed a little to see them back in their "good" place and couldn't help the tiny feeling of hope that was building in my stomach. Who knows? Maybe they'd make it work for longer than six months this time?

"Yes." Bassano focused his attention on Lisa and I saw Valerie narrow her eyes viciously at Mal as Bassano forgot about them both and started to make doe eyes at my future sister-in-law. "Like who is this enchanting creature?"

"Lisa." She held out her left hand to shake his, flashing her engagement ring.

"My fiancée." Tolliver grabbed Lisa's hand, bringing it to his lips before Bassano could touch her.

"Ah, well aren't you a lucky demon?" Bassano smiled at Lisa and ignored my brother.

"Exceptionally." Tolliver's voice was so dry that you could've struck a match against it, and we could all feel the black power he was barely holding in check.

"Personally…" Valerie leaned forward and rested her chin on her upturned hand. "I'm more curious about why Faith didn't want to move in with Matt. Are you having second thoughts, Faith? I know demons have a problem with, oh, what is that word?" She glanced over at my father and then back at me. "Fidelity?"

My mother sucked in a breath and I watched my father grab her arm, trying his best to keep her in her seat.

"I don't know." Mal cut in, leaning closer to Valerie and mimicking her pose. "I'd say that's more common in Matt's family than Faith's. Or don't you remember—"

Val's hand shot out and connected to Malachi's cheek with a sickening crack as everyone stared at the two of them in horror. Oh sweet Alpha protect us, Mal was going to lose his shit and annihilate Matt's mom right here in the restaurant. This was definitely not going to get me on the Angale's Christmas card list.

"Thank you, darling," Mal purred, and Valerie's face went deathly pale. "Perhaps later you can give me another. Just like…" There was a rattle of glasses and Malachi fell silent, smirking at Valerie again before he sat back in his chair.

The waiter came back with a beer and a glass of water and

froze when he saw Lisa and Tolliver sitting at the table. He closed his eyes and took a deep breath, probably trying not to lose it. Not that I blamed him. With as dysfunctional as this group of immortals was, they'd test the patience of a saint. Hell, most the time J skipped our family dinners so he could enjoy his peace and quiet. What's that tell you?

"Valerie." Bassano smiled at Malachi and then ran his finger carefully across the red mark marring her pale cheek. "Shut up. Our son is happy. Quit trying to ruin it for him and by the by—if you ever so much as think about marring Mal's face again I'll personally pluck your wings bald, feather by feather."

"But—"

"Leave your son alone. That's an order." He snapped his fingers underneath her nose and her mouth clamped shut while her eyes bugged.

I looked over at Mom and raised my eyebrows. As someone who'd been bound into silence during a family dinner you'd think she'd be against the practice, but it looked like some things beat out female solidarity. She laced her fingers through my father's and kissed him on the cheek before smiling at Valerie in a brief show of spite.

"So, what did you boys have planned for today?" Mom glanced first at Dad and then at Bassano, her eyes twinkling. "I'm sure you weren't getting together for some little meeting without planning to do something together. Besides, Valerie and Brenda will want to catch up and the girls and I have some wedding arrangements to work out. How about you guys go out for a game of golf?"

"Can't." Tolliver shrugged. "I have a thing."

"A thing?" Lisa turned to look at her fiancé. "You have a thing that's keeping you from playing golf? Really? What?"

"Nothing important." Tolliver swallowed. "Just a thing."

"Something he's helping me with," Matt added quickly. Why in the name of Evil and Chaos would Matt ask *Tolliver* for help? "For work."

Matt squeezed my hand and widened his eyes, a bolt of calm reassurance shooting from his hand to mine. I felt a solid jolt of *don't ask* running through the link between us.

"Right," I agreed. "That thing you were telling me about with work."

"Well whatever this mystery thing is, if Tolliver doesn't join us we're short a fourth player," Bassano said. "But I could be up for a stroll around the golf course."

"I bet Harold would love to go," Mal said. "You could make him corporeal, Your Majesty, so no one would question his presence."

"Harold?" Bassano asked.

"My ghost." I grinned at Malachi for thinking of a way to cheer up my currently depressed poltergeist. "He's having a rough time of it right now. A game of golf might do him some good."

"Wait, you have a ghost to do your bidding?" Bassano asked.

Dad ignored Bassano's question and focused on me. "What's wrong with Harold?"

"They found his body," I said.

"Ouch." Dad winced and then nodded. "I think a round of golf might be the answer. What do you two white wingers say?"

"The Devil and a depressed ghost?" Bassano looked over at Matt. "Shouldn't be too much effort on our part. How do you feel about a little wager?"

"I live for them." My father rubbed his hands together.

"You," Bassano turned to stare at Matt's mom, "will find a way to bond with your son's new girlfriend. You will be nice. You will be polite. And at the end of the day the girl will be ecstatic at the idea of becoming a member of this family. Or I will hand you over to Mal and make you do the demon's bidding for the next century."

"You wouldn't dare." Valerie hissed.

"Dad, I don't think that's a very good—" Matt was cut off when Bassano waved his hand at him.

"We made a deal," Bassano said. "You kept quiet about my courting my last two wives and didn't tell your mother until I decided to announce my engagement. In return I promised you a life free of the Angale and your mother's interfering. I couldn't keep her away but I can make sure she doesn't complicate your life now that she's here."

"I have duties to attend to in managing your flock," Valerie said. "I don't have time to bond with a demoness. No matter how much my son is infatuated with her."

"Are you sure about that?" Bassano asked. You could have heard a feather drop at our table.

"Positive."

"Fine, I Bassano, Cherub of the Celestial Order, repudiate you, Valerie Andrews. You are no longer my wife. You no longer have a place in my heart or my home. Your presence is no longer welcome amongst my tribe—"

"Wait." She reached out to cling to his upper arm.

"Wait?"

"I'll reschedule some things," Valerie said, her shoulders slumping in defeat. "If it is that important to you I can juggle my other responsibilities."

"That's not necessary." I tried to smile, even though I'm pretty sure it ended up coming out more like a grimace.

"Why are you willing to accommodate me?" Bassano raised an eyebrow at Valerie, both of them ignoring my protests that Valerie and I really didn't need to bond.

Valerie swallowed. "Why?"

"Say it," Bassano said.

"Because you're right," Valerie said, the pent up rage in her voice evident. "I need to be nice to your son's love interest. No matter how short of a time they may be together. I'll devote the rest of my day to getting to know her better."

Hope was right—this guy was a bully. If it weren't for the fact that Matt said they were evenly matched I might have felt sorry for her.

"You know that's not such a good idea." I tried to throw her a lifeline. Sure, she was a bitch and I was pretty sure she hated me, but that didn't mean I wanted her to be miserable. She was the woman who gave birth to Matt, and for that reason, if nothing else, I wanted to make sure she was at least somewhat happy. "I have plans to go for a bridesmaid's dress fitting after lunch. I'm sure it will be boring and I would hate to put you through that. Hell, I don't want to go through that. So, maybe we should get together the next time you come to town?"

"Or you could come with us?" Mom asked, her baby blue eyes sparkling. It didn't take a mind reader to tell that she wanted the other woman to come so she could needle her. "I'd love to have someone else's opinions on the dresses we chose. You and Brenda could both come if you like. We'll do the dress fitting and then all go get our nails done. How does that sound?"

"Mom." I tried my best to keep my voice light. The last thing I wanted was to spend the afternoon with Valerie, Brenda, and a room full of hideous taffeta. After all, it was bad enough to go dress shopping with Mom. "Are you sure that's such a good idea? You've been keeping these dresses under wraps for weeks. Aren't you worried that it might leak what we're all wearing?"

I looked over at Valerie and tried to keep my tone convincing, hoping the old dragon would just play along. "Not that I think you'd go blabbing about things, but Mom's so secretive she wouldn't even let her bridesmaids see the dresses before now."

"Oh well." She rolled her eyes at me and I could tell that she was going to play along. "Bridesmaids' dresses are a big deal. A mother-daughter bonding moment. I'd hate to intrude."

"So why don't we do lunch tomorrow?" I grinned at her and we both knew that was never going to happen.

"Sounds perfect," Valerie agreed.

I smiled at her, then sprung my clever trap. "And today, while I'm with Mom, you and Brenda can pack all her stuff up and move it from my apartment to wherever the two of you are going to be staying here in Pittsburgh."

"I think that's an excellent idea." Valerie smiled back.

Fear niggled at the base of my spine, causing my tail to itch. Why did I have that sinking feeling that when I got home Brenda was going to have raided all my candy stashes?

Chapter Eleven

"Mirror, mirror, on the wall," I muttered to myself as I stared at my reflection in the mirror and mourned the loss of good taste in wedding apparel. "Who's the worst dressed demoness of all?"

Could my mother have picked anything uglier? Pink was bad enough but taffeta and hoop skirts? I wasn't expecting miracles or Donna Karan or anything, because let's be serious, nobody looks good in a bridesmaid's dress from a place called Kate's House of Brides, but this might be the worst dress in the entire building. Possibly the entire state.

"Have you put the hat on yet? Mom called out. "The hat really completes the look that we're trying to go for."

I snatched up the hideous white straw sunhat by the pastel pink ribbons trailing off the back of it and jammed it on my head, my eyes flaring at my reflection like two tiny red torches of pissed off. Between the hat, the ruffles on the off-the-shoulder bodice, and the tiered hoopskirt, I looked like a throwback from a bad seventies wedding. Oh yeah, I was riding that retro wave.

"Are you three done yet?" There was a pounding on my

dressing room door and I knew that Mom was getting impatient to see the hot mess of ugly she'd managed to put together for her bridesmaids. "I'm dying to see how beautiful you look."

"No," Hope said, the frustration clear in her voice.

"Not even close," Lisa added.

"But you've been in there for ten minutes. Surely you girls have your dresses on by now?"

"Maybe you could send some tequila in to help speed it along," Lisa suggested. "Because right now I could really use a drink."

"There's been a mistake," Hope said. "Our dresses were switched with some other, horribly tacky wedding's dresses. Antje needs to go find the right ones immediately."

Wow, Antje the wedding planner extraordinaire would have steam coming out of her ears at hearing Hope try to give orders. All of us, except for Mom, had suspected she might actually be a demonic wedding planner. But she scared Dad, so that meant being a demon was out. Antje was just a psychopath with a fixation on flowers and proper seating arrangements.

"There's been no mistake," Antje said in her clipped German accent. "Those are the dresses your mother and I have chosen to complement the storyline of her wedding. Now, out you come, and let us see what alterations need to be made."

"On three?" Lisa said from the dressing room on my other side.

I looked at the god-awful gown and closed my eyes, sighing. My mother had done a lot of things to torture me, but this might be the worst. I mean really, how hard is it to find a bridesmaid's dress that doesn't suck? "Can we try three hundred?"

"No," Antje said. "Out you come on three. One…two…"

Alpha help me they better make this attempt at marriage last because this was the last time I was going to be one of my mother's bridesmaids. Three times was two times too many as far as I was concerned. *At least this groom wasn't going to be naked for half the ceremony as he communed with nature*, I reminded myself. I turned and grabbed the door handle.

"…three."

"Don't you girls look stunning?" Mom clapped her hands like an overexcited toddler. "Look at all of you. You're just…visions."

"Yeah, visions of the ghosts of Tacky Weddings Dead and Gone," Hope said.

I snorted, trying to mask my laughter.

"They aren't *that* bad." Lisa plucked at the fabric of the skirt, wrinkling her nose. "They're just a little more *retro* than you're used to, Hope."

"There's a reason this fashion trend died and hasn't made a comeback." I gave Lisa's yellow confection the once over. The dress itself hung better on her than it did me, but then again everything hangs better on a tall, skinny succubus than it does on a shorter, curvier demon like me. But nothing took away from the margarine color. Her tanned, olive skin seemed ashy and washed out next to that much pastel sateen fabric.

"Yeah, the reason this fashion trend hasn't come back is that it sucks." Hope looked down at her mint green version and shook her head. The hat cast shadows over her face and made the lines around her eyes stand out.

"You look lovely." Our bride-to-be popped one of the complimentary brownie bites they'd left as a snack into her mouth. "Very summery. You just radiate feelings of 'Garden Romance by Twilight.'"

"What are you spouting now?" Hope asked, hands on her

hips. She hadn't been part of the conversation in mine and Lisa's apartment last week about the themes Mom and the wedding planner had worked through before settling on Garden Romance by Twilight. All of the wedding planning they were doing made me want to gouge my eyes out and swear off marriage forever, but the whole garden idea was by far the best idea for a theme they had. For $100,000, Antje wasn't exactly a risk taker in her planning abilities.

"That's your mother and father's nuptial theme." Antje held her hands in front of her, palms up, before she flourished them dramatically. "We're going for a story line of Everlasting Love inside a romantic twilight garden and you three will be our fairies of matrimonial bliss in a fairytale entitled Love in the Garden."

"Mom, have you ran this whole thing by Dad?" I looked at my sister, then my soon-to-be sister-in-law. "He's not really a garden person."

"We'll provide him with antihistamines." Antje gave me a tight smile.

"I don't think that's going to help," I said.

Lisa's shoulders were trembling, and Hope was looking at the ceiling, probably so she didn't lose it. All it would take is one spark, and we'd all be in hysterics.

"I'm sure he'll be fine." Antje looked at the three of like she was the Mother Superior of an order of wedding planning nuns and we were her unruly novices. "Now if you could let the shop attendants look over your dresses and determine what alterations need to be made instead of taking up mine and the bride's valuable planning time…"

"Dad really sort of has this thing about gardens." I tried to make her see reason without actually making her see *the reason* it would be such a bad idea. I really didn't want to think about how Mom would react to bringing up memories of Dad's former consort and their relationship. "So you might want to change the theme."

"The theme stands," Antje said. "Now moving on to the dresses."

"You need a new storyline," I said. "First of all, this one sucks."

"I think you'll find—" Antje pushed up from her chair and stalked toward me.

"I think *you'll* find that it might be better to allow my sister and I to choose our own dresses, and you can tailor *your* storyline to fit." I let my horns curl upward. My eyes flashed red and Antje's widened in shock. "Since this storyline is a bad idea to begin with. My father has already had one wedding in a garden. Maybe you've heard of it? Eden? Demoness named Lilith? Their pet snake was present. They served apples."

"I—" Antje backed away slowly and swallowed. "I think perhaps you'll be better served by a wedding planner of a different caliber, Ms. Bettincourt. No worries of course, our firm will reimburse all of your fees. In fact, I'll just go ahead and write you a personal check right now."

"But Antje." My mother looked at the wedding planner, her eyes pleading. "What will I do without you? You are the glue that holds this event together. Without you I have nowhere to even begin."

"Try Wenslow & Wapperly, they take on all the alternative wedding planning in Pittsburgh." Antje reached into her red leather purse—rather cute for a Chloe, actually, and completely unexpected given Antje's personality—and tossed a brown wallet at my mother. "Here, take it. No hard feelings. Just, I'm going to go. Now. If you don't mind."

She turned on her high-heeled boot and tried to scurry out of the room, catching her foot on the carpeted runner on the entryway stairs, and stumbled. She bounced against the glass door and didn't even stop.

"Well." Mom sighed. "That wasn't what I had hoped would come of today's shopping trip. Really, Faith, what were you thinking?"

I tugged at the ribbons holding on my overly large plantation style sun hat and threw the monstrosity down into the chair Antje had been sitting in. "I think I'm tired, and stressed out, and I have way too much going on. And most important, I think these dresses suck like a hardcore vampire on a three day hunger strike and offered a sacrificial virgin."

"I think they're absolutely lovely." My mother tried to make her tone pleasant but it was easy to see she was pissed off. Then again, so was I. It had been three weeks of nonstop wedding talk, wedding planning, wedding strategizing, and I for one was more than a little tired. "But if you're going to make a scene like you used to do when you were two then I guess I'll just have to handle all the details on my own time. I'm not going to make you stay here and behave civilly. Even though this is the most important day of my life."

"That right there is why I never intend to get married." I turned back to my dressing room. "Because it turns women into complete idiots."

"Faith!" Mom sounded stunned.

"What?" I turned around to look at her. "It does. Just look at yourself. You have two grown daughters. You went to college as a single mom. None of us have spent more than a night in jail, and considering our special circumstances, that's pretty amazing.

After all of that, you want to look me in the eye and say that the most important day of your life involves a game of dress up and a catered dinner? Really?"

"If you'd ever gotten married you'd— "

"Mom!" Hope grabbed my shoulder and pushed me toward the dressing room while she turned to stare down the pain of our combined existence.

"But I'm just trying to— "

"Go finish up with the bridal shop people." Hope growled as I closed the door between us and tried not to let my mother get the better of me. Leaning back against the mirror, I took a deep breath and beat my head against the glass, trying to keep myself distracted by the dull pain so that I wouldn't cry.

"I was only explaining that if Faith— "

"Mom!" Hope yelled. "Go deal with your shit. Now."

"Faith?" Lisa asked a second later. "Are you okay in there?"

"Yeah." I sniffled and tried to keep myself from losing it at the thought of the wedding I had missed. I tried not to dwell on it, but remembering my own dress, and the groom who was supposed to have been waiting for me that day, made that tiny spot just below my heart burn like an imp was trying to roast my internal organs for dinner.

"It's Mom." Hope pounded her fist against the door once. "Don't let her get to you."

"I won't." I swallowed and stepped away from the mirror. I reached behind me and started tugging at the dress's zipper.

"Let's just get changed and get out of here," Hope suggested. "I'm feeling the urge to go mess with someone's head."

"Can you still do that?" Lisa asked, her voice further away than before. "I mean now that, well *you know*."

"First rule of demonhood, DeMarcos," my sister retorted. "The power just amplifies the natural talent. Not vice versa. Even now I'm still the most evil bitch on the block. Given my lack of powers I've just had to become more creative about it."

I chuckled and shook my head as I heaped the dress in the corner of the dressing room and grabbed my own clothes. Leave it to Hope to be a glass is half full kind of girl. At least when it came to doing evil.

"Ma'am," a perky voice said from the other side of the door. "Are you sure that you and your bridesmaids are finished? They've barely had time to try their dresses on. Don't you want to have some last minute alterations done?"

"The dresses each girl had were perfect. They fit wonderfully. Everything is perfect. If you could just arrange for everything to be sent to La Pomponee Spa by three p.m. on Saturday then we'll be set. Is that going to be an issue?" Mom's voice was muffled and I heard her gulp. "Oh, and do you mind if I take another plate of these brownie bites to go? They are absolutely delicious."

"Of course not, ma'am." The young woman sounded confused. I slipped my shoes on and I came out of the dressing room to see her looking at Mom, obviously perplexed at her sudden decision to bail on her girly day of wedding delight. The girl smoothed her long auburn ponytail as she looked first at the clipboard in her hand and then back at Mom. "There's some paperwork we'll need you to fill out, and we'll make all the arrangements."

"I'll be back to do the paperwork." Mom patted the girl on the hand. "My younger daughter is…"

"Hypoglycemic," Hope said, stepping out of her dressing room and putting herself between Mom and the perky attendant. "And she hasn't eaten yet. Very bad situation. She could go into a coma and die right here in your store. Think about the news coverage. Not to mention ruining our parents' wedding."

"Oh." The girl's eyes widened. "That does sound serious. You know what? Why don't I just go ahead and fill out all the paperwork for you? We've got your information from the wedding dress papers and I can just copy all the information for your bridesmaids over. I'll call you when it's done."

"Perfect." Hope leaned forward and pretended to peer at the girl's name tag. "Tiffany. You're just an absolute peach."

"Well." The girl smiled at Hope and fluttered her eyelashes. "Anything for a customer."

"Scrounge up better snacks next time," I called out over my shoulder as I stomped toward the door.

"Down, girl. She was just being helpful." Hope followed me out of the store with everyone else hot on her heels. Not that I cared too much.

"Here." Lisa grabbed a Milky Way Dark bar out of her purse and handed me an emergency ration of chocolate.

I knew there was a reason I loved her. I peeled back the wrapper and sniffed the candy bar, letting my toes curl in anticipation.

"Are you better now?" Hope asked.

"It depends." I took a greedy bite of chocolate. "Are we still going to have to wear those awful dresses?"

"I don't see what your problem is with the dresses. Not that it matters, because they're already paid for and I'm not buying new dresses because you're being picky," Mom huffed.

"Then no, I'm not better." I scarfed down the rest of the snack in two bites. "Lisa and I both have to work tonight and, to make matters worse, tomorrow morning I have to spend part of my morning with the guy I didn't marry. Plus Brenda is still here, and who knows if I'm going to get rid of her now? Bassano could decide to keep her here in Pittsburgh and I don't know what with her. And Matt's mother has shown up and if you haven't noticed she doesn't like me very much. So no, better is not the word I'd use to describe me right now."

"Wait." Hope held a hand up in front of my face. "Dan's in Pittsburgh? Does Matt know?"

"Not yet." I sighed.

"Oh my goddess." Mom gasped. "You're seeing someone else behind Matt's back? Faith, how could you?"

"I'm not having an affair on Matt," I yelled, and then froze as everybody in the parking lot and standing on the sidewalk in front of the various shops in the strip mall all turned to look at me.

"Dan works for MEDTECH." I lowered my voice. "They sent him to the hospital to do some work on our security systems. Not that it really matters, since he doesn't remember me."

"At all?" Hope looked at me, her eyes filled with pity, and I felt my stomach plummet. How pathetic had I become that even *Hope* felt sorry for me?

"Why haven't you told Matt?" Mom asked. "I mean you can't keep this a secret from him. Trust me, I've tried to keep the men in my life from your father at times and it always ends badly. Always."

"I'm not trying to keep it from him." I rubbed my face, suddenly much too tired to deal with all of this. "But with everything going on right now there just hasn't been a good time to tell him. Between Brenda, and the weddings, and I've been working double shifts and twelve hour shifts and—"

"About those twelve hour shifts..." Lisa shrugged when we rounded the corner of the bridal shop and started toward the shaded area where I parked my Civic. "I've got one tonight and

I want to spend some time with Tolliver before I go in. So if you don't mind me bailing on you guys…"

"You don't need to ask my permission." I waved my hand at her. "Go forth and get your demon nookie on."

"More like argue over wedding locations again." Lisa popped out of sight without bothering to open a phase portal, leaving nothing behind but a faint whiff of brimstone. She'd gotten a lot better at controlling her powers since the engagement and I knew Tolliver's mom, Lilith, had been helping her get the hang of things. Lisa had even become somewhat comfortable in Hell. She still wouldn't leave Dad's villa except to phase, but hey, at least she was going there willingly now.

"So what are we going to do now?" Mom asked. "Oh, I know, you can help me finish the wedding favors. I'm still terribly behind on those. Or we could even discuss the surprise 'Welcome Home' party you're hosting for me after your father and I get back from Hawaii. I've been thinking about all the things I want."

"Lisa and Tolliver are both off the mortal plane and out of my apartment." I unlocked the car. "I am going home, changing into my jammies, and then I'm taking a nap. No calls. No interruptions. Just me and my pillow snuggled up together in sleep's sweet embrace."

"But it's the middle of the day and there are so many things we need to plan. I mean really, neither of you have even started on the hand calligraphied thank you notes for all my wedding presents. Those will need to go out the minute I get back. We don't want Lilith to accuse me of not following proper etiquette."

"Neither of us care," Hope retorted. "You heard Faith—her apartment is empty and I just don't want to bother doing all that other stuff. It sounds boring and so instead I'm going shopping."

"I don't see what the big deal is about having an empty apartment," Mom insisted.

"Do you know what it's like with those two as roommates?" I put my key in the ignition, starting the car.

"Lisa's been your roommate for years," Hope pointed out. "What's the big deal?"

"The big deal is that Tolliver is a screamer. And the walls in our apartment aren't very thick. All night long I have to listen to the two of them going at it."

"So stay at Matt's." Hope pulled on her seatbelt. Now that she could no longer enchant her way out of a ticket my sister had gotten a lot more diligent about the law.

"He's been working late and comes home exhausted. Besides, with Brenda on my couch the past couple of days even my fantasy guys are saying 'Not tonight, dear. I have a headache.'" I looked pointedly at my mother. She stared back defiantly for a moment before huffing and putting on her own seatbelt. The only mortal being in the car, and she's always the one I have to fight with about it. You'd think she would be more careful about those sorts of things.

"Agh." Hope shuddered. "Even that guy from that television show? You know, Hot SyFy Channel Guy, the one with the eyes and that suit he always wears?"

"He shows up in my head and all he wants to do is talk about his feelings. I'm thinking about relegating him to TiVo until I can get my head on straight. " I turned onto Cochran Road and merged into traffic. Mom and Dad had bought a fabulous 1940s stone mansion in the older part of Mount Lebanon that was entirely too big for the two of them, but was absolutely amazing. Or it would have been if they hadn't turned their pool house into a portal to Dad's realm. I mean, really? Nine bedrooms, a study, a media room, two gyms, and a heated garret over the garage, and they turned the *pool house* into the portal?

The phone started singing "I'm Too Sexy" and I narrowed my eyes and punched my foot down on the gas pedal in response. Dad never called about good things.

Hope picked it and pressed the Talk button. "Hello?"

I strained my ears and could just make out the sound of Dad on the other end but I couldn't understand what he was saying.

"No, I don't think she'd mind," Hope said suddenly and smiled at me. "I'm sure she'll be fine with it Dad. Okay. See you soon. Bye."

"What?" I asked when she ended the call and put my cell phone back in the cup holder.

"That was Dad. They couldn't get a tee time at the course so they've decided to cheer Harold up with some Wii Bowling."

"Shit," I muttered. There went my nap.

Chapter Twelve

I made it through four hours of Wii Mario Cart and a heated battle of Modern Warfare 3, six come-ons by Bassano, and one very disgusting moment when he put his hand up Malachi's skirt, before I threw everyone out of my apartment. Malachi had planned on staying but Bassano assured everyone that he'd set a protection on my apartment to keep both Valerie and Brenda out so I could get some sleep.

Matt packed Brenda's clothes and they were gone, but not before I overheard Bassano whispering something in Mal's ear about a strip chess game in his hotel room. Dad had offered to stay until my bodyguard got back but I sent him home to Mom. Right now all I wanted was some privacy. Besides, him and Mal were both a phone call and a quick phase between spaces in reality away. I'd be fine. I was cool. I was collected. I was a demoness damn it, and two psychobitch nephilim were not going to get in the way of my nap.

I took a scalding hot shower, groomed my feathers to keep them shiny, and reveled in the quiet of an empty apartment. I sang along with the radio, my tail swinging back in forth with the beat, relaxing for the first time in a month. Brenda was gone, the apartment was empty, and as soon as I finished my nap I was going to make Matt sit down so I could tell him about Dan. Not that my ex had invited me to dinner and seemed unconcerned about me having a boyfriend—I was totally going to edit that part out—but that he was in town and I'd seen him and any feelings I might be having were just regrets about the way the past had played out. The past was just that—the past—and no matter how much I didn't want to say "I love you" and take the chance of jinxing us, I did love Matt and he needed to know that nothing would change that. And I needed to tell him that, as much for me as for him.

My phone buzzed on the vanity. Crap. Why was it every time I got a little bit of quiet time someone had to call? Knowing my luck Harold had been spotted at the hospital. Or even worse, Bassano and Mal had done something to get arrested. An angel with indecent exposure charges—really not something I wanted to contemplate right now.

I used my tail to hit the Power button on the radio and picked up my phone. "Hello?"

"Faith?" Dan asked, sounding agitated.

"Dan?" I tried to piece together why exactly it was so wrong for him to have my phone number and couldn't come up with anything.

"Do you have a minute? I'm not disturbing anything, am I?"

"No, but you do realize that I'm going to be on duty at seven tonight, don't you? I can turn you down for dinner then. You didn't have to call me at home."

"I know you've got to work tonight but I was wondering if we could get together and talk now. Outside of Roger's."

"Look, Dan, you're a nice guy..." I tried to keep my voice pleasant. This new persistence on Dan's part would be hot if I was single. "I've told you before I have a boy—"

"I know who hacked the MEDTECH system," he said. "It wasn't your head of pediatric surgery and I can prove it. But I want to discuss my evidence with you before I go to the police. They might want to talk to you after I'm done."

Shit. Another round with the Pittsburgh Police Department. Just what I needed. Detective Kastellero, who was in charge of the MEDTECH investigation and the still-unsolved case of who planted explosives underneath a car I was meant to be in, hated me. Like, seriously, *I Want to Throw You in Jail and Lose the Key* hated me.

If Dan thought the police could somehow tie this back to me that meant Kastellero would see it as an airtight case. Whatever evidence he thought he had I was going to have to persuade Dan he was mistaken. Or get Malachi to mind warp him so he'd forget the whole thing. I'd do it myself but mind warps were tricky in the best scenario and I'd never heard of anyone going through two of them. Definitely not something for a novice to try. Either way, my relaxing afternoon had just been ruined.

"Repeat that for me?"

"I know who hacked the MEDTECH system and it wasn't someone on the Roger's Hospital Staff. But you know the person who did it."

"I do?"

"Look," he said. "I'm still at the hospital. I'm actually hiding in the stairwell of the parking garage so no one can overhear me. This is huge, Faith. I mean seriously huge. I need someone else to see this before I take it to the police."

He sounded nervous. I knew Dan. No matter what the memory wipe had done to his personality, I knew him. If he said it was serious then it was. He wasn't the type to over exaggerate.

"I'm home by myself," I said. "532 Carson Street. Apartment D. If you can't find parking on the street then we've got a lot behind the building. Do you need directions or can you manage it?"

"I've got GPS," he said.

"So, I'll see you and your conspiracy theory in twenty minutes?"

"I can be there in eighteen." The line went dead.

I put the phone back on my sink and climbed back in the shower to rinse the rest of my conditioner out of my hair. So much for the past being the past. Especially with the way mine kept shoving himself back into my life.

I peeled myself out of my super-comfy *home-by-myself-all-day* pajamas, hurried into my closet, and grabbed a pair of jeans and a long-sleeved, peach tee. I scrambled into my clothes and stopped, looking down at my outfit. Dan had bought this for me. Back before the whole *Losing His Mind* thing. Definitely not appropriate.

I pulled the shirt off and grabbed another one off my pile of clean laundry. Loyola Nursing. Not much better but I didn't have time to go through my entire wardrobe to find something that didn't have a connection to Dan. Given how much I hated clothes shopping there wouldn't be much there besides scrubs that he hadn't seen me in at one point or another in our relationship.

I finished getting dressed and looked down, making sure my black bra didn't show through the light gray fabric. So far so good. I hurried over to the dresser and brushed through my damp curls, trying to tug them back into a ponytail. My horns kept causing bumps, though, and instead of trying to camouflage them, I gave up and let my hair hang down my back instead.

I heard a knock at the door and froze in front of the mirror. Moss green eyes stared back at me and I swallowed, trying to ignore my wings' instinctive pull to unfold. There was no need to panic. Dan didn't know who I was. More importantly, he didn't know *what* I was. I ran a hand through my frizzy blond curls again and took a deep breath.

He didn't suspect. He couldn't suspect.

There was another knock on the door and I let my breath out in a shaky burst. If he didn't suspect something was up already, acting crazy wasn't going to keep him in the dark for long. I needed to seriously get my shit together. Now. Which I could do. I was the Daughter of Satan. I was calm. I was cool. I was a professional.

I hurried into the living room and threw open the front door.

I was so totally fucked.

Dan was standing there in the black leather jacket I'd bought him the first Christmas we'd lived together. Which matched with the motorcycle helmet he had tucked under his arm. The one I'd picked out, fussing that I didn't care what his friends said about helmets being for sissies. There's a reason ERs had a specialized code for motorcycle accidents. We didn't call them brain donors for the hell of it. I wondered how he remembered getting the helmet and his jacket. Another girlfriend, perhaps? Some girl who didn't exist but had replaced me inside his mind?

"Loyola, huh?" he said. "I didn't know we were alumni from the same school. I wonder if we were there at the same time."

"Who knows? Loyola's a big school, lots of people there." I swallowed and clamped my mouth shut to keep from rambling. Way to be cool, Faith. Way to keep it together. "Come on in. Do you want something to drink? Something to eat? I'm not much of a cook but I could manage something."

"Could I get a glass of ice water maybe?"

Instead of answering I hurried into the kitchen, trying to put some space between us. He set his helmet on the table next to my front door and made his way into the living room. I fixed two glasses of ice water, trying to stall for time long enough to compose myself. It was now or never.

"So you said on the phone that you think you might have found something?" I handed him his glass and sat down on the couch.

He took a seat beside me and set the glass on my coffee table. "I've found the guy who hacked the MEDTECH system," he said. "Or should I say the *guys*?"

"Are you sure?" I took a drink of my water, trying to keep my composure. He knew two guys were involved. Matt's brother Levi and my sister's ex-husband Boris. Shit, this was worse than I'd thought. I didn't want to mind wipe Dan again. He didn't deserve that. He'd just gotten his normal life back after his time in a mental hospital. What if the second mind wipe went wrong and he ended up back in an institution?

"Yeah," Dan said, looking down at his hands, "and I've got the proof."

"So how do you know who did it? How did they bring down the MEDTECH system and the security cameras all at once without anyone noticing? You can't be in two places at once."

"They weren't," Dan said. "Well, they were, but not in the sense that you mean."

"So how did they do it?"

"Simple—one of them killed the two systems and the other waited until Bernice was distracted. Then he walked into the medication room and walked back out with your morphine."

"So how do you hack two systems at once?"

"From inside MEDTECH headquarters in Chicago."

"Excuse me?" My stomach dropped. We sat there staring at each other for a few minutes, or more precisely, I stared at Dan and he kept his eyes trained on his hands. If the person responsible had hacked the system from Chicago that meant it hadn't been Levi and Boris. Levi had been here, stalking me, and Boris had been with my sister in Idaho. They hadn't been involved. It also meant I wouldn't have to steal Dan's memories again.

"My boss hacked my system," he said, not looking up. "When I started digging it was logged into the system like routine maintenance on his part, which would have been strange enough because my boss doesn't do system maintenance since he's a manager and not a tech. Then I remembered something he told me just after he got promoted last year and I took over his service area."

"What?" I leaned closer to him, trying to appear sympathetic, but close enough not touch him.

"He told me about this little restaurant down in Washington County. A place called Soloman Brothers. He said every time he came to town on a maintenance call he met his brother there for dinner. He told me it was one of those out of the way places you had to try." Dan tugged at the collar of his shirt.

"I've heard of Soloman Brothers," I said. "But a love of fried catfish doesn't predispose people to being drug traffickers. Heart attack victims, maybe, but not drug traffickers."

"No, but it told me that he had someone here to do the physical stealing when he killed the system back in Chicago. Divide and conquer. It's ingeniously simple." His shoulders slumped forward.

"So one brother broke into the system from Chicago and the other swiped the medication? Once again I have to ask you how? We don't just let anyone on the PICU unit. You can't just wander in and steal medication without someone noticing. Maybe it was a routine maintenance matter and someone else got lucky? I mean it's a sucky coincidence but that could be it." I knew the likelihood that it had been some random stroke of thieves' luck was almost nil.

"That's what I thought, but it kept nagging at me. So I hacked into the MEDTECH human resources system," Dan said. "Not exactly ethical on my part but right then I didn't care. My boss had just finished a six weeks family leave before the break-in. Last week he took leave again."

"So?" I said and leaned back, trying to keep space between us now that he didn't seem on the verge of crying.

"The first leave was to help care for a sick niece. This one is for funeral leave. I dug a bit more and I found his brother listed on the faculty page of the local university in the English department. Except, according to their website, his brother has taken the year off for a sabbatical." Dan sank back against the cushions, crossing his arms. He looked miserable, like his faith in humanity had just died. Which it might have, considering how he'd always respected his boss.

"And the niece?" I asked, connecting the dots on the path he'd laid out for me. Medical care was expensive. Especially in a place like the pediatric intensive care unit.

"Emily Cosgrove."

"I remember her. Nine years old. She had a seizure during a community league soccer game. They found a brain tumor the size of a grapefruit attached to the back of her brain. Due to its placement, it was considered inoperable. ”

He pulled a folded up piece of paper from his inside jacket pocket and I looked down at the little girl staring back at me in the obituary. The picture was so much better than my memories of her. I instantly felt relieved—Harold hadn’t been her physician. He had signed over her care to Dr. Woo since she had a specialty in pediatric oncology. They couldn’t connect Harold to the drugs or the people that may have stolen them. That meant there was no way to connect his death to the stolen drugs. So all those nasty rumors I knew Sally had been spreading would be put to rest and Harold could be remembered as an amazing doctor whose life had been cut short; not as a monster who had stolen pain medications from dying kids.

I studied the picture again and my relief disappeared. If we gave Harold any say in the matter I knew he’d tell us to let it go. Let him take the blame and leave the Cosgroves to mourn in peace. Because, the thing is, he was the type of doctor who’d have willingly given her family the drugs and never said a thing about it if that morphine could have somehow saved her. Which was all the more reason for me to find a way to make sure his memory wasn’t dragged through the mud because of this. Then I’d get on the phone to J and see what could be done for Emily’s family, and her ghost for that matter. He’d know how to make sure she was taken care of properly.

“Yeah.” Dan began picking at his thumbnail, refusing to meet my eyes. “I found that in her medical records. Sounded like it was Hell on Earth for everyone involved.”

“She didn’t go easily and, now that I think about it, Dr. Cosgrove was a pacer. Bernice said he drove her nuts.”

“A pacer?”

"While his daughter was asleep, he'd pace. He could never sit still. He used to go up and down the halls a dozen times, not bothering anyone. Just pacing. A lot of parents are that way. Which means the hallway in PICU becomes a walking track between two and four a.m."

"So he'd pace the halls, and no one would pay him any attention because he did it every night?" Dan took my hand in his. Sharp jolts of human energy, and more than a little longing for the past, coursed through my fingers and I thought about pulling away from him, but the way he held my hand wasn't meant to be romantic. It was a simple need for human connection.

"Every night. Every day. Every time she was having a treatment. I know for a fact he lost at least twenty pounds while she was there. The wife was more withdrawn."

"But I don't understand." Dan took a drink of his water, pulling his hand away from mine. "Why steal morphine? What possessed them to start selling pharmaceutical grade drugs for cash?"

"Hospitals cost money and they had a sick little girl so they were desperate. When people are desperate they do very, very stupid things." I drank from my own water, using the move as an excuse to shift further away from him.

"I guess." Dan grabbed my hand again, clinging to it like I could somehow make this right. Meanwhile all I could think when he tightened his fingers around mine was that if Matt walked in right now there'd be no way to convince him that this wasn't what it looked like.

"But it seems like such a waste," Dan continued. "In the end it didn't do them any good. If there wasn't any hope to begin with…"

"If Emily was on the PICU unit, she was still alive," I said, feeling vulnerable just talking about the harsher realities of my job. “And the one thing I’ve learned, if absolutely nothing else in this line of work, is that where there is life, there’s hope. Any nurse in my position will tell you, you don’t give up fighting until there isn’t any hope left.”

“So you think they did it, hoping that because she hadn’t died yet she might what? Somehow pull through? Do you think they were that— ” Dan pulled our linked hands into his lap and instead of letting him, I pulled away.

“Delusional?” I shifted to the other side of the couch, putting as much room between us as possible. “Absolutely. When you’re dealing with sick kids that’s how you have to be. As long as those kids are alive and still fighting then so is everyone else around them. You don’t for one single second even think about the fact you might not beat death. Once they’ve died you can lose your shit but until they’re dead you keep your head down and you keep doing whatever it takes to keep them alive.”

“Losing your shit? Is that what you call slamming your car into a tree on an empty road? Because right now I call that a tragedy brought to you by the combined forces of cancer and the American health care crisis.” He grabbed another piece of paper out of his jacket pocket and tossed it at me. It was the front page of the *Washington Chronicle*, the local newspaper for Emily Cosgrove’s hometown.

LOCAL COUPLE KILLED IN SINGLE CAR ACCIDENT

Beneath the headline was a picture of the entire Cosgrove family that looked like it had been taken during a family get together, along with a brief article that explained how Dr. and Mrs. Cosgrove’s car had veered off a curvy local road and hit a tree Tuesday. Police believed they might have swerved to avoid a deer in the road. Or at least that was what everyone was agreeing to say.

I shifted on the couch, unable to get comfortable while my heart broke over what the Cosgrove family had gone through. I knew for a fact that we'd reduced the grief counseling staff at Rogers to only two counselors and they were both overworked. Regardless, someone should have seen the warning signs when it came to the Cosgroves. Someone should have cared about how desperate they were. The problem was, as a nurse I didn't have time to help their daughter and take care of them, too.

"What are you going to do?" I grabbed a throw pillow and hugged it to my chest so that I didn't instinctively scoot closer to the man I'd once been in love with.

"I'll go back to Rogers and finish updating your systems. Then I'll gather my documentation and hand it over to the hospital administration and MEDTECH upper management. The rest is up to them." He set the paper down, tapping his fingers against Beth Cosgrove's face.

"So why did you come to me?"

"You seemed like the only other person who would see how much this sucked. The only other person who would care more about these people's death than you would about the fact they broke the law. I don't know why I thought that but—"

He looked up at me through his eyelashes and all I could think about was how vulnerable he was. The Dan I'd known had been a smart guy but he'd always sort of had this naïve belief in the natures of good and evil. He was what Malachi had always called one of those "silver lining idiots." To see that sometimes, in some cases, there just wasn't a silver lining, or a miracle, or someone to save the day had to hurt.

"I do," I said. "I do get it."

Instead of answering, he grabbed the side of my face and

crushed his lips to mine, kissing me like he was looking for some sort of truth that could be found in the pressure of his lips against mine.

Chapter Thirteen

He pushed his tongue into my mouth and I jerked backward, brought my hand back, and smacked him as hard as I could. The crack of my palm against his cheek echoed through the apartment.

"What the hell are you doing?" I jumped off the couch and glowered at him. I knew the guy was suffering from a whole *fallen-mentor-vulnerability-of-life* moment but that didn't mean he needed to invade my personal space and make my resolve weaken to keep things professional between us. Which was a bad thing, not just because of Matt, but because in the end I couldn't be the one to *fix* the pain Dan was feeling. Not without hurting him worse.

"You come over here, tell me that two people with a dead child stole my morphine, then killed themselves, and then you decide that's a good time to make out with me? Are you insane?" I shifted from one foot to another and tried to keep anger coursing through my veins so I could keep being irrational about his moment of weakness and get him out of here for both of our sakes.

"I'm sorry." He stood and ran a shaky hand through his hair. "I shouldn't have done that. I didn't intend to do that. You have a boyfriend and I respect that."

"Yeah, well respect that by keeping your face at least a foot from mine, because your lips haven't gotten the memo."

"I'm sorry."

"So am I. You should leave."

"Right." Dan sighed and nodded. "Sorry again. If the Pittsburgh Police call, trying to get under your skin, or they try to get you to link yourself to this in any way—"

"Why would they do that? There's no connection between me and the Cosgroves."

"True, but when I talked to that guy in charge of the case… what's his name?"

"Detective Kastellero." My heart started to pound and sweat trickled down my spine just at the mention of the guy's name.

"Yeah, Kastellero." Dan rolled his eyes as he said the detective's name. "When I talked to him he seemed all fired up that you had to be a part of this. If he comes to see you get a lawyer, and no matter what he says, there is no evidence connecting you to this break in."

"If he contacts me I'll make sure I take my boyfriend with me to the station." I held my arm out, motioning toward the front door. "Matt's a lawyer, He'll have no problems handling Kastellero."

"Matt the Lawyer. Sounds intimidating." Dan walked to my door.

"He can be, if you piss him off." I grabbed the door handle and pulled it open.

He grabbed his helmet and stuck it under his arm before sticking his hand out for me to shake, not meeting my eyes. "So I'll see you at the training tomorrow?"

"Of course." I shook his hand. "I couldn't think of a better way to spend my day off than sitting in a classroom with fifty other people, discussing computer software. Can you?"

"That sounds like my own personal version of Heaven," Dan said. "And I'm sorry about kissing you. If you tell your boyfriend make sure you put all the blame on me. "

"Don't worry about it." I waved a hand at him in what I hoped looked like a dismissive gesture. "Like I said, he's a good guy…for a cage fighter with homicidal tendencies."

"Good to know. I'd hate to have to hurt him," Dan continued. "Those mixed martial arts guys always get so touchy about things after they get their asses kicked."

"You keep telling yourself that." I stepped forward, crowding him. Sure, he was sweet for trying to stick up for me but I'd dealt with a depressed ghost, several cranky nephilim, the Devil, and my mother today. Testosterone-based posturing was not how I intended to end my afternoon. "I'll see you tomorrow at the training."

"Nine sharp," Dan said.

"What's at nine sharp?" Matt stepped onto the landing and looked between the two of us. Oh shit. Why did I have a feeling that this was going to be a lot harder to explain than I'd first expected?

"Training for work." Dan gave Matt the once over and then shrugged, clearly not believing the part about the mixed martial arts. Which goes to show that no matter how book-smart a man might be sometimes he could be a lousy judge of character. "I'll see you then, Faith."

"Bye." I watched him brush past Matt.

"Coworker?" Matt asked once Dan had disappeared, turning to follow the other man's departure with curious eyes. He raised an eyebrow in my direction.

"MEDTECH software engineer," I corrected. "He's in updating our systems."

Matt watched Dan disappear down the stairs and then leaned against my doorjamb, his face skeptical. "He felt the need to make a house call?"

"He had some information about the MEDTECH incident last month." I twisted my fingers together, silently debating how much I should tell him about the whole situation. Especially considering we were standing in the middle of the hallway. "They've found the culprits."

"Oh." He nodded, slipping immediately into lawyer mode—which was way sexier than it should have been, given the circumstances. "So does he expect us to be talking with Detective Kastellero soon about your nursing staff?"

"He thinks I might have to do a follow up conversation with the Detective but there's no link to the nursing staff so I should be fine. The medication was stolen by one of the patient's families." I leaned against the opposite side of the door and looked at the ground, my stomach still in knots about what had happened a few minutes before.

I should tell him that Dan had kissed me. It was harmless. Okay, it wasn't harmless but it wasn't my fault. That didn't mean I wanted to discuss it right now. Or ever. Because no matter how much it wasn't my fault the fact that I hadn't told Matt about Dan before now made me look like a really crappy girlfriend. It made me feel like one, too. Despite the good intentions I'd had, I hadn't acted on them, and a few minutes ago my ex's tongue had been trying to probe my tonsils.

"Dan plans on finishing his paperwork up tonight and handing everything over tomorrow after the funeral. I figure hospital administration will have it forwarded to the Pittsburgh Police Department by the end of the day." I looked up at him and tried to come up with the best way to tell him the rest without completely destroying his trust in me—in us—at the same time.

The door to Matt's apartment flew open and Brenda and Valerie crowded the doorway, both of them staring at me with—poorly faked—shocked glances on their faces.

"Funeral?" Brenda asked. "Why is there going to be a funeral? Oh Heaven protect us you killed someone? Faith, you take care of *children*. How could you? They're harmless innocents."

"I didn't kill anyone," I said and rubbed my temple. "I had nothing to do with any of this. I was only questioned because they talked to all the charge nurses who worked on the PICU. Not that it's any of your business, but cancer killed the patient in question two weeks ago. The collision of a moving car with a stationary tree killed her parents a couple of days ago. Their joint funeral is tomorrow."

"Damn." Matt wrapped his arms around me and pulled me close. "Does the MEDTECH guy think the family Angel of Deathed their own daughter?"

"They'll probably look into it." I cradled my head against his chest. I could smell the burnt toffee stink of anger coming off both Brenda and Valerie, but right then I didn't care. "Even though that isn't what happened. I was there the night she died. It wasn't a morphine overdose. Those are easy deaths. Most likely her parents stole the drugs so they could sell them and use the money to pay her medical bills. It's been known to happen."

"Now they'll suffer eternal damnation for their crimes," Valerie said, her face grim and the smell of righteous indignation wafting off of her.

Matt stiffened.

"I'd think you'd be pleased about such a thing," she continued. "Isn't enlarging your legions of the damned something every demon strives for?"

"Damnation doesn't exist." I pulled away from Matt to face his mother. I stepped forward and my horns curled upward while hellfire prickled along my skin. Outside thunder rumbled and the light in the hallway exploded. "You create your own Hell and you imprison yourself in it by your own choice. We merely serve as gate keepers, harvesting the souls given to us willingly."

"That's not—" Brenda said and I turned towards her, my wings fighting to be unleashed so I could use them to beat her senseless.

"Enough." Matt stepped between me and the two harpies crowding his doorway. "Mother, Brenda, we will not be having a theological debate in the middle of the hallway right now. We will also not be attacking Faith. Especially while she's feeling vulnerable. Go inside. We have to leave in about five minutes so we can meet Dad at his hotel. Then the three of you can go back to Biloxi and stay there. But right now I need to talk with Faith. So go inside. Now."

"But—" Valerie said.

Matt pointed at the door to his apartment. "You wanted to come and check up on me so badly, here's your chance. You have five minutes until we leave. Go root through my drawers, poke about in the fridge, and make up a list of complaints. But if you're going to snoop through my life then I think it's fair to warn you that I keep my midget porn stashed in a file folder called tax returns."

"Your *what*?" Brenda gasped and I buried my face in his chest, trying not to break into hysterical giggles.

"Midget porn," Matt said, enunciating each word. "Now, go. You're going to follow the rules Dad set down for this little field trip of suffering."

"You're presuming to enforce rules over me?" Valerie's voice was venomous and her scent reeked of pure fury. "I am the leader of the Angale. Not to mention your mother. The Holy Testament says 'Honor Thy Mother and Father.'"

"And my father specifically told you to leave Faith and her family alone. While you're here you can pester me to your heart's content but you have to stay away from Faith."

"What about me?" Brenda asked, her voice dripping with innocence. "Those were the rules your father laid down for your mother. Surely they don't apply to me?"

"Oh yes they do," Matt said. "If you don't get in that apartment right this second so help me I will have Faith's father bind you into the Grey Lands for the next thousand years."

"B-b-but—" Brenda spluttered. "You wouldn't dare!"

"Watch me." Power crackled around his entire form.

"Faith?" Brenda looked at me, her eyes wide. "You aren't going to let him threaten me that way, are you?"

"You bet your creepy angelic ass I am." I smirked at her.

"This is unacceptable." Valerie dropped her bags and pointed at Matt. "I will not allow you to order me around like I'm some sort of commoner. Or threaten Brenda, for that matter. She is your future bride and I will not allow you to disrespect her by choosing to side with some demonic concubine against your own family."

"Excuse me?" I pulled back from Matt and stared first at him and then at the two other women. Valerie looked like she was in the middle of some sort of psychotic fit, her eyes glowing and golden light sparking out of her fingertips in erratic bursts. Brenda just gave me a smug smile and the satisfaction rolled off her in sugary waves. "What did you just call me?"

"My son's concubine," Valerie repeated. "The willing sexual submissive he indulges himself with when his lawful wife is otherwise occupied."

"Lawful wife?" I stared at my boyfriend, waiting for an explanation. Apparently there was a breakdown in communication taking place somewhere. Last I checked, Matt had told me his mother *wanted* him to get engaged to Brenda. He didn't mention that engagement had taken place or that they'd followed through on it.

"Mother..." Matt sighed. "I'm not marrying Brenda. It's never going to happen. No wedding will be taking place. She is not my wife. She is not my fiancée. She is not my intended. Or any other term you want to use for it. She's just some sad little girl whose hopes you've raised to impossible levels before you sent her here to cause trouble."

"But—"

Brenda's devastated look said it all. Whatever she'd expected to happen when she hatched her little plan, this wasn't it. If it hadn't been my boyfriend she'd been trying to steal, I'd almost feel sorry for her. It had to hurt to find out the person you thought you were in love with couldn't stand you.

Valerie looked over at the other woman and pursed her lips in annoyance, obviously waiting for Brenda to say *something* to defend herself. When Brenda just sniffled, she grabbed the stunned girl by the arm and dragged her into Matt's apartment like a domesticated imp fighting against the leash for the first time.

She turned around to face us and her eyes were glowing so brightly that I couldn't even see her pupils. "I hope you're happy with yourself," she hissed and then slammed the door.

Matt wrapped his arms around me. "Maybe I'm a bad person but yeah, getting her out of my life for good makes me exceptionally happy."

"I'm just happy I don't have to worry about driving Brenda to Philly. The toll road is not where I want to spend my day off."

"Apparently, she never had any intention of taking you up on that trip." Matt dropped his forehead down against mine. "She told Dad that she and Mom cooked this plan up to get between the two of us before she ever left Biloxi. If I get my hands on Tony I'm going to pluck his feathers one at a time."

"Do you think he knew she was planning to cause trouble when he took off?"

"I think that's going to be the first question I ask him when I finally track him down. But, before I can do that I have to get the three of them on their way back to Biloxi and out of our lives. Then things can go back to normal. Or as normal as they ever are around here."

"About that…" I took a deep breath in and let it out slowly. It was now or never. I had to tell him about Dan and I had to tell him about all of it. Even the kiss. No matter how much he freaked out. "We need to talk."

"I know." Matt brushed his lips against mine and tightened his arms around me in a brief hug. "I haven't forgotten that you said you wanted to talk. I promise. But can it wait?"

"Wait?" I swallowed and tried to keep my voice even.

"Just until they're really gone?" He asked wearily. "We can talk later but right now I just need to get rid of them and reconnect with you for as long as I can. Is that okay?"

I ran my fingers over the exhaustion lines that had etched

themselves into his forehead and let my thumbs trail over the dark bruises underneath his eyes. I'd waited this long to tell him Dan was back in town, what did a few more hours matter anyway?

Chapter Fourteen

"Miss Bettincourt." Dan smiled and opened his arms to me in mock welcome the next morning as Lisa and I stumbled into the hospital's basement training room. "You're five minutes early. I'm impressed."

"Oh, stuff it, tech boy." I waved my cup of coffee at him and then gave him a tight smile. "I'm not required to be chipper or pleasant until the caffeine has completely entered my bloodstream. All you get for the next five minutes is coherent. Got me?"

Lisa yawned and took a slug of her own coffee. "We've both had long shifts and this training is keeping us from going home and going to bed."

"That makes three of us who'd rather be home in bed," Dan said. "I finished all the security updates last night. Plus I finished my paperwork on the security breach and handed it over to your hospital administration. I was hoping they would wait a few more days before acting on it but I think that redhead, Sally, might have the police department on her speed dial."

"Great." I rolled my eyes and took a big drink of my latte.

The guy at the coffee shop across from the hospital had added two double shots of espresso to it to help perk me up this morning when I told him I had to stay over on my day off for a training seminar. *Alpha, bless helpful young baristas.* "So I should expect Detective Kastellero to show up during lunch—"

"Or now," a snide, masculine voice said from behind me.

Crap. I turned to find the detective leaning against the open doorjamb, staring at me.

"Miss Bettincourt. Why am I not surprised to see you here?"

"Because I work here?" I said. "Much like you often find yourself working out of the local Dunkin Donuts if that jelly belly you're sporting is any indication of things. What do you want, Detective?" I took another drink of my coffee and sighed. "I have a training that this guy says I can't skip out on. No matter how much I want to."

"I wanted to let you know, personally, that we've looked at the paperwork Mr. Cheswick provided us and I don't think we'll need any further information from you regarding the robbery that took place last month. But we're investigating the attempts on your life. So I'm sure we'll be seeing each other again soon. Unless you have something else you need to share?"

"Not a thing." I had to give the man credit. He was persistent. He had no evidence to link the car bombs that had destroyed my father's, Matt's, and Tolliver's cars last month to anything else, but he wasn't about to let it die, either. He intended to find something, and Alpha save us all when he finally did.

"What about any information you might have on the death of Dr. Harold Winslow?"

"Not a thing."

"Are you sure?" Kastellero leaned closer to me, so we were

almost nose to nose, and narrowed his eyes like he had suddenly become Kojak and I was about to go away for a very long time after beating someone's granny to death. "Because it seems very convenient to me about the timing of all these incidents. You file a harassment complaint against Dr. Winslow and the next day he comes up missing along with a whole batch of morphine. But no one sees anything and I do mean *no one* because even the security cameras were down."

"That has nothing to do with me." I straightened so that I was standing at my not-so-impressive full five foot two height and narrowed my eyes at him in a way I hoped looked more like annoyance and less like a sudden urge to confess to everything but stealing morphine—including accessory to murder after the fact. Especially since I didn't think he was going to buy my defense of "my best friend the succubus did it. I was just the poor innocent schmuck that got pulled along for the ride."

"I'd believe you but that very same week you suddenly gain a stalker who decides to go from threatening notes to explosives in record time." The burnt coffee smell of irritation mixed with the peppery smell of suspicion wafted off of his clothes and I had to try my best not to sneeze as it tickled my nose.

"Crazy people, who knows what they're thinking?"

"Now we find Dr. Winslow and the man who stole that morphine, except both of them are rather inconveniently dead. With no visible connection to you." Kastellero took another step toward me, forcing me to take a step back.

"Because there is no connection to me," I said, my voice shaking slightly.

"Of course there is. I just have to find it and when I do you, me, and your lawyer are all going to sit down together for a chat."

Kastellero stepped back and gave me a predatory smile.

"Lucky us." I took a drink of my coffee and rolled my eyes at him, like I was totally not pissing myself at the idea of being trapped in a room with him. Not that any sane person could blame me. The guy had tried to accuse me for the missing morphine even though I hadn't even been in the hospital when it was stolen. Then, he'd tried to somehow tie it to the whole *Stalker Blowing Up My Car* incident and even went so far as to suggest to the ATF that maybe it was tied to drug trafficking on my part. Which was totally bogus, and thankfully the ATF had seen that after only a little bit of subtle mind fuckery courtesy of the Son of God.

"Have a good day, Miss Bettincourt. Try not to kill anybody. Or get yourself killed, either." Kastellero turned on his heel, and walked away.

"Same to you, Detective, and do try not to wrongfully accuse too many innocent people today. I'm sure the paperwork is killing your superiors."

"Okay, you two obviously have a history," Dan said.

"He tried to blame me for the MEDTECH incident. Plus he scared off Bernice by coming in here every single night to grill her for more details on what happened. Now guess who has to cover her shift until they can find a replacement nurse who's willing to work midnights? One hint, it's not Detective Kastellero."

"But now that this is settled, maybe he'll quit screwing with the staff so much and you can all get back to your normal routine."

"Your mouth to God's ears." Lisa grabbed my arm, pulling me up the stairs to one of the back rows in the auditorium.

"I'd like to get hold of God's ear," Harold muttered, appearing in the seat next to me. I raised my eyebrows. I wasn't sure if my ghostly companion could manage to not make a scene in a room full of doctors and nurses who couldn't see him. It was a huge temptation to cause trouble and the fact he'd been divorced four times—all of them for adultery—should prove that temptation wasn't something Harold was good at resisting.

"Relax. I promise I'll be good. No matter how much fun it might be to mess with these guys, I can control my more juvenile urges." Harold rolled his eyes. "I just thought I'd come keep you company today. You know me. I like to stay up on all the new medical devices. Amazing the stuff they've come up with in the past twenty years. You would be shocked if you had to work in the conditions we used to when I was in medical school. Compared to you guys we were trepanning skulls and applying leeches."

"They're actually finding that leech thing is pretty effective," Lisa said.

"Really?" Harold raised his eyebrows. "I can see it, I guess. There had to be a reason all those people used to use them before the advent of modern medicine. Not something I'd want to play around with, but then again I always hated dealing with slimy stuff."

"Enough, you two." I opened my notebook and uncapped my pen. "He's getting ready to start and we should be paying attention. We're professionals, remember?"

"Says the girl who brought in three turkeys and a dozen two-liter bottles of soda last year on Black Friday so her patients could start the First Annual PICU Holiday Turkey Bowl," Harold said. "You're not exactly a model of professional behavior, Faith."

"They all had a blast and it didn't hurt anyone for those kids to have some fun," I whispered, glad no one sat in front of us. "This is actually related to patient care so I think maybe we should try to pay attention."

"Oh please," Harold said. "Why are you so concerned with being teacher's pet today? Matt's not going to like it. You should have told him you were going to be here with Dan today."

"He already knows." I tapped my pen against the side of my foldout desk. "He met Dan last night."

"Wow," Harold said. "The engineer doesn't have any black eyes. I expected Matt to kick his ass. I bet Malachi twenty bucks he'd knock him out in less than five minutes."

"Matt didn't touch him. He had no reason to. Dan just came over to tell me about the Cosgroves and then he left," I said and rubbed my temples. I wasn't about to tell Harold that Dan had kissed me last night. Which could be uncomfortable since I still hadn't gotten the chance to tell Matt. Not that I hadn't tried but it seemed like he was allergic to the phrase "*we need to talk*."

"Did you tell Matt who he was?" Harold asked.

"I told him Dan was the software engineer MEDTECH sent to investigate their system failure and install an update. I also told him that Dan had stopped by to tell me what he'd found out during his investigation. That was actually pretty good thinking on his part because Pittsburgh's Most Annoying was waiting for me here this morning."

"Did you happen to tell Angel Boy the software engineer's *name*?" Harold asked. "Or illuminate for him that, even though he doesn't remember it, Mr. MEDTECH has seen your naked boobies?"

"I'm not even going to answer that."

"So you didn't tell him, which would be why Cheswick is still able to walk today."

"Matt wouldn't have punched Dan for something that, one, happened years before I even met him, and two, Dan can't even remember."

"Doesn't matter." Harold put his hands up in the air. "It's this thing with guys. We can't help it. There's like this short circuit that happens when we see another guy who might have seen naked breasts that belong to us. We don't want to hurt that other guy but the reptilian part of our brain takes over and we have to punch them in the face until we cause enough brain damage that they can no longer remember what the breasts we have in common look like."

"That is the most immature, childish—"

"Tolliver wants a list of all my ex-boyfriends so he can have them tortured by imps when they die," Lisa said.

"Like I said, immature, childish, and so very much something that someone like Tolliver would do. Matt is a reasonable adult." I narrowed my eyes at Harold and reached for my coffee.

"And he could come up with much better ways to torment Mr. Cheswick," the Alpha said, His voice sounding like melted chocolate poured over ice cream.

My uncle and my cousin stood in the aisle, wearing scrubs and white lab coats. The Alpha's white hair was cropped close to His head and when He smiled the lines around His eyes deepened.

"What are you doing here?" I asked.

"Lisa called me." J ran a hand through his dark brown hair and the muscles in his arms rippled underneath his lab coat. Which was so wrong in my opinion. The Son of God really shouldn't be such a hottie. It messed with the whole scheme of things. "She said you got some bad news last night before work and I thought we'd come spend the day with you for moral support."

"You can sit right here next to me," Harold told J, motioning to the empty seat beside him. He looked at my uncle and raised an eyebrow. "You can go sit next to Lisa. I have nothing to say to you. Except to tell you you're an asshole."

"I have been accused of that a time or two." The Alpha nodded, His white hair glowing underneath the fluorescent lights. "Did I do something particularly asshole-like today to upset you, or is this just a general philosophical decision on your part?"

"Emily Cosgrove," I muttered and looked down at my notebook.

"Right." The Alpha nodded and covered my hand with His. Warmth traveled up my arm and my fatigue from a long night on duty dissipated like the clearing of morning fog when the sun rose each morning. "I know it doesn't help to remind you, but they do say that I work in mysterious ways."

"Don't give me that bullshit." Harold squared up against my uncle and shoving his phantom finger underneath the other man's face. "I'm dead and that means there aren't any mysteries left for me. So I don't need to hear a bunch of platitudes and excuses. Sometimes you just suck. Case closed."

"Right." The Alpha nodded. "I'll just go sit next to Lisa. Son?"

"I think I'll sit next to Harold." J gave his father a sour look. Harold wasn't the only one who disagreed with the Alpha's hands-off stance. J was fiddling with the cuffs of his lab coat and had pulled them down to cover the tops of his hands. He reached up to scratch at his hair and shuffled his feet, rubbing the bottom of one against the top of the other. I reached around Harold, my hand sliding through his phantom clipboard, and took my cousin's hand in mine, giving it a brief squeeze of reassurance.

He glanced at me and smiled. A bolt of warmth and love shot through the length of our connection and my energy levels were back to normal. If I were a mortal I'd feel like I'd just spent a week on the beach being pampered instead of just off an overnight shift where everything that could go wrong had.

"Feel better now?" he asked and glanced toward my coffee cup. "Because I have to tell you I'm bushed and I didn't get a chance to stop for a drink."

I smiled, grabbed my coffee cup, and waved it at him. "Nice try, but I'm not giving you my latte with a double shot of espresso."

J winked. "It was worth a try."

"Everyone..." Dan stood at the front of the room and clapped his hands. The medical personnel jammed into the conference room took their seats and quit gossiping. One thing you could say for people in a hospital—some of us were pains in the ass, but we all had excellent listening skills.

Dan went into his introductory spiel, and I glanced at the Alpha and Lisa, who were having an intense conversation, their heads bent low together. He peeked over at me and Harold before whispering in her ear again. I turned back to Dan. Whatever those two were up to, I didn't want to be involved.

Chapter Fifteen

Four hours later, I was so sick of hearing about the not-so-revolutionary advances that MEDTECH had made in hospital security systems that I was willing to barter my powers for a reprieve. Chaos protect me, I was ready to barter everyone's powers for a chance to get out of here.

"So everyone." Dan clapped his hands together at the front of the room. "I think that's everything. If we have no further questions—"

Before he could even finish what he was saying medical personnel stood and started gathering their stuff. I rose and stretched, pulling my arms up over my head and cracking my neck. I was slowly reaching the point in my demonic lifespan where I didn't actually have to sleep but right this second that was all I wanted to do. I wrinkled my nose at a flaky looking stain on my scrub shirt. Scratch that. I wanted a shower and then I was going to bury my head underneath a pillow and stay there till I had no other choice.

"I'll see you later." Lisa grabbed her stuff and brushed past me like her tail was on fire.

"Wait, where are you going?" I asked. "I thought we were going home?"

"I have somewhere I need to be," Lisa called out over her shoulder, bolting out of the room.

"But how are you going to get home? We carpooled," I called out, even though she was long gone. My stomach twisted as I watched people stream out of the room behind her. It was probably wedding planning, or something like that, but the thing was, Lisa'd never blown me off before now. Somehow, I knew it wasn't because she'd decided to go looking for a cake topper.

"Bettincourt. Paging Faith Bettincourt," the PA system blared. I groaned. Two other nurses gave me sympathetic grins and then beat a hasty retreat. Not that I blamed them. If I'd heard them page someone else I'd have gotten out of there, too. Who knew which person they'd page next?

I walked over to the phone sitting on the top of the podium Dan had been using earlier and picked up the receiver. "This is Faith Bettincourt. What can I do for you?"

"Faith?" Sally simpered on the other end of the phone. "Do you have a few minutes?"

"Sure, Sally." I held back a sigh. "What do you need?"

"Well, Detective Kastellero stopped by my office and told me that he'd seen you this morning…"

"Of course he did." Detective Kastellero was totally the grown up version of that tattle-tale you went to grade school with. Except this time I wasn't going to lose my recess for not sharing the red crayon. If he pushed his suspicions enough, the hospital could request that I take a leave of absence to investigate any possible connections between me and the Cosgrove family.

"So for legal reasons," Sally continued like I hadn't even spoken. "We need you to stop by the human resources department and schedule a meeting with the hospital's legal department."

"I have to go talk to the lawyers?" I heard my voice go unnaturally high and sucked in a breath, trying to calm down.

I felt a hand on my shoulder and looked up to see Dan standing beside me, his eyes filled with concern. "You okay?" he mouthed.

I put my hand over the receiver and nodded. "Kastellero," I whispered.

"Ass." Dan picked up the last of his stuff and gave me a sympathetic smile before leaving me alone in the now empty conference room.

"You're not in trouble or anything," Sally reassured me. "They just need to talk to you."

"Fine." I ran a hand through my messy hair. "I'll come on over."

"Oh, well, actually…" Sally gave a light laugh that I knew meant she was going to screw me over further. "I'm on my way to a meeting. So if you could just come on over and wait for me I should be there in a bit."

"A bit?" My heart sank. I knew how long those administrative meetings could go. Mainly because those people loved to talk.

"A half hour tops," Sally assured me.

"A half—" I heard a click and then the phone line went dead. Damn it. Not only was she keeping me from going home and taking a nap, now she'd hung up on me!

Two hours later I was tired, cranky, and not in the mood to wait around for an elevator. Pushing the door open to the Northeast stairwell, I let myself inside the tiny landing and looked around. Just like I expected. Completely empty. I glanced around once more, just to make sure, and then opened a narrow phase portal and stepped from the stairwell to the corner of the parking garage where I'd left my car way too many hours before.

"Faith? Is that you?"

Crap. Had I really just phased in front of man who was not supposed to ever learn that paranormal creatures existed? Now I had no choice but to mind wipe him. My day was getting better by the minute.

"What are you doing here?" I smoothed my fingers over my bun, then pulled out the pins so my hair hung in a low ponytail at the nape of my neck. "I thought you would have left already. Didn't you work graveyard shift last night?"

"You did, too. But here we are." Dan sauntered over to my car, and leaned against my rear driver's side door. "I was taking a call from senior management at MEDTECH. The Chicago Police just took my boss in for questioning."

"Damn." I leaned against the back of my car. "I'm sorry."

"Me, too." He stood next to me, and ran his fingers down my back.

"I have a boyfriend." I jerked away and gave him a dirty look. "Remember?"

"Right. Matt the Lawyer, who does mixed martial arts and has homicidal tendencies. He looked like a tool."

"He's not a tool."

"Oh yeah, definitely a tool."

"Look, it's just been a long day and I've got an even longer one tomorrow. I get to come in early and meet with Legal so they can dissect everything I may have inadvertently said to Detective Kastellero in case the hospital finds itself in court for some reason."

"Great." Dan smirked. "That's why you look like you're about ready to cry."

"I'm not ready to cry." I undid my ponytail and ran my fingers through my hair, trying to keep my horns firmly inside my skull. "I'm just tired."

"Faith." He grabbed my other hand. "You know you can talk to me, right? I mean, besides my constant flirting I'd like to think I'm a good guy."

"Except for when your lips get a mind of their own and decide to attack me."

"Yeah, besides then." He gave my fingers a squeeze. "So look, whatever is bothering you, you can tell me about it. It'll be our secret. I promise."

"I can't." My phone vibrated and I snagged it out of my scrub top pocket. Lisa. I sent the call to voicemail, but it rang again.

"Well whatever it is..." Dan took my phone out of my hand and answered it. He pressed the phone against my ear and stepped back when I took it. "I hope you can talk to someone about it."

I nodded at him and then swallowed. "Hello?"

"Faith!" Lisa sounded frantic.

"Lisa?" I felt my heart begin to pound. "What's wrong? What happened?"

"Is Tolliver with you?"

"No." I shook my head even though she couldn't see me and Dan reached over to touch my shoulder, trying to comfort me. "I'm still at the hospital. Why would Tolliver be with me?"

"He's missing," Lisa said, her voice panicky. "No one knows where he is."

"He's what?" I asked.

"Tolliver is gone."

Chapter Sixteen

"What? What do you mean Tolliver is gone?" My heart was pounding and a prickle of fear ran up my spine. Children of the Devil didn't just go missing. Not because we were paranormal creatures, but because our father thought our safety required us to be within reach at all times. If Tolliver was actually missing, that meant that whoever had taken him wasn't messing around.

Dan looked at me and raised an eyebrow.

"Where are you, Lisa?" I asked, trying to keep my voice calm.

Her voice was thick and I could hear the echo of her pacing across the hardwood floors in their new place. "Our new apartment. We were supposed to grab something to eat before he went to your dad's baseball game for a bachelor party thing. But the door was wide open and he's not here."

"Maybe he's out getting something and just forgot to latch it behind him? You know Tolliver. He never thinks about that sort of stuff. Have you tried his phone?" I asked.

"There are feathers everywhere," she said and her voice cracked, "and a big black spot from where he threw hellfire at someone."

"Shit." I turned my back on Dan, trying to keep my composure. "Get everyone together at my apartment. I'll be there as quickly as I can."

"Should I call Matt, too?" she asked. "I mean normally I would but…"

"We don't know if that crazy mother of his might have had something to do with it," I said. Shit. My parents' wedding was in two days, my brother was missing, my boyfriend's family might be involved, and I was trapped here with the one guy whose mind might crack if I said the wrong thing. "Don't call him. Let me handle it. Let's just keep it in the *family* for right now."

"Right," Lisa said. "Just demons. Gotcha. Please get here, Faith. If something's happened to Tolliver…"

"Lisa, we'll find him. I promise. I'll get there as soon as I can."

"Okay." Lisa sniffed. "Promise me you'll be careful?

"You, too." I hung up my phone and turned to Dan.

"Is everything okay?"

"No." I shook my head. "That was Lisa. There's been an emergency and they need me at home."

"Then you better go." He opened the driver's side door of my car for me and stepped back. "Give me a call if there's anything I can do to help."

"I will." I slipped behind the wheel and pulled the door closed.

Once I reached an empty alley next to the Health Department, I focused every bit of my energy on opening a portal big enough to drive my car through. The fabric of reality shredded with a loud, whip-like *crack* and I punched it, sliding the car into a parking spot on the street in front of my building. After throwing it in park, I rushed inside, not even bothering to wait for the hole between spaces to stitch itself back up.

I sprinted up the front steps and threw the door open, skidding to a halt in the front vestibule. Dad, Malachi, Harold, and a few high-ranked demons clustered around the open doorway.

Mom and Hope were sitting on the steps with Lisa wedged between them. One look at Dad's clenched jaw and the tight line of Malachi's shoulders told me that she'd been right. Tolliver hadn't just popped out for a gallon of milk and left the door open.

"What happened?" I asked.

"I came home after we split up and found the door standing wide open," Lisa looked up at me with red-rimmed eyes and sniffled. "The place is trashed. He's not here. So I tried his cell phone and got his voicemail."

"And?" I prompted.

"Then I called him again. That's when I heard his phone buzzing on the kitchen counter," Lisa whispered. "Tolliver would have never gone anywhere without his phone. Not by choice."

"Sprites," my father said from the doorway, his mouth set in a grim line and his eyes blazing.

"What?" I asked.

"Sprites," he repeated, motioning me to come to him. His hand was shaking. "I'd say a full pack, guessing from the amount of feathers we've found."

"Sprites? You're talking about the angelic version of imps?" I moved to stand next to him. "Those little green things with shiny wings that like to play in flower gardens and bite your fingers?"

There was no reason for sprites to even be in Pittsburgh. They attached themselves to angelic creatures for protection and they never—voluntarily—strayed into demon-controlled areas. It would have taken someone with an immense amount of charisma to convince them to appear in Pittsburgh with the Bettincourt-Morningstar family taking up residence.

"You're saying my brother, the Crown Prince of Hell, was taken by a group of do-gooder imps?" They should have been shitting themselves in fear of an Archdemon. Not hunting him for sport. "Those things are only like three inches tall, and they squish like modeling clay when you step on them. I remember watching Ba'al beat one down with a fly swatter when I was a kid. You're telling me something like that managed to snag Tolliver?"

Nahamia, one of Dad's demon lords, pushed his dreadlocks over his shoulder as he approached. "Sprites hunt in large packs so they could have blitzed him from multiple sides. He wouldn't have a chance to fight back. I'd say there was somewhere around seventy-five to a hundred, easy."

I craned my head to the side and looked past Dad into Tolliver's living room. Holy shit. No way could only one being, supernatural or not, inflict this much damage to a room. Furniture was flipped on its side. Holes were punched into the drywall. Black smears still smoldered on the carpet, leaving an oily residue on a few patches of the walls. Tolliver hadn't gone down without a fight.

"So what do we do?" I asked. "Where would a group of sprites keep Tolliver?"

A puff of smoke curled from Dad's nostril and his horns popped through the skin on his forehead. "His presence would be detected in the Celestial Kingdom, and they can't access my realm. The only place left to look for him would be…"

"The Grey Lands," I finished. Purgatory. Man I hated that place. Absolutely hated it. It was gray. Miles and miles of endless gray. Aside from the gray, there were hundreds of millions of couches and chairs that looked like they'd all been stolen from hospital waiting rooms sometime in the early Sixties. It was also huge and easy to get turned around in if you didn't know where you were going, since everything looked the same. Which, if you thought about it, made Purgatory the perfect place to stash someone.

"Okay." Dad clapped and looked at each of us in turn, his eyes flaring red. The air around him crackled with dark energy and the entire building hummed with evil. Thunder sounded, and the sky outside the window turned green and hazy. "Here's what we're going to do. Lisa, Faith, Hope, and Roisin, I want the four of you to stay here. Get Lisa's apartment fixed up. If anyone calls or shows up, get in touch with me immediately. If there's any sort of ransom they'll start here."

"I think I should go with you," Mom argued. "Tolliver is my stepson and I want to help."

"Stay here," Dad said. "The rest of us will find Tolliver."

"But I can help," Mom protested. "I can call upon my sisters in the coven and together we can cast a spell to divine his location. Then we'll cast another one that compels whoever has taken him to send him home to us."

"Roisin," my father said. "Stay here. Help the girls. Don't talk to anyone else. I'll call Lilith."

"You're going to call Lilith?" Mom yelped. "Why are you calling Lilith? We don't need to call that woman. She'll just make this worse. Let me help instead. *Please.*"

"I'm calling Lilith," Dad said. "She's Tolliver's mother. She'll have a link to him that no one else has."

"B-b-but are you sure that you have to call her?" Mom asked. "I mean she's your ex-wife."

"Roisin…" Dad sighed. "My son is missing. He could be hurt. The last thing you have to worry about is me suddenly deciding to start back up with my ex-wife. Besides, after the last time we broke up I can promise that she would rather castrate me than kiss me."

"Are you—?"

"Stay here." He walked to her and kissed the top of her head. "Protect our girls."

He opened a portal and ushered the rest of them through it.

"Wait!" Mom called out before he managed to follow the others through. "What should I do?"

"If it comes down to it I know you'll think of something." He stepped through the portal, sealing it behind him.

"He's wrong you know," Mom muttered.

"About what?" Hope asked.

"Lilith would take him back in a heartbeat if she had the chance."

"It's not likely," Lisa countered, her voice hollow sounding. "Especially since she just moved in with Baziram, the Archdemon delegate to the International Court of Justice."

"Lil is dating someone?" Mom's eyes lit up. What woman wouldn't be insecure about having Lilith, the Archdemoness of Lust, as a rival? She had the whole Sophia-Loren-gone-British thing going on, and man she made it work for her. I'd once watched the woman stop eight lanes of traffic on the L.A. freeway with nothing but a smile and a double whammy of pheromones.

"I wonder if Dad knows?" Hope asked, widening her eyes at me. I knew she was thinking about the way Dad had reacted every time he saw Mom with another man. One particular instance with a canning jar, a goat, and three voodoo priestesses was an especially vivid reminder of how territorial Dad could be when it came to the women in his life. Or the women that used to be in his life. Same difference.

"He doesn't." Lisa looked at her open doorway, gnawing on her lower lip. "She said it's not any of his business and she doesn't want to make things awkward by fighting with him about it before the wedding."

She started to sniffle again, and I could see tears clinging to her lower lashes. I draped my arm over her shoulders. "It's going to be okay."

"No, it's not," she said and hiccupped. "A group of sprites took Tolliver and now he's missing. They're going to hurt him or banish him or…I don't know, something even worse than that."

"Nothing is going to happen to Tolliver," I said. "They'll find him, they'll get him back, and you'll get married, just like you planned. I didn't endure all this wedding planning crap for you to just chicken out now."

"But what if they don't? What if those things have already done something horrible to him?" Her eyes were wide and filled with tears. Even devastated the girl was drop dead gorgeous. If I didn't love her so much I'd hate her guts.

"He's going to be fine," I insisted.

"How do you know?"

"Because we know." Mom stood up. "Now, if you girls will excuse me. Even if your father won't let us search, my coven and I can still start laying protective spells over Tolliver to keep him from harm until your father arrives."

"Faith?" Lisa looked at me. "Are you sure he'll be okay?"

I wasn't. That was the problem. I'd never heard of imps attacking someone unprovoked before now, and if imps didn't do it then I doubted that sprites would, either. I couldn't imagine my brother somehow pissing off a sprite and not mentioning it to anyone. So that meant someone had sent these particular creatures to target him. That made this whole mess a lot more complicated than it should have been.

Sprites wouldn't be able to kill Tolliver but if they were clever they'd be able to hide him somewhere and hand him over to another, more powerful creature to use in a whole host of unholy ways. Possibly leaving him trapped outside the mortal realms, and in the thrall of another being, for the rest of time.

My phone buzzed. Matt had texted me. *Have you seen your dad today?*

Yes, I texted back. *Why?*

My dad is sending Mom and Brenda to the Grey Lands and Mom's sure your dad put him up to it.

Doubt it, I typed. Dad would never have suggested banishment as punishment for anything but an unpardonable act. Exposing the Celestial realms to mortals. Stealing the souls of children. Blowing up his car and trying to take over the mortal realms. Really jaw-droppingly bad shit that even demons didn't consider to be a good way to kill time on a Thursday night.

But what if Valerie thought he had? What if she thought Dad was responsible for her banishment? How desperate would she be to bargain her way out of the situation?

I took Lisa's hand. "Why don't you stay out here and help Hope keep Mom reigned in on the 'protective spells' while I get your apartment cleaned up?" I didn't like the direction my thoughts were taking and cleaning would take my mind off a certain duo of women who would have access to sprites and a motive for taking hostages.

"But what if all that malicious power sucks you dry?" she asked. "It isn't safe. You could get zapped and then you'll be helpless if the sprites come back."

"That's why you're going to stay out here and watch my back." I wiggled my fingers at her. "Besides, you shouldn't be in there working with this stuff. One, with the way your emotions are right now it could backfire and make things worse. Two, it's just better if you don't have to see it all again."

I remembered going back into mine and Dan's townhouse one last time to clean up after the EMTs had taken him away. Filtering through the wreckage had made the situation so much more painful. It wasn't going to be like that for Lisa, though. Dad was going to find Tolliver, and they'd get their happily ever after.

I nudged Lisa toward Hope.

"Hey." My sister bumped Lisa's shoulder with her own and then pulled out her cell phone. "I've been stockpiling pictures of the ugly people who come into the library. Want to point and laugh with me? It'll take your mind off things."

"Why not?" Lisa sighed. "Someone else's ugly shoes always have a way of making you feel better about things."

Leaving them to snark about the rampant abuses of fashion that tended to crop up in Pittsburgh I stalked into Lisa's apartment and closed the door. Or tried to close their door, since someone—or several tiny someones working together—had ripped it off its hinges. Somewhere in that apartment dead sprites were starting to decay and the smell was horrible—rotting meat and vanilla cookies rolled into one thick, all-encompassing stench that had saturated the room, seeping into the tiny nooks and crannies. I fled back into the hallway, leaning over and bracing my hands on my knees, taking in deep, cleansing breaths.

"You okay?" Hope looked up from her phone.

"It's fine," I wheezed. "The mess is just bigger than I'd first expected. I needed a second to regroup and strategize."

"I can help clean up." Lisa tried to stand and Hope grabbed her arm again, keeping Lisa in place.

"No, no." I closed my eyes, and a crackle of power crawled along my skin. I pushed it outward, forming a protective bubble around myself. "I'm fine. You sit out here and try not to worry. Find something really cringe worthy to show me. Like people who dressed to match their dogs or something."

With my force field in place, I crossed over the threshold and took a deep breath. Nothing but clean, deliciously fresh air. Not the slightest stench of burnt cookies and death penetrated my exterior. Good. Now I could get to work.

Chapter Seventeen

I'd found forty sprites underneath various bits of furniture in the living room and one wet towel shoved under the couch. My guess was that the sprites had ambushed Tolliver when he was getting out of the shower and he'd never had a chance. A naked demon is almost as vulnerable as a naked human. Maybe even more. Humans don't have wings for an attacker to tear at or a tail to grab onto for leverage. Plus, male demons have all the same sensitive areas to protect that a regular man does, and a sprite would play dirty by going for those first.

The upside was, if he'd managed to take out forty of the little nuisances, they'd be wary about trying anything else until they replenished their numbers. The downside was that he'd managed to take down forty sprites and they still had enough members in their pack to kidnap him. I'd finished setting the living room to rights when the vestibule door opened and I waved my fingers, letting the furniture drop back onto the floor with a thud. The last thing I needed was the neighbors to see a levitating living room set.

"What happened?" Matt asked, peeking his head inside the open door. "Why are Lisa and Hope sitting on the steps? And why are you cleaning Lisa's apartment…inside a bubble?"

"The bubble cuts down on the stench." I'd gotten rid of the sprites and cleaned up the hellfire residue so I let it dissipate. In fact, the only thing I had left to do was draw out all the energy swirling about the room. It was like a seething mass of pink cotton candy left too long in the machine, reduced to a giant nest of ick. Yeah, that was going to be fun.

"The stench of what?" Matt twitched and rubbed his hands up and down his arms. He scratched behind one ear and then ran one foot up the back of his opposite leg. "What the Hell happened? And why does it feel like we're in the middle of one of those giant static electricity balls?"

I motioned around me. "A pack of sprites attacked Tolliver."

"Not possible." Matt shook his head and scratched at his arms, this time harder. "Sprites would never attack unprovoked."

"Well, these ones did."

"No way," he said. "It couldn't have been sprites. We had them as pets when I was a kid. I'm telling you, it wasn't sprites."

"Are you sure? So what are those? Butterflies?" I motioned to the garbage bag I'd used as a makeshift body bag for them. Not that I wanted to keep the nasty things, but I wasn't sure of how to dispose of them. They were too big to flush, and the garbage disposal just seemed sort of sadistic. Well, more sadistic than I was comfortable with anyway.

Matt pulled the bag open and peeked inside, recoiling in horror. "What did Tolliver do to them? They're just simple creatures."

"It looks to me like he defended himself. Besides, those *simple creatures* ambushed him, Matt. Now he's missing and we've got half a dozen demons scouring the Grey Lands for him right now."

"I can't believe a pack of sprites would do this." He turned to me, eyes wide and face a faint green. "The sprites we kept at home would have never behaved this way. Not unless they were specifically ordered to attack in order to defend the community."

"If they only attack at someone else's command then maybe you should worry less about the poor, simple creatures, and more about who decided to sic them on my brother."

I knew that seeing dead sprites bothered him on an elemental level, and I understood where he was coming from. He was part angel and he believed desperately in the sanctity of all life. But right now I needed him to focus on the fact that my brother was missing and that was bad. Sure it sucked that a bunch of sprites had to die, but I could only have so much sympathy for the little buggers. Especially since all the evidence seemed to point to the fact that the sprites had started it.

"You're not suggesting the Biloxi pack was involved?" His eyes were instantly wary.

"That's precisely what I'm suggesting. Your mother is desperate and she wanted some trump card to keep your father from banishing her to Purgatory. She'd see hurting my brother as a logical solution that had the added bonus of giving her a chance to screw with the Devil."

"Why Tolliver?" He blew out a long breath and crossed his arms over his chest. "What possible advantage is there for my mother to kidnap the Archdemon of Gluttony? Of everyone she could have attacked, why *Tolliver*?"

"I'm sure she was hoping to get me instead, but hey, one demon is as good as another to the Angale, isn't it? We're all just interchangeable little bits of evil for those people to attack, unprovoked."

"Faith." Matt took a step toward me and then stopped. "I know you're upset but you have to know that not all of the Angale are like that. There are those of us who realize that the world needs both sides of the Celestial Order to keep the world in balance."

"Name five besides you."

"Well there's..." Matt stopped. "That doesn't mean these sprites are from Biloxi. Just because my mother and Brenda were here..."

"And they left in a huff," I pointed out.

"They were upset when they left. But that—"

"Then your father threatened to banish your mother into Purgatory."

"Leaving that aside." He pinched the bridge of his nose. "We have no definitive proof that these sprites are from Biloxi. They could be—"

"The minions of some other apocalyptic cult full of militant nephilims?"

"It sounds really bad when you put it that way," he huffed.

I bit my lower lip and looked at my shoes, scuffing them together. I knew this had to be hard for him to accept and I couldn't imagine what it felt like to realize that your mother wasn't just harmlessly crazy, she truly was a beyond the pale level of evil. Which was sort of surprising actually since I didn't know that angels, or their offspring, could go quite this level of bad. Impulsive, sure. Dangerous, even I could get behind. But she had sent innocent creatures to attack someone for no reason other than her desire to cause pain. That was a pure, premeditated evil that even my soul, dark as it was, shied away from.

"Do you recognize any of them?" I opened the mouth of the

bag so that he could look inside.

"Sprites are just like imps—carbon copies of each other. The only difference is sprites are green and imps are blue." He turned his head away from the bag and closed his eyes. "I couldn't identify them even if I wanted to. Which I don't. If they are part of the Biloxi pack at one point and time these creatures were my friends."

"I'm sorry." I closed the bag and stepped toward him but stopped. What was I supposed to say? His pets had attacked my brother and he'd protected himself. I couldn't blame Tolliver; I would have done the same thing in his place. All I could really be sorry for was the fact that someone had put all of us in this situation. "But, you said yourself, your mother has a pack of sprites that she could have ordered to attack my brother. Doesn't she?"

"Yes but we have no proof this is the Biloxi pack," Matt said, snapping into attorney mode. "That's the thing you seem to have forgotten. You have no proof that your brother's victims are from my mother's pack of sprites. You don't have anything more than suspicions and an act of mass murder on your brother's part."

"This isn't a court of law and it's not mass murder if you're defending yourself." I shook my head and turned away from him. I knew the magic swirling around the room had us both on edge but I wasn't going to let it give me an excuse to act irrationally and say something I'd probably regret later. "Besides, you really think the demons who are looking for Tolliver are going to care about proof? My father is currently out of his mind with worry and surrounded by a pack of demonlords who each command their own legion. Including Malachi. And if you haven't figured it out, that three foot grim reaper disguise of his hides a whole lot of scary underneath it. They'll do whatever it takes to get Tolliver back."

"The Alpha isn't going to allow your father to just—"

"There's no *allow* to it." Black power surged along the length of my spine and I tried my best to shake it off and focus on Matt instead of my sudden, irrational desire to zap something—or someone. "We don't take orders from Him. We're demons. Like my patients would say, the Alpha is not the boss of us."

"So you're saying that they can just do whatever they want and no one is going to stop them?" He crowded me backward, against the island, and loomed over me. His wings unfolded and golden light sparked across his skin. Obviously the malignant magic that had filled Tolliver's apartment was affecting his emotions just like it was mine. It was time to make him see reason and then we could figure out how to deal with this.

He came closer and the green of his eyes disappeared behind the gold filling them. Energy crackled along his skin and I had to move away from him as it arced between his hands.

Oh, hell no. Just because this place was filled with bad juju didn't mean I was going to let him turn himself into the Celestial version of Chernobyl. I moved toward him so that we were nose to nose. My wings spread and my horns shot upward, tearing through my scalp. My tail dropped loose and curled around my ankle, the end flicking back and forth. "Look, I know this sucks and I'm guessing that you really don't feel like yourself right now because the Matt I know wouldn't be this stupid."

"So now I'm stupid?"

"You have to help me figure out where your mother stashed Tolliver because if we don't come up with something soon they are going to pull it out of her by force. Trust me, I don't like your mother, but I've heard stories of some of the things these demon lords can do and none of them are something I'd wish on anyone.

Not even her."

"They wouldn't dare." His wings beat in an angry staccato and a bright golden glow enveloped him, the edges rough and spiked with anger. The air was perfumed with a mixture of cookies and the sulphuric tang of brimstone.

"You want to test that theory?" I made my eyes flash black. "If she doesn't tell them what they want to know, they could come after you and I may not be able to keep you safe. So please, whatever you're feeling right now, push it aside and *help me.*"

"So my mother was right. You're all just a bunch of mindless killing machines. All of you." He pulled away from me, stalked toward the door, and threw it open.

"It's better than the alternative," I whispered as he stormed out, slamming the door behind him. I picked up the glass candy dish sitting on the island and hurled it at the door, shattering it into dozens of tiny pieces.

Damn it. Why did relationships have to be so damn complicated?

I looked around the rest of the room and made sure it was back to the way it had been before. The only thing left to deal with was the sticky residue of malevolent magic that had turned my normally rational boyfriend into a testosterone-fueled pair of well-muscled wings. Then I could go upstairs with Lisa and a pint of chocolate ice cream to wait for news of Tolliver.I stretched my powers, probing the magical goo saturating the room. It shrank away when I pressed against it. Good. That should be easy enough to clean up. I could just draw it up into a big ball-o-gunk and give it a blast of dark magic. I opened my body up to its full power, focusing on the room. I tried to draw all of the magic toward me, and watched it seep across the floor and pool around my feet.

Yuck. Why couldn't my brother get kidnapped by somebody

normal? Like a drug cartel. They'd have just chopped off a few of his fingers and he could have healed himself with no problems. Instead, he got nabbed by someone who liked to leave behind a magical version of toxic sludge.

I shivered when the gunk latched onto my tail and absorbed into my skin. The magic inside of me tried to contract into a tiny ball, fleeing the thread of Celestial power seeping into me. The lights flickered and the sides of my vision darkened.

This was so not good.

"Faith?" I heard Lisa from a distance, calling for me and pounding on the door, as the world went black.

Chapter Eighteen

The phone rang and I rolled over to answer it. Whatever was in the magical energy that I'd absorbed, it packed one hell of a punch. "Hello?"

"Faith?" Dan asked, sounding concerned.

"Dan?" I hurt too much to care that he had crossed over into stalker territory with his phone calls.

"Are you okay? You sound like you're hungover."

"What? No, just tired." I snuggled closer to my pillow. "What time is it?"

"Ten in the morning."

Okay, what was the big deal? Ten wasn't all that late for me to sleep, honestly. Hello? I worked the midnight shift.

"On Monday," he added.

"Monday?" That wasn't good. Tolliver had been taken on a Thursday. My parents' wedding was scheduled for Saturday. There was no way today was Monday. Because even if I was on my deathbed my mother would have dressed me up in that ugly bridesmaid's dress so she could have the wedding of her dreams.

Unless they'd canceled the wedding, and there was only one reason I could think of that Mom would allow that to happen. Tolliver must still be missing. But that didn't explain why they'd let me pull a Rip Van Dyke, or Winkle, or whatever his name was. The door flew open and Lisa rushed into the room, flinging herself onto the bed beside me. She hugged me so tight that I was thankful that I didn't actually need to breathe. "Faith! I've been so worried about you."

"So have I," the voice in the phone said, sounding amused.

"What?" I pressed the phone back to my ear and tried to squirm free of my best friend's grip of death.

"You didn't show up to work last night. Andrea said Lisa had called you in sick and that it had to be something serious because you never missed your shifts. So I did a little hacking into the computer and found out you've never taken a sick day, in the four years, eleven months, and twenty-two days since you were hired at Rogers Hospital."

"I hesitate to ask this but why were you so concerned about seeing me?" I croaked.

"I have your purse."

I sat up and pulled the phone away from my ear, staring at it for a second before pressing the receiver back to my ear. "You have my purse? How did you get my purse?"

"You left it sitting in the conference room. I found it when I went back to teach my next security seminar," he replied.

"Oh. Well when and where can I meet you to pick it up?"

"Don't worry about it," he said. "Since you're sick I thought I'd be a nice guy and deliver it myself. Nice shade of peach, by the way."

"What?" I looked over at Lisa and then at the curtains. What the hell was he doing outside my building?

"I'd have expected blackouts since you worked the graveyard shift but those are much prettier. Very feminine," Dan continued.

I scurried out of bed and threw back the curtains he'd just called feminine. I saw him leaning against the side of his black Triumph motorcycle and he held my purse up, waving it at me.

"What are you doing here?" I shrieked, still feeling about three seconds behind in this conversation. Which was pretty good considering I'd been without coffee for almost four whole days.

"Returning your purse, of course." He dropped it back onto the motorcycle's seat. "What else would I be doing? Are you busy?"

"Am I what?" My jaw dropped and I stared as he smiled back up at me from the window.

"It sounds so much better than *what are you wearing*?" He sat on the bike and crossed his ankles, his smile going from charming to downright smug.

"Agh!" I backed away from the window and threw the curtains closed, then got a look at myself in the mirror. My hair looked like a tornado had ripped through it, and I was in rubber ducky pajamas. Green rubber ducky pajamas.

"Now don't be that way," he said. "All I want to do is return your purse. Possibly talk a bit."

"Talk about what?"

"You haven't read the papers? Or talked to the police?"

"Look." I combed my fingers through my blond tangles. "It's not a good time right now. With my brother missing and everything. I'm just—"

"They've found a suicide note in Dr. Cosgrove's personal effects. He confessed to killing that pediatrician who was found in the Dumpster. They also found the stuff to make bombs that link him to some other case here in Pittsburgh. It looks like Emily's poor, bankrupt parents might have been into something more sinister and unpatriotic than we first thought."

"What? Dr. Cosgrove was a terrorist?" There had to be some mistake. Dr. Cosgrove, the guy who quoted poetry and wore a Professors for Peace button, was supposed to be some nut trying to overthrow the government?

I looked over at Lisa, whose eyes focused on my comforter, and whose shoulders curled inward, and suddenly I just knew. My stomach curled up into a knot and all I wanted to do was throw up.

"According to my administrative assistant there are federal agents all over MEDTECH looking for clues to link the Cosgrove brothers to any number of criminal organizations. She says she can't sneeze without one of the government guys trying to test her for viral pathogens. "

"I still don't believe it," I said and narrowed my eyes at Lisa. "You said that he confessed to killing Dr. Winslow? Maybe Dr. Cosgrove killed him because he was afraid of getting caught with the morphine. Maybe Dr. Winslow confronted Dr. Cosgrove and he killed him to get away. I don't know. But I just can't believe he was a terrorist."

"Why? Because he was a middle class white guy who taught English Literature?"

"No, because terrorists aren't the types of guys who comfort the nurses when a child dies. They don't sit up with other parents keeping vigil over terminally ill kids. I don't care if he had a PhD in Chemistry and every piece of clothing he owned was covered in gun powder, Dr. Cosgrove was a good man." Tears welled up in my eyes. "He was a decent guy and I refuse to believe he was a terrorist."

"I don't want to argue with you and for what it's worth I think you're right. I never got the whole terrorist vibe from his brother, either, and I've worked for him since I was a junior in college." Dan said. "Look, why don't you come for a ride with me and we'll talk about it? Maybe, between the two of us, we can figure out something that the investigators might have missed."

"I can't." I shifted my weight from one foot to another. "I need to stay here in case we hear something about my brother. But thanks for the offer."

"What about your purse?"

"Give me two minutes to get dressed and I'll be down to get it."

"If that's really want to you want."

"Yes, it is." I hung up the phone before he could argue. I turned and saw Lisa staring at me, her face filled with guilt.

"Faith, I'm sorry about Dr. Cosgrove. I know he was a good guy and we all felt terrible about what happened to his daughter. But you've got to understand—"

"I don't have to understand anything." I put my hands on the top of my dresser and bent my head, unable to even look myself in the mirror even though I didn't have a part in this. "Just tell me that you let me sleep because you found Tolliver."

"Nope." She picked at the seam of my peach comforter. "No luck yet. But your dad and the rest think they've narrowed down a trail to follow. He said to let you sleep until you had your power back. Plus he was worried that you might get upset about the whole thing with Dr. Cosgrove."

"And you agreed? I should have just slept while my brother was missing and you were smearing the memory of a dead man?"

"I couldn't have woken you up even if I'd wanted to." She hopped up from the bed, pacing. "Your mom and I tried and you didn't even move. Hope and Malachi both said you were drained. Whatever that stuff was, it was nasty. We finally had to get your uncle in here to help. According to Hope, He may have saved your life."

"What do you mean?"

"Whatever that stuff was the Alpha said it wasn't meant for Tolliver. It wasn't some sort of residual gunk left behind by the sprites," she said. "He said it was some sort of nasty hex, specifically tuned to attack you. Whoever left it behind meant for that magic to take you out."

"Shit." I walked over to my closet and searched for a pair of clean sweatpants. What was it with people and trying to kill me all the time? I'm the most harmless demon there is. I pay my taxes and donate to the local fire department. Hell, I work with sick kids for a living. I even buy Girl Scout cookies. In bulk. But no, it's always me people try to kill.

"Yeah," she said. "After the Alpha had finished taking care of you your dad sent Malachi and a few other demonlords to find Matt's mom and Brenda. Mal's got the two of them separated, questioning them."

"What?" I turned to look at her, my search for clothes abandoned. She stopped pacing and sat on the side of the bed, staring at her hands.

"The Alpha and your father think the Angale had something to do with the attack on you and Tolliver. Malachi and Jesus have Brenda in Hope's apartment, and Karathian has Matt and his mom locked up together in his apartment. They don't think Matt had anything to do with it but they're hoping he can somehow make her see sense before this turns into an all out war."

"Damn it," I muttered and turned back to my pile of clean clothes. I grabbed a T-shirt and a pair of black sweatpants and hurried into the bathroom, not bothering to close the door all the way. "I have to get over there."

"You don't want to do that," she warned me.

"Why? What haven't you told me?" I stripped out of my pajamas and hurried into my clean clothes.

Lisa came over and leaned on the doorjamb. "Trust me on this."

"Why?"

"When your dad found out Valerie and the Angale might be behind Tolliver's disappearance, and your accident, he had one of those…what's he call it? Oh yeah. A moment of anger. Matt was the closest Angale he could get to."

Oh great, first I'd gotten into an argument with him, and now my dad beat him up? The odds of salvaging this relationship were dwindling into single digits. I should have stayed unconscious. "How bad?"

"Not *terrible.*" She reached over to pat my shoulder, still avoiding my eyes. "Your dad just picked him up and shook him, yelled a bit."

Liar. "What aren't you telling me?"

"Then Matt lost his temper and essentially told your dad off."

"Oh brilliant." I grabbed my sneakers and pushed past her to sit on my bed and put them on. "Anything else?"

"Then he said some rather unflattering things about demons, so your father told him if he felt that way he should just stay the hell away from you. Matt told him that wouldn't be a problem in the slightest. To consider the two of you through. That was when your father pretty much kicked his ass. The Alpha tried to stop it. He's sure that Matt was under the influence of the same gunk that was affecting you and it was making him irrational, but you know how your father is—he tends to punch first and ask questions later."

Great. I'd been dumped via a conversation with my father by a guy who may or may not have been under the influence of a nasty bit of magical mischief. You'd think that wouldn't be such a surprise given my life, but nope, this was actually a first. Well at least it didn't end with the guy in question in a psychiatric ward. Score one for me.

"Shit." I finished tying my shoes and stood, leaving my shattered heart scattered across the floor. "Is he okay? Matt, I mean? Dad didn't kill him, did he?"

"He was a little bruised but he healed quickly. But how are you? Are you going to be okay?"

"I'll be fine. Let me go get my purse from Dan and then I'll go talk to Matt. I'm sure with a bit of screaming and a few smacks to the head I can make them both see reason. Then, instead of beating each other up, they can get back to trying to find Tolliver."

"Do you think that will work?" She followed me out of my bedroom and down the hall to my empty front room.

"I doubt it but I'm all out of better ideas right now. So if you've got another suggestion…"

"Nope."

"Right." I hurried out of the apartment, ran down the steps, and pushed open the front door of the building.

"That might have been the longest two minutes of my life," Dan said when I stopped in front of his bike. He held out my purse and waved it back and forth.

"I'm running short on clean clothes that match." I took my purse and slung it over my shoulder. "Thanks for dropping this off. I appreciate it."

"No problem." He grabbed my free hand. "Are you sure about the ride?"

"I need to stay here in case we hear something about my brother. But thanks for the invite. Maybe next time."

"Sure," he brought my hand up to kiss the back of it.

I pulled away from him and turned away, not bothering to look back. Dan was my past and—even if my relationship with Matt was over—no good had ever come out of regretting the life you didn't get the chance to live.

I ran up the front steps and entered the front door to my building, my head down. Inside I smacked into a solid, muscular chest. I looked up and found Matt staring down at me, his face filled with hurt.

Chapter Nineteen

"Must be one hell of a software update if the computer guy's got to drive over here a second time to see you about it." Matt's shoulders were tense and his jaw was clenched.

Guilt flooded through me, and I tried to remind myself that I'd done nothing wrong. I'd told him we needed to talk but we hadn't actually had the chance to. Our relationship was strained already and he'd caught me in what looked like a really compromising position. Which was not how I wanted this conversation to go, but now I didn't have a choice anymore. I had to tell him the truth. I'd put it off for way too long and now it was so much worse than it should have been. "That's Dan."

"*The* Dan, I take it?"

"Yeah. I'm sorry. I tried to tell you that he was in town before but we never sat down and just talked. And nothing happened between us. I mean he wanted something to happen but—"

"Well at least I know I never had a chance with him in the picture. Maybe it'll make it easier knowing the game was rigged before someone bothered to tell me we were playing for keeps."

He looked out the door, refusing to meet my eyes, and I could see that he was grinding his teeth together.

"Maybe that's the real problem, Matt. You can't seem to understand that I'm not a prize to be won." I walked past him and Nahamia, who had been watching him from the first step. "Besides, you didn't want me anymore. I'm just like the rest of them, remember?"

"One mistake and there's no coming back from it, is there? One bad reaction to a spell that was loaded down with negative energy and that's it. We're through. Why? Because Faith Bettincourt's tender mercies don't rain down upon those of us who might not live up to her standards of perfection?"

I didn't even bother reminding him that it was him that dumped me, not the other way around. What was the point? He'd already decided who was to blame in this situation.

Besides, what was he doing lurking in the vestibule anyway? I thought he was under lock and key with his mother inside his apartment.

I walked upstairs and opened the door to my apartment. My father sat on my couch next to Lisa, while Hope tinkered around in my kitchen and Malachi and Jesus talked quietly on my couch. Everyone turned to look at me, and almost as one, they all found somewhere else to look, like they wanted to do anything else but make eye contact.

"So." Jesus looked around at everyone else and shifted his weight on the couch like he was trying to find a way for this to not be a massively uncomfortable moment for all of us. "Are we going to discuss the big white elephant in the room, or are we going to pretend it doesn't exist?"

"If you're talking about the fact none of you can bother to call before you drop in, then sure, let's talk about it. If you want to talk about my love life—"

"We don't want to talk about your love life," Dad interrupted. "But we do need to talk about Matt."

"Why?" I asked.

"Because Matt may know where Tolliver is," Lisa said.

"Excuse me?" I stared at her, stunned. Did she say what I thought she just said?

"He knows where they're keeping Tolliver," Hope agreed. "Once he quit being pissed off at Dad for kicking his ass he started thinking about it and put the pieces together. He thinks he might know where the Angale have hidden Tolliver. So, the two of you are going to go get him. Together."

"You want me to do what?" I stared at my father. He'd beat Matt up yesterday—or was it the day before?—and now he wanted me to tag along with him on the off chance that we might find Tolliver? I wasn't the darkest demon in the flock, and I could see serious issues with this plan.

"We're going to Biloxi together," Matt said from the doorway. "Actually, about five miles outside of Biloxi. If they're keeping Tolliver anywhere, it will be close to Neaveh."

"Neaveh?" I asked.

"The Angale compound," Jesus said.

Matt nodded. "The others figured since the two of us had phased together a few times before it would be easier to control if you were the demon they chained me to."

Nahamia opened his hand and a pair of blue-black bracelets appeared. He grabbed Matt's wrist and slapped the first cuff onto his left hand and then stepped forward and lowered his head in front of me. "Your Highness?"

I lifted my arm and he fitted the bracelet around my wrist. Celestial power surged through the link and I sucked in a deep breath, shocked by how intimate it was to be able to wield Matt's powers.

"The Angale's power is yours to control," the archdemon said, and backed toward the door. "Should he do anything unwise, my recommendation would be to drain his physical body, banish his soul to the Grey Lands, and then leave the carcass for his own kind to deal with."

"Noted." I felt imps fluttering in my stomach.

"Are you ready?" Matt asked, acting like he hadn't heard Nahamia's advice.

My heart clenched at the dull look in his eyes. "As I'll ever be." I closed my eyes, focusing on the place he was picturing in his mind. A phase portal slid open and the image on the other end wavered, then solidified. "Is that the right place?"

"Yeah." Matt walked through the window between realities, and I followed.

We were in the front yard of a white farmhouse with boarded up windows. The paint was faded and the mailbox next to the front door was covered in rust. A swing in the front tree rocked back and forth idly in the breeze and the grass shifted against my knees.

"This is the headquarters of the fearsome Angale army?" I asked, skeptical.

"No." He shook his head. "This is where it all started for us. This is where my mother grew up."

"So you think she stashed Tolliver here because…?" I glanced at the house and then back at him.

"If she was going to hide him anywhere it would be somewhere she felt safe. Somewhere her madness made sense." He kept his eyes fixed on the house and lifted the latch on the chicken wire fence.

"*This* is that place?" I looked around the yard and tried to picture Matt spending time somewhere like this. It was…well it definitely didn't scream "idealistic childhood home" that was for damn sure.

"Strangely enough." He pushed the gate open and walked into the yard. "Yes, this is that place. Why?"

"I don't know." I shrugged and followed him up the cracked, concrete walk toward the obviously abandoned house. "I just expected something—I don't know—*more*."

"Sorry to disappoint you." He reached for my hand but pulled away. He grimaced at me and shook his head before he started up the front steps. "Come on, let's get Tolliver and go back to your place. The sooner this is done with the better."

"Fine." I followed him up the steps, my heart feeling like it had been shattered into a million pieces and was currently being ground into dust by a pair of vengeful imps. "I couldn't agree more."

"Whatever gets the two of you home," he said.

"I think you'll find that your count is off," I said. "There are three of us that will be going back to Pittsburgh. I can't release you without my father's permission."

"Who said anything about release?" Matt turned around to loom over me, his green eyes burning. "Didn't you hear Nahamia? They don't want you to release me. They want you to drain my powers and banish me somewhere so they don't have to deal with me anymore."

"Well then, they'll have to learn to live with disappointment," I said. "I'm not banishing anyone. Especially you. I don't want you to get hurt."

I pushed past him into the house and looked around at the empty room with its dank, dingy looking walls that were once probably white but now a sort of soggy yellow. The floor was covered in dust, and with the boarded up windows the place had a sad, lonely feel to it. Like its people had left one day and never bothered to look back.

"I said something I didn't mean in a fit of anger." Matt followed me into the main room, standing close enough so that we were nose to nose. "Which, if you haven't heard already, was brought on by your father kicking my ass, and just so you know, he doesn't fight fair."

"Of course he doesn't fight fair. He's the Devil. Fair is not a word in his vocabulary."

"Then I find out you've been seeing your ex-fiancé behind my back." Matt started toward another room. I followed him into what had once been a kitchen, judging by the cracked black and white checked linoleum and dust-covered green counters, and put my hands on my hips.

"I wasn't *seeing* Dan." I brought my fingers up to make air quotes. "I'm with you. Or I was with you. Besides, I tried to tell you what was going on."

"Yeah well you didn't try too hard, did you?" He turned and stalked out of the empty room and into another one. Hellfire tingled between my fingers and I had to bite back the urge to give him a solid zap in the ass. With the way he had his head crammed up there it might cause brain damage.

"Let's just get my brother and get out of here." I pushed past him and into another empty room. We made our way upstairs and found it deserted as well. Tolliver wasn't here.

I lifted my nose and sniffed, pulling on Matt's power through the link between us. He drew back and I could feel him trying to resist the control my mind had over his. I tugged harder and felt my control of his powers strengthen.

Sunshine and chocolate chip cookies. Dust. I could smell mothballs in one of the closets downstairs. But nothing in the place smelled like Tolliver. I stretched my powers and tried to locate him. Nothing. There were no demons anywhere nearby and from the smell of things, there hadn't been demons around here for a very long time. If they'd ever bothered to check this place out at all.

"Wherever they're keeping Tolliver, it isn't here." I slumped down on one of the stairs.

"He has to be," Matt said. "This is where she hides everything of value."

I motioned around the first floor and then pointed upstairs. "What of value do you see in this house? Unless she's found a way to spin dust to gold there's nothing here."

"I know." Matt sat beside me and dragged his hands over his face. "That's what I can't understand. This was always Mom's hiding place. If she was going to hide Tolliver anywhere, this would be it."

"So your hypothesis is what? Because he's not here she's not responsible for stealing him?" I nudged him with my shoulder. "Or do you think she turned him into a garden gnome and stashed him outside?"

"No," Matt whispered. "She confessed to me that she sent the sprites to attack Tolliver and that she'd cast a trap to kill you. She kept telling me how she'd done it for me. Like this was something I wanted."

"Didn't you? You did dump me after all."

He rubbed his hands over his face again. "For the last time, I was mad when I said that thing about breaking up with you."

"But I'm just like they are. Just another demon."

"No." He lunged forward and grabbed me around the waist, pressing his forehead against mine. "You're mine."

I felt my heart flutter and I leaned into him, my lips seeking his like they held the answer to life, the universe, and the all-important question of why the heck no one could make a low-calorie chocolate ice cream that actually tasted like chocolate ice cream was supposed to.

Then I remembered that this was the guy who walked out on me while I was unconscious and apparently fighting for my life. "You left me." I kept my eyes focused on his and swallowed. "I need to be with someone who thinks I'm worth fighting for. Someone who wants to be in with me no matter what it takes. If you truly want me, the real me and not just some idea of me, you'd have fought for me."

"He may not want you," a reedy voice said and I turned around to see a green sprite hovering in front of my face. "But I do. In fact, I want you both."

He snapped his fingers and a swarm of sprites appeared out of nowhere, surrounding us. Shit, we'd walked straight into an ambush and I'd been too distracted to even notice.

Chapter Twenty

"Oh, God damn it." I reached for my power and my brain slammed against the mental equivalent of a brick wall. My magic, straining toward me through the block, was no use. Crap. So much for smiting the damn things with hellfire. It seems they'd learned from their experience with Tolliver and weren't taking any chances.

"I thought you said they were simple creatures." I smacked at the sprite clinging to my left arm and tried to pull on my powers again. Instead of retreating the little bastard bit down on my right thumb.

"They are." Matt's face had gone pale, like he'd been sucker punched.

"I swear to all that's evil I'm going to kill your mother for getting me into this mess. I should have known that she'd figure out that you were going to come here and leave an ambush behind."

"I thought you said you didn't believe in murder?" Matt reached out to snatch a sprite out of the air, and when he caught the little monster he flung it across the room.

"I'm reevaluating my belief system on killing right now. Ask me again later," I said. Half the sprites surrounded me, wrapping silky threads around my legs. Flying imps crossbred with spiders. Perfect. Just what you want in a heavenly creature.

They cocooned my body up to my chest and wrapped my arms up to the elbows to pin my sides. Within seconds I was standing like a half-finished mummy. They had Matt wrapped up, too. Efficient little buggers. I'd give them that.

"Reevaluate silently," the sprite from earlier said, flying close to my face. "Your prattle annoys me."

"Hey!" Matt yelled. "Talk to my girlfriend that way again, and when this is over I'll get the weed killer out and bathe you in it."

"Your threats of murder don't scare me, traitor." The sprite made a show of sticking his nose up at the two of us like we were shit on his tiny little shoes. "Daharack is the High Emperor of the Sprite Kingdom. When he is successful in his task he will be given power beyond all reckoning. Even the loathsome Tailed Ones will quake in fear at my reign."

"Tailed Ones?" I raised my eyebrows at Matt.

"Cats," he said, his face pale. "Sprites loathe cats."

"Murderers," the tiny megalomaniac screeched. "The evil beings hunt us down and perpetrate genocide amongst us. They would strip us from our rightful place and exterminate us. They are devil's spawn."

"No they aren't," I said. Okay, so he was a crazy little monster who had ambushed me and now had me tied up. And yeah, I was going to smite the ever-living hell out of him once I was loose. But I could sort of understand his whole *Hatred of Cats* thing. Dan's cat Copernicus had loved bringing me presents when we lived together, and birds were her favorite since they were airborne targets. If I had to guess I'd say sprites were a whole new level of difficulty, which meant serious bragging rights for one of the more competitive cats out there.

"Do you say Daharack lies? Do you suggest that I, Daharack, would play my pack false?" He thumped his scrawny chest like an angry war chieftain from one of those old school spaghetti Westerns.

I tried to hold back my smile. "No, but I can tell you for certain that the feline species was not created by the Devil. They aren't demon spawn."

"They are!" he insisted.

"They aren't." I hopped closer to him so we were nose to nose—or as close to that as we could be since my nose was bigger than his entire face. "Trust me, I'd know, I'm devil spawn and we can all identify each other. Besides, the Devil's allergic."

"What?" Daharack flitted back from me. "What lies spill from your evil mouth?"

"My father is allergic to cats," I said. "Totally allergic. Can't even be in a house where one lives. It makes his skin go all blotchy then he swells up and starts to wheeze."

"You lie." Daharack pointed his tiny clawed hand at my nose.

"I do not." I jerked my head toward Matt. "Ask the nephilim."

"I refuse to recognize that the race traitor is among us," Daharack said with a sniff. "He offends my eyes. His mere presence disgusts me."

"Why? Because he's been dating the Devil's daughter? You can sit here and argue with me, but *he* offends you?"

"He is a traitor to our kind!" Daharack yelled. "You, demon child, cannot help the unfortunate circumstances of your birth but that thing chose his own fate. He's chosen to cast himself out of the light. For that he must die. Our law decrees it!"

"What? That's the stupidest thing I've ever heard. He's offended you and so you've just decided to kill him? Why? Because he doesn't think that the Apocalypse is a really nifty idea?"

"Because I love you, stupid," Matt answered softly.

"What?" I whipped my head to the side so that I could look at him. We were being held captive by psychotic sprites who were experts in mummy wrapping. I couldn't feel my toes or my fingers, and this is when he decides to declare his love for me? For the love of all Evil, someone had to talk to this man about his timing.

"Daharack cares not for the traitor and his words." The ugly little sprite flew closer to me. "Daharack wants to know of this allergy the Woman of the Forked Tongue speaks."

I turned to the overgrown dragonfly. "The Devil has hounds. Hell hounds. He has big black dogs that howl and chase down wicked mortals on moonless nights. They also go ape shit for cherry-dipped chocolate ice cream cones from Dairy Queen. Get over it already. Can you not see that we're having a moment here?"

I thought the people on my side of the arrangement were a pain in the ass. At least our pets didn't back talk. I reached for my powers and winced as a sharp electric current raced along my spine instead. Matt hissed and the bracelet on my wrist heated as his pain flowed back through the link between us.

"The Devil has no Tailed Ones," Daharack said, putting the pieces together in his tiny cracked out mind. His eyes sort of lit up and I thought he had that look primitive guys had when they figured out they were supposed to bang the rocks together instead of beating each other over the head with them.

"The Devil has The Ones That Bark. The Ones That Bark hate the Tailed Ones. They declare war upon the evil beasts and chase them from their lairs."

"Yes," I said. "The Devil prefers dogs. Congratulations, you're catching on. Meanwhile, God has a big white fluffy Persian named Magdalene. And Jesus has two Tabbies, Mark and Matthew."

"The Light and The Glorious Return own Tailed Ones?"

"Yes, so I highly doubt they're going to let you declare war upon their pets. But if you let me go and lead me to my brother, I'm pretty sure my dad will reward you with a whole animal shelter full of cats to slaughter. Fluffy death for everyone."

Another sprite flittered forward and whispered to Daharack. The two of them huddled and whispered, waving their tiny arms in the air like they were arguing. Perhaps Daharack wasn't quite the unquestioning king of the sprites he thought he was?

"Your offer intrigues me." Daharack turned toward me with an appraising look on his face.

"Good. Take me to my brother and once I know he's safe I'll work out a deal for you with Dad." Finally we were getting somewhere. Now if the freak would just unwrap me I could squish him like a bug so we could get out of here.

"No." Daharack flittered close enough that I could smell his nasty mulch breath.

"No?"

"I said your deal intrigues me, Woman of the Forked Tongue. I did not say I would accept it. We take our chances with the Beings of White. Bring them!"

Well crap, so much for negotiation.

The sprites swarmed around us and I was lifted off the ground, tilted backward so I was staring at the ceiling. Perfect. All they needed were bones through their noses and a couple of cooking pots for this to become a messed up, angelic version of a Bugs Bunny cartoon.

"Oh, come on," I yelled and tried to kick my feet. "Give me a break. I'm offering to cut you a deal and you're still taking me to the dungeon? When I get free, I swear to everything that's evil I'm buying an industrial sized thing of RAID and a flyswatter. You think cats are bad? You just wait."

"Faith," Matt's voice was resigned.

"Then I'm gonna throw you in a hamster cage and leave it in the Grey Lands."

"Faith," Matt said, and I turned to see him giving me the "*you're so stupid I wonder how you've managed to survive this long on your own*" look. I wasn't the one who led us into an ambush by sprites. Sprites! Did he realize how much shit I was going to take for this later? Especially if I didn't manage to rescue Tolliver.

I squinted at the bright sunlight and tried to come up with a plan as the sprites took us out the backdoor of the farmhouse and into the forest crowding the back of the house. Sprites and imps weren't high enough up the food chain to phase between spaces in reality, and Tolliver wasn't in the Grey Lands. Matt had been right all along. Shit. There'd be no living with him if we made it out of this with our powers intact.

I stared at the trees as they passed above me and my spirits sank. I was being held prisoner by a bunch of garden sprites. With my ex-boyfriend. *Boyfriend.* I wasn't sure what our status was right now. Either way he was a guy the sprites had no problem taking along with me to have our powers sacrificed. Or be banished from the mortal realm. Or hell, have the physical bodies we were using butchered and our consciousness fragmented to the wind. How was I supposed to know what a bunch of garden sprites had in mind to torture us?

No matter what they decided to do to us they were taking Matt along on this little adventure with us. Which meant he probably hadn't known this was going to happen. That wonderful conclusion left me with nobody's ass to kick for this stupid mistake except my own. And kicking your own ass is always difficult. Especially when you lack flexibility like I do.

"Faith," Matt whispered.

"What?"

"Are you all right?"

"What do you think?"

"It's going to be okay."

I looked over at him, raising my eyebrows. He was joking, right?

"Sprites aren't aggressive. They're cowards by nature. Once they realize your father and the Alpha will get angry about your disappearance they'll turn us back over and grovel on their knees to keep from being punished. The trick is not to rile them up before someone comes to save us."

"So the whole *Going to War With House Cats* thing? You don't think that's aggressive?"

"Well okay, so this group is a little more peeved off than usual but I still don't think they'd hurt us. If you don't piss them off I think we might be able to negotiate our way out of this."

"No more talking," Daharack said. I gritted my teeth and fantasized about all the ways I was going to make him suffer once we were free. "The prisoners will be silent."

I rolled my eyes at Matt. Sprites weren't aggressive? So what? Our miniature ringleader was an outlier with a bad attitude? And a name. Which, come to think of it, when did sprites start taking names?

"Hey, Matt?" I whispered.

"Yeah?"

"No talking!" Daharack shrieked again. "I am Daharack, High Emperor of the Sprites, and I forbid the Woman of the Forked Tongue and the Race Traitor from speaking."

"Never mind." I turned my face forward.

"I said—" Daharack screamed, flying over to levitate in front of me. Instead of flipping down to face me, though, he gave me a clear shot up his tiny loincloth. I cringed. I'd been assuming Daharack was a male sprite. But apparently, unlike imps, sprites were genderless. No wonder he was so cranky.

I closed my eyes to avoid seeing his tiny ass again. "Hey, Daharack."

"What?"

"You know what I'm going to do before I throw you in that hamster cage in the Grey Lands? I'm going to rip your wings off and tape them to my bedroom window like some sort of sun catcher a serial killer made in art therapy class."

"You don't scare me," Daharack said. "You have to escape first."

My toes went cold. Picking my head up, I looked at the wavering bit that had appeared in front of us and watched my legs disappear beyond it. That couldn't be good.

"They've got a reality bubble," Matt said, groaning. "Like the one we have at Neveah. Great. Just what we needed today."

"Somebody will find us." I bit my lower lip. The air around my ears turned icy as they carried me through the wall of their bubble. "When we don't come back they'll send out a search party."

"Except for the whole reality bubble thing," Matt said. "The only way you can find one of those is if you know where it is to begin with. They aren't just invisible. Unless you know one exists it doesn't manifest in this version of reality."

"So nobody's coming for us?" I asked. "But, even if they do, this place doesn't exist for them?"

"Yep." Matt said, popping his "p."

"So we've got to get out of here ourselves is what you're saying?"

"That's exactly what I'm saying."

I picked my head up and looked at the sprawling, seething mass of sprites filling this hidden space. Matt's mom had struck up an agreement with a pack of feral sprites. Who had us trapped in a place that didn't actually exist unless you knew it was there. Great. My day was getting better and better with every passing moment.

"No worries. We'll be out of here by dinner." I looked back over at Matt and tried my best to smile. There was no reason to let him see that I was scared. I was the only one who had access to our combined powers and that meant it was my job to get us out of here.

Chapter Twenty-One

"Tell me again how I had to be mistaken about the sprites taking Tolliver?" I squirmed my back against the rough bark of the weeping willow tree Daharack's minions had propped us up against, trying to find a way to get clear of my bindings and not getting anywhere. I looked out at the sprite camp and tried to kick my feet. No luck there, either. "How they weren't aggressive? Simple creatures you called them. Think you might want to reevaluate your position, Mr. Andrews?"

"Would it help if I said you were right?" Matt rolled his eyes. "You were right. I was wrong. Okay? I…was…wrong. Does that make you feel better?"

The swarming mass shifted and pulled at each other, flittering to and fro, a high-pitched wail reverberating from their constant motion. It was like being trapped inside a giant beehive filled with very large, homicidal bees.

"No," I said.

"No?" He raised his eyebrows and I could tell he wanted to reach up and tug at the ends of his hair. But he couldn't. Because

Daharack had us trussed up like a bunch of Christmas hams. "Why not?"

"Because this is the fucking icing on the cake. Think about it. We've had almost no time alone in the past month. Or sex life is nonexistent. Then, just when it seemed like things were settling down, your crazy ex-girlfriend shows up and moves her ass onto my couch." I knew I was being irrational but right now I didn't see how that could make things any worse.

"You were the one who insisted she stay at your place. I wanted to put her ass on a bus the minute she got there," Matt said, and I felt a surge of power through the link bonding us.

"I know I did but you shouldn't have listened to me. You know damn well and good I make decisions without thinking them all the way through."

"Now you tell me. Or is that your excuse for snuggling up with your ex-boyfriend the minute my back was turned?" Power surged through the link again and I stretched my mind toward it. If I strained I could just about wrap my mind around the edges of it. I gave an experimental tug and Matt's face paled. Crap. So much for that idea.

"I wasn't *snuggling up* to anyone. The only person I even want to snuggle with is you, you big, stupid jerk. The problem is people keep interrupting just when it's starting to get good."

"So there's nothing going on between you and Dan? You're being serious? Nothing happened between the two of you?" Cautious hope filled his eyes.

"Of course not." I huffed and shook my head, trying my best to channel the unspoken "*you stupid, stupid man*" vibe. "Nothing has happened between us and the one time he tried to make something happen I smacked him across the face. I don't want him. I want you."

"Even though I'm a big, stupid jerk?"

"Yes, even though you're a big, stupid jerk and we're stuck underneath a tree like a couple of second rate mummies at a really crappy flea market. I love you."

"You know that's the first time you've ever said it?" Matt shifted closer and licked his lower lip, his eyes filled with intent. "I should have known you'd have to call me a name first and say something off the wall immediately afterward. But that doesn't change the fact that—"

"Well, if we're going to end up stuck in the Grey Lands, or something worse, I thought I should say that first."

"You're not going to get banished to the Grey Lands," Matt said.

"Why is that?"

"Because we're not going to let that little shit Daharack beat us. You're Satan's daughter and I'm a nephilim. We're not getting outsmarted by a bunch of flying twerps."

"So how are we going to stop them?"

"You can feel my powers." Matt smiled. "I felt it when you tried a minute ago. You can touch them. Can't you?"

"Yes." I wrinkled my nose at him. "But I don't see what good it will do. There's got to be a million sprites in here. We aren't going to be able to sneak past all of them."

"Who said anything about sneaking?" Matt asked. "You're going to get the two of us free from these webs and then we're leaving here fighting."

"But—" My stomach clenched. He was right. If we could get free, and if I could manage to channel his powers—both of which were huge ifs—we might be able to get out of here. Or we could get our asses kicked.

Even worse, I could be forced to drain him off all of his powers and that would take his mortal form apart at the angelic equivalent of the molecular level—which would leave his soul trapped in the Celestial realms, unable to manifest in a human form. If we were lucky he'd end up like Harold. If not? He'd be trapped in Heaven—the one place I couldn't follow.

"Concentrate," Matt said. "You're going to get us out of here, Faith."

Damn it. I hated when he decided to trust me. Because the thing was, if there was one creature on Earth you shouldn't trust it was a demon. We didn't deserve it.

I closed my eyes and tried to still my mind. Near the top of my head, dark power tickled the inside of my skull. I reached for it mentally and the power sparked, flaring into life. It slipped through my mental fingers, smooth as silk, and I managed to grasp it. I tugged and my wings began to twitch. Now we were getting somewhere.

My horns inched upward of their own volition and my tail itched, confined inside my cocoon. I focused on releasing my wings and the silken bonds gave way, allowing me room to breathe. The wings had torn the wrappings down far enough for me to pull my hands free and I ripped through the bindings around my legs. My tail shot free and I sighed in relief at how good it felt to not be cramped up like an elephant inside a wine bottle anymore.

Matt groaned, and I looked over at him, my heart racing. He was still wrapped up tight, his face a sickly gray and sweat beading on his forehead. Shit. I was draining him through our link. I concentrated on the dark energy swirling through me and tried to push some of it back toward him through the link. But it was like there was a faucet between us. Power flowed out of him to me, but I couldn't send it back.

"Matt?" I knelt to pull him free of the bindings. "You okay?"

He lay there, sucking in deep breathes and trembling. I wrapped an arm around his shoulders and helped him to sit up. He rubbed at his cuffed wrist and I could see ugly red blisters forming underneath the blue-black metal. I laid my fingers over the skin and the blisters disappeared, but his skin was still an ugly, raw red.

"Okay maybe try to pull a little less power? Jesus, I feel like I just ran a marathon and then got my ass kicked at the end of it."

"I'm so sorry." I grabbed the wrist cuff on his arm, prepared to yank it off and give him complete freedom. Besides, if we had to fight our way out of here it would be better if he had control of his own powers. If we got separated somehow he needed to be able to save himself.

"Don't." He jerked his arm away from mine and cradled it against his chest. "The only person who can take the cuffs off of us is Nahamia."

"What?"

"They've been bonded to us," Matt explained. "They're held in place with dark power. If you try to remove them, they go boom, my body goes boom, and I'm trapped outside the mortal realm."

"Are you kidding me?" I yelped. "You let them put a handcuff on you that has an explosive inside it? So what? If you take it off then you basically die?"

"In the mortal sense…" Matt shrugged. "Using your way of putting it, yes, if I take the cuff off my body dies. If you die, I die. If you pull too much power through our link I die. If back in Pittsburgh, Nahamia gets hit by a bus and somehow dies, I die. In short, if this doesn't go perfectly, my body is toast."

"But—" I looked first at my wrist and then at his. I let go of my grasp on our powers and retreated into my own mind. "How are we supposed to fight our way out of here if you can't use your powers?"

"You'll use them."

"But I could drain you."

He gave me a sad smile and shook his head, so much better than me at conveying annoyed amusement at the fact that I'd just now caught up with what he'd been saying from the beginning of this craptastic little adventure. "If we stay here they'll kill me. Given the way this plan is going right now let's just say I'll be lucky to join Harold on the phantom golf circuit before the day is out. Otherwise it's an eternity of harp lessons. Not my idea of a good time."

I smacked him on the shoulder and scooted closer, so that our sides were touching. "Nobody is dying, or leaving the mortal realm, or whatever you want to call it." I pulled my knees up to my chest and wrapped my arms around them.

"Somebody's going to have to," Matt said. He scooted back into the shadows of the willow tree. I followed him and we huddled together, his arms wrapped around my shoulders, holding me close. "They aren't going to let us walk out of here like nothing happened, and let's be serious, that's all my fault."

"It's not your fault. I was the one who told you to let Brenda stay."

"True, but I know how close Brenda is to my mother. I should have known better than to believe that she had suddenly decided to make a life of her own. But none of that matters now. All that matters is figuring out how to get you out of here and make sure you're safe. Although you might be late for dinner."

He was right. We were screwed. But what I wanted to know was why here? If Valerie didn't have Tolliver stashed here, why was the place covered by such mad levels of security? Emphasis on the *mad* part.

"Matt?" I lifted my head.

"Yeah?"

"What gave you the idea to come here?"

"I told you." He pulled me closer as he ran a finger around the neck of his T-shirt. "This is where Mom always hides the things she doesn't want people to find. Like that stupid necklace Grandmother left…"

"What?" My eyes widened.

"It's where she hid the necklace that my Grandmother had left for Aunt Ruth, my mother's younger half sister. She's a full mortal and when Grandmother died she left Aunt Ruth this cross necklace. It's nothing expensive, just a cheap silver cross that Grandmother had always worn. But Mom stole it before the funeral. I was a kid, but I remember watching her take it off Grandmother's neck before the funeral home people came, and hiding it in the floorboards upstairs. She told me it was 'our secret' and that I shouldn't tell anyone else."

"So?"

"That's the last time I was here." Matt said, his voice more insistent, like there was something I should be seeing but very obviously wasn't. "The day she hid that necklace from Aunt Ruth."

"And once again I have to ask… *so*?"

"She was wearing it at my apartment." Matt grabbed my shoulders and turned me so that we were facing each other. "She kept playing with it while we were talking."

"The necklace?"

"We were talking about Tolliver and about how she tried to hurt you. How you didn't deserve me. That's what she'd always said about Aunt Ruth. How she was a pure mortal and didn't deserve to be Grandmother's favorite. The whole time she's telling me about how you'll never find Tolliver, she's playing with that necklace so that I'd see it. She knew that I'd see it and I'd remember this place."

"And if you remembered…"

"She knew I'd bring you here. She set a trap she knew I'd walk you straight into."

"But she had to know you'd come with me. Why would she set a trap for her own son to get caught inside?"

"Because she disowned me." Matt huffed and then shook his head. "I told her that I loved you and that wasn't going to change. No matter what she wanted. No matter how much she begged and pleaded and threatened, I refused to give you up. I love you, stupid."

"I love you, too, jerk." I leaned my forehead against his and tried to still the fluttering in my chest. This was so not how I'd expected this conversation to go. For starters, I'd always figured a big bed would come into play at some point. And chocolate. Because there's nothing quite like mixing chocolate and corrupting a member of the Heavenly Host when you're throwing a private celebration for two.

I pulled away from him and turned to look at our less than ideal setting, my heart sinking into my toes as I stared at the hive full of sprites mid war dance. "You think she played us? You?"

He ran a trembling hand along the curve of my cheek. "All things considered, I probably should have expected it. Mother's not exactly the maternal sort. Not when it gets in the way of world domination at least. So yeah, I should have probably come up with a better plan than stumble in and get ambushed. Especially since there's a chance I'm going to get ripped to shreds by garden pests now. Which, for the record, wasn't how I intended to retire from the mortal world."

"That's not going to happen." I grabbed his hand and pressed my lips against his knuckles. "We're walking out of here together."

"Faith," Matt said and shook his head. "For once in what will be a very long life on the mortal realm for you, can you please quit arguing with me?"

"I'm not arguing with you."

"Obviously that's a no." He stood and gave me an exasperated smile, brushing the dirt off his jeans. He gave me a brief kiss on the nose and straightened. "I just have one thing I have to know."

"What?" I asked, standing beside him.

"If this form dies, and I manage end up a ghost like Harold, can we still have sex?"

"What?"

Instead of elaborating, he grabbed my shoulders and hauled me toward him. He brought his lips down on mine for a kiss that made my toes curl. Heat roared between us and it took all I could do not to pull on the dark energy fighting to escape from me. I wrapped my arms around his neck and tangled my fingers in his hair, pulling him closer.

He let me go and I stumbled backward, landing hard on my ass. When I looked up he had sprinted off, straight into the swarm of sprites.

"What in the name of Evil are you doing?" I screeched, chasing after him.

"Saving you," he called over his shoulder. "Now run!"

"I am running!" I seriously regretted my previous avoidance of exercise. He'd have probably outpaced me anyway because of his height, but he ran every day and I hadn't been near a track since tenth grade gym class. And back then I'd gotten myself a note from the doctor claiming I was allergic to aerobic exercise so I didn't actually have to do anything.

"The other direction, you dipshit!" he barked over his shoulder and I swear on his mother's grave—I know, I know, wishful thinking on my part—the bastard sped up. On purpose. I *so* needed to get to the gym more.

He disappeared inside the swarm and the sprites froze, stunned at the intrusion. They fell silent for an awful moment, not moving, and then seemed to implode toward the nephilim in their midst.

Damn it. Damn it. *Damn it!* So much for sneaking out while their backs were turned. Now I'd be lucky if they didn't tear his physical body apart before this was over. There was no choice left—I could either run for my life or save his ass. I felt a sharp zap through the bracelet and then an agonizing pain that I knew was coming from Matt as the sprites bombarded him with magic.

I watched, stunned, as a sprite flew past my head, tumbling head over heels as it went, and heard several loud crunches before another sprite went speeding past me and the entire mass began to howl. Matt backhanded another one of the creatures like it was nothing more than a fly and I had to resist the urge to kick him. Stupid man. Stupid, brave, honorable man who was trying to distract them with his bare hands so I would have enough time to escape.

Like I was going anywhere without him.

I felt another sharp jolt. Matt's knees buckled. He dropped to the ground and the swarm covered him completely, cutting me off to nothing but their howls and the pain-filled shrieks of the man caught in their midst.

I stopped, kicked off my shoes, and dug my toes into the moist grass. I closed my eyes and drew as much power through the link as I could. It rushed through me, dark and electric, tingling as it raced along my wings. I threw my head back and lifted my hands, hellfire crackling between them. Blisters had formed on the palms of my hands, cracking open from the intense heat when I launched the hellfire over my head and into the swarm.

There was no time to waste building more fireballs. I needed something a bit more immediate. Something able to fight the sprites at their own level. Dad had always warned that imps were fickle—almost impossible to control—but right now I didn't see where I had a choice.

Another fireball crackled between my hands and I tossed it overhand into the center of the swarm, hoping it would be enough to distract them and give Matt the chance to get free.

As the swarm rose up, turning toward me instead of Matt, I stamped my foot, focusing all of my anger and hatred into the Earth beneath my toes. The ground rolled sickeningly, splitting open along the length of their meadow and between my feet. I hopped to one side as brimstone fumes billowed out of the chasm. An angry, roiling mass of blue appeared, and I smiled. If they wanted a fight, it was time they got the chance to pick on someone their own size.

The problem with concurrent evolution was this: for every creature we had, the Celestial Kingdom had one that was similar. Demons had rock imps, little blue creatures who lived in craggy bits of rock and basically caused mischief. The angels had little green flying sprites that tended flowers and worried about cats.

The crucial thing everyone forgot was that *similar* and *identical* were not interchangeable words. An imp and a sprite might look alike but there was one crucial difference—imps were Hellborn, a twisted mutation of demon stock. Those pint-sized buggers loved a good fight. They didn't need a reason. Just an enemy.

"Imps," I yelled down into the Earth and they all turned to me as one, their wide, black eyes on me. They scurried into a swarming mass, their teeth bared, howling and pounding on their tiny chests, ready to go where I ordered them. "To war! Take no prisoners but leave the nephilim alive."

The imps poured out of the chasm, screeching like bats, attacking anything and everything in their path. I watched four of them stack themselves up like circus performers and pluck one of the sprites out of the air, ripping off her wings and tossing her to the ground for the others to dispatch before moving on.

The imps charged at the swarm of sprites surrounding Matt and the whole mess exploded into chaos. The blood-curdling screams of sprites blended into the war cries of the imps and the whole clearing burst into a fury of carnage. I skirted around the battling creatures and took off toward Matt, who was standing stunned in the middle of the battlefield, all of his weight on his left side.

"Jesus Christ," he said, coughing as I ran toward him. He was covered in grass and mud, his shirt soaked in blood and hanging in tatters. His jeans were ripped and I could see a long, bloody gash down the length of his inner thigh. He'd lost his left shoe and, given the angle of his right foot, I was pretty sure his ankle was broken.

"Had nothing to do with this," I said when I reached him. "But will completely approve of my methods."

"I doubt it." Matt doubled over and wheezed, his knees buckling. He crumpled to the ground and I dropped onto my knees beside him. He fought for breath and I knew he was in agony. "But I will admit it was one hell of a show."

"Yeah, well, you ain't seen nothing yet." I wrapped my arm around him, trying to keep him upright. I couldn't see any serious injuries but his face was pale and his muscles trembled. You didn't have to be a nurse to know that neither of those were good signs. "Let's just get you home and I'll knock your socks off."

"I don't think that's going to happen. You can't get me out of here on your own." He nodded and gasped as a spasm wracked his chest. He struggled to breathe, blood splattering across his hand as he tried to suck in some much needed air. Damn it. I needed to get him home and I needed to do it now. No matter how big of a risk it was.

"I'll open a portal," I said, fighting to keep my composure. Now was not the time to cry. Now was the time to get him somewhere safe. Do triage. Crying would have to wait. I reached for my powers and the portal opened, less of a rip in reality and more like the slow ease of a Band-Aid. "I'm so sorry, Matt. There just isn't any other way."

Instead of answering, Matt groaned and went limp, his face gray, and his chest still.

CHAPTER TWENTY-TWO

I grabbed him by the arm and dragged his unconscious body through the hole, and into my apartment.

"You are not allowed to die! Or shuffle off your mortal form, or whatever you want to call it! Don't even think about it, Matthew…Andrews." I wiped my eyes and grimaced. "See, you can't die yet. I don't even know your middle name, and that means I can't cuss you out."

An angry shriek sounded behind me on the other side of the portal, and I turned to see Daharack glaring at me. "A curse on you, Forked Tongue. I lay a curse of— "

I pointed my right index finger at him, giving a solid jolt of demonic power. The sprite exploded like a grape in the microwave.

"Oh, go to Hell," I yelled. The imps, who were busy tearing the clearing to pieces, turned to look at me *en masse*. "All of you. Back to Hell. And clean your mess up before you go."

The imps let out a high-pitched cheer and swept back across the meadow, pulling tiny green bodies behind them. The portal closed with a *snap* and I turned to the man lying on my floor.

I dropped to my knees and put one hand on his chest and the other at his throat. Still not breathing. No pulse. Damn it. Years of medical training kicked in. First things first: get him breathing. We'd deal with the other injuries after that. I pressed my fingers into his mouth and swept the airway, making sure there were no obstructions.

"You are not going to die," I snarled and started CPR. Not here. Not now. And definitely not over me.

A portal tore open behind me but I didn't stop. Whoever it was could either help or come back later.

"Faith, move," Lisa said behind me. "We need to—"

"*MOVE*!" J yelled and dropped onto the floor next to Matt. I noticed that, for once, he wasn't wearing scrubs. Instead, he was actually dressed in his regular people clothes. Crap, the one time I needed him to have it together and this is what I get. "Nahamia, get the cuff off of him."

Nahamia rushed over and fell to his knees beside J, across from Lisa who had planted herself on the other side. He snatched Matt's arm off the floor and tore the cuff open. He dropped it onto the floor, and turned to J. "What do you need?"

"Dad. Whatever he's doing tell him it can wait." He looked at me and then at Dad. "Uncle Louis, take her and go. Now."

Dad grabbed my wrist and started to pull. When I jerked away from him, grabbing at Matt's body, he let go of me and stood. Strong arms wrapped around my waist and he hoisted me into the air like a sack of potatoes.

"Let me go." I batted at my father with my hands. "I'm a nurse, I can help. He's not going to die because of me."

Instead of answering he carried me into the hall and slammed the door shut behind him. "Hope!"

My sister came barreling down the stairs, her shoes clopping on the bare wood, and her horns curling up out of her hair. "What happened?"

"Matt's injured." Dad shifted his weight, trying to keep hold of me even though I was smacking at him and kicking my feet.

"Let me go." I squirmed until my head could turn into his arm and I sank my teeth into his bicep. He lowered me to the floor, and held me against his chest in an iron grip.

Hope hauled her arm back and slapped me.

I blinked through the stars swarming in front of my eyes. "What the hell?"

"You're hysterical. Everyone knows you slap someone who's hysterical." Hope grabbed me and pulled me away from Dad, giving me a good shake. "Besides, if something didn't snap you out of it you'd have tried pulling on your power and then you would have killed him for sure. And, I've got to admit, smacking the tar out of someone felt pretty good. Even if it was you."

"The bond doesn't just click on and off like a switch." Dad gave me a tight hug before plopping down on the stairs and dragging me into his lap. I let my head drop onto his shoulder and he began rubbing circles in my back. "It'll take a bit for the links between you to break down. I know you want to help Matt but right now the best thing you can do is stay out here, sweetheart. Let your cousin and your uncle work."

"He's going to die because of me."

Instead of answering, he began rocking back and forth like you would to soothe a tiny child. He started to hum softly, patting my back, and I let myself sink into the soft warmth of his shoulder. Sometimes even demonesses needed their daddies.

"It's not your fault." Hope took my hand in hers, squeezing

my fingers. Which only made me feel worse. Hope bitch-slapping someone was her standard operating procedure. Comforting was something she could only bring herself to do during an utter catastrophe.

"It is." I buried my head further into the crook of my father's neck. "Everything's my fault. He ran into the middle of a swarm to save me. But I couldn't let him do that. So I called up balls of hellfire and caused an earthquake. I released a tribe of imps. What was I thinking?"

"You were trying to save him," Hope said. "If you wouldn't have done those things those sprites would have torn him apart and you'd be right there with him. Matt gave you the only chance at escape you were going to have. You had to take it. And what do you mean, you called up an earthquake and a pack of imps? I've never even called up a pack of imps before. No one can control imps."

"I don't want to talk about the imps." I sniffled. If J wouldn't let me in the room that meant he didn't expect Matt to walk out of my apartment on his own. Matt probably hadn't expected to make it even that far. He'd died trying to give me the chance to escape and all I'd done was drain him. "Matt's going to die and all you care about are the imps."

"He's going to be all right," Dad said. "Your uncle and your cousin aren't going to lose him. He means too much to you. To all of us. He's part of this family.

"What if they can't manage it?" I stared into his emerald green eyes. "What if they can't save him? What if he ends up trapped *there*? Where I can't be with him?"

"Do you know," Dad said, "that I think you might have the most trust issues of any person I've ever met in all my long life?

It's ironic, if you think about it. A woman named Faith, who has seen the Alpha Himself perform miracles, and you don't think they can manage to heal a man who's been mugged by a group of overgrown honeybees."

"Yeah, well, maybe Mom should have tried for Charity or Prudence as a virtue to name me after instead of Faith."

"What I want to know is why?" Hope asked.

"Why what?" I asked.

She was chewing on her lower lip and picking at her nails. "Why send your son out to die? Valerie set an ambush in the one place she knew he'd look."

"We figured that out." I nodded. "She set this all up for a reason. I just don't know what it is."

"She's sending a message," Dad said quietly and his hand quit moving, pressing down in the middle of where my wings would be if they were out. "You girls heard Brenda at the Church Brewworks. They consider the Crucifixion to be a good thing. They think the message is something to be celebrated like a badge of honor. 'For he so loved his followers he gave them his only son.' Matt's not her only son but he's what she had available to sacrifice at the time."

"So you're saying his mother is a fucking nutcase," Hope replied.

"Tell me about it." I rested my head against Dad's chest, and tried not to think about the fact that there wasn't any noise coming from behind my apartment door. The places where healthy people battled to stay alive were never quiet.

"Don't try to explain it to yourself," Dad said. "There's no point in trying to understand why crazy people do the things that they do. Even when they have reasons, they're never good ones."

"How am I not supposed to try? We didn't even manage to

find Tolliver. We're going to lose them both now."

"We know where Tolliver *isn't*," Dad said, "and that is almost as good as knowing where he is. Now we know where not to look to narrow things down considerably. Plus, I still maintain that the nephilim isn't going to step into the light. I won't allow it and neither will your uncle. They will find some way to heal his body. He's part of this family and we aren't going to take a chance of losing one of you ever again."

"But—" I froze. Dad had said they weren't going to lose Matt. Not that they wouldn't let him die. Only that they'd somehow manage to heal him. Which would be the same thing—if Matt was being taken care of by mortal doctors. But he wasn't. And you didn't need to be a Sunday school addict to know that J had more than one trick up his sleeve when it came to keeping people alive.

The problem was, Dad and the Alpha hated to perform resurrections. Tolliver had told me once that the Alpha hated resurrections so much that they were the reason he'd taken a hands-off stance related to the mortal world. He believed resurrections were his sign that he needed to butt out and let mortals deal with things on their own.

I can't say that his stance didn't make sense. Bringing people back from the dead was a nasty business. Resurrections never worked like they should and the people who suffered through them never spoke about the experience. Whatever happened was something dark and terrible and no one who had been a part of one would ever talk about it.

"For now, the only thing we can do is wait," Dad continued. "Wait and try to find out where your brother is. Just because Matt is injured and in our possession doesn't mean the Angale will hand Tolliver over to us."

"What about their compound?" I asked.

"We couldn't find it. It's trapped in some sort of bubble and no matter what we tried we couldn't find an entrance." Hope rose and stalked across the length of the landing, kicking the railing of the stairway when she got to it. "It's like the place isn't even really there."

"A reality bubble," I said. "Unless you know exactly where it is, it doesn't exist on this plane. Not even for Dad."

"Damn," he muttered. "But I can't understand why Bassano would allow something like this to happen. He has to know the Alpha isn't going to sit idly by and let a group of nephilim take your brother hostage."

"Who said he has any idea what's going on? It's not like Bassano and Matt's mom were on the best of terms after all." Lisa slunk out of my apartment, shutting the door behind her.

"Are they done? Is he okay?" I pulled myself out of my father's grip and hurried over to her, hoping to hear something—anything—that would assure me Matt was going to be all right.

"They said it would take time." She closed her eyes and dropped her head back to let out a long sigh. "So they sent me out to tell you everything was going to be fine."

"Liar. They wouldn't have just sent you out here to reassure me. Besides, I saw him. I was there with him in that place. He's not fine, he's dying. You're a surgical nurse. Get your ass in there."

"They told me to come out here and talk to you. Then they told me not to come back."

"Right." Dad nodded and clapped his hands. "You know what this means?"

"He's never going to forgive any of us?" I slumped back against the stair above me and Hope wrapped her arms around me in what I suspected was supposed to be a hug.

"No," Dad said. "Your uncle has given us something to hold over Valerie, and now, to add insult to injury, we're going to go steal back the demon she kidnapped."

"How do you propose to do that? We still don't know where they're keeping Tolliver."

"Simple." Dad gave me a grim smile. "You and Lisa are going to make her tell us where he is."

"What makes you think she's going to tell *us* anything?" I looked at my father but he wouldn't meet my eyes, keeping his head turned toward Matt's apartment door, and like that I knew. The Alpha wasn't the only one who was inclined to play fast and loose with people when he needed to clear up loose ends. He'd learned that particular skill from Dad.

"Oh, I expect she won't tell you much of anything at all to begin with." Dad's voice was forbidding and his shoulders were so tight that muscles in his back trembled. "But your uncle and I also don't care what it takes for you to get it out of her. Just don't kill her. If you kill her and she's given you bad information our chances of finding your brother decrease."

"Right." I was not going to feel sorry for this woman. She'd planned to kill her own son. That should have been enough. Her homicidal tendencies aside, I still wasn't looking forward to what was about to come. I'd never killed a person, not intentionally anyway, and until today I'd never wanted to, either.

"Leave it to me," Lisa muttered. "You don't need to be in there with her."

"The hell I don't." This was a woman who had taken my brother hostage and tried to destroy the man I loved rather than let us be together. "Besides, I think I know a way to make her talk."

"How is that?" Hope asked.

"Don't worry about it." I rubbed my palms over my eyes to wipe away the last of my tears. "If I have to use it, you'll have plenty of time to be appalled later."

"You're going to do something that will appall *me*?" Hope asked. "Do tell."

"Later." I strode toward the door to Matt's apartment and popped my knuckles like a barroom brawler getting ready for a fight. I tilted my head first to one side and then to the other, cracking the vertebrae in my neck, and shook my legs to loosen them.

"Are you ready for this?" Lisa asked, her voice cold and businesslike. Her wings were out, and her horns curled upward like two very ugly, demonic hair bows.

"Are you?" I asked.

"That woman intends to use my future husband as a sacrifice." Her tail whipped back and forth and thunder rumbled in the distance.

I watched the dark energy around her flare while the lights above us dimmed. "You used to cry and make me take bugs out of our apartment in a scrap of paper rather than squashing them."

"That was back when I had a soul," Lisa said. "Now I have a groom to save. So are we going in there together or do you want me to handle it on my own?"

"We're going in there together."

She pushed the door open. Inside, two demons stood guard over Valerie. They turned to us, their eyebrows raised.

"Out." I jerked my head toward the hallway.

"But your father—" the younger of the two demons started.

“Do I look like I’m in the mood to be argued with?” I made my eyes flash black.

“No, Your Highness, but…” He looked over at the older demon, his eyes wide.

“I’m not my father,” I said.

“Oh be gone already,” Lisa said and snapped her fingers in his direction. The two demons in front of us disappeared in identical puffs of brimstone.

“Well that makes things simpler.” I sauntered into Matt’s living room and leaned back against the island that separated it from the kitchen. I crossed my arms and made a show of crossing my ankles. My gaze traveled over my arch nemesis.

She was sitting upright on the couch, her chin raised and her eyes blazing. Her hands were clamped down on her knees and I could see that her ankles were pressed tightly together. The bonds woven around her caused the air to shimmer like an oasis in the desert and the garlicky smell of pure fury rolled off of her.

“Far be it from me to judge.” I gave her my bitchiest smile. “But the look of total failure doesn’t seem to suit you.”

Chapter Twenty-Three

Valerie sneered. "I'm not telling you anything, you worthless bastard of the Devil."

"First," I replied, "my father recognized me as his own. Second, my parents would be married right now if you hadn't stolen my brother and made them postpone their wedding. So if I were you I would be very glad that it's me who came in here and not the bride. She's pissed, and let me tell you, my mother is not a woman you mess with when she's pissed. My dad won't even cross her. Third, telling me you aren't going to tell me anything might be the most clichéd thing I've ever heard come out of someone's mouth. It screams cartoon villain. Now, try again."

"Go to Hell."

"Been there." Lisa inspected her fingernails and then yawned. "Done that. Planned on leaving with a T-shirt, and walked out with a husband."

Valerie gave her a vicious grin. "Not yet you haven't."

Lisa's eyes flashed red as dark power flared to life around her. She smothered it, but clearly Valerie had gotten to her.

Unfortunately, for the nephilim sitting across from us, that probably wasn't a good thing.

"Oh, you're going to tell me where Tolliver is." Lisa slinked into the living room and sat in the easy chair across from the couch, acting like this was something she dealt with every day. "The only question is, how much fun am I going to get to have with you before we get to that point?"

"You can't do anything to me," Valerie said, directing her rage at me. "Not beyond what you've already put me through in your attempts to destroy my son."

What *I* had done to destroy her son? Hello? Someone was four or five beers short of a six-pack, wasn't she?

"You were the one who did that." I glowered at the madwoman in front of us. "You sent him to be attacked by feral sprites, not me. You sent him to his death."

"Sacrifices had to be made."

The madness rolled off of her in an almond-scented cloud. I sniffed, trying to find the lower, flowery notes of regret or sadness, but couldn't detect them.

She felt nothing when we talked about her son and his death. He was nothing more than a pawn for her to use as she saw fit and, when he quit being useful, she sacrificed him.

"Besides, I couldn't have my own son doubting my rule in such a blatant fashion. The others were beginning to talk because of his dalliance with you." Her scent flared to a bitter burnt toffee smell, intermingling with the madness.

He wasn't toeing her party line so she had him killed? She couldn't be happy to just have him out of her hair? No, she came into our homes and destroyed him instead. Then she thought she was going to walk away from this without any lasting consequences.

Well, she could think again. I might be the Devil's nice daughter but nice was relative, and she'd worn out my last nice nerve.

"Well, so you know, I intend to inform every single one of your followers that he died trying to save me," I said.

Her eyes widened. "*What?*"

I couldn't help but wonder how she had planned on explaining the cold-blooded murder of her own son. Had she even cared about it before now? She'd probably intended to let them believe I'd killed him for the fun of it. Or because I was bored. Or any other reason she thought might fire them up so they would be ready for war against all demonkind.

"He almost killed himself to save me," I repeated. "Now, do you want to take a guess on how fast I can turn your sacrificial lamb into a martyr? Then what happens? A martyr of your own making is a tough act to follow. Ask the Romans. Oh wait, you can't. They're all dead."

"My son wouldn't dare," Valerie gasped, her mouth hanging open. "He would have never given himself for you."

"Believe it." He'd been stupid. Foolish. And utterly without fear the entire time. Not that I was going to give her the comfort of knowing that.

"He wouldn't." She glared at me and the smell of almonds filled the room, saturating the air around us like a cloud of nasty smelling perfume.

"Because she's a demon?" Lisa looked up from her fingernails and glanced first at Valerie and then at me.

"No, because he's a coward." Valerie was so angry the hairs on her arm were standing on end. "My youngest son is nothing but a coward. He feared the coming war and ran from it like a child. He ran from his duty and hid behind a demon's skirts. His death at your hands will make him the hero he would have never been in life."

"But he didn't die by my hands." I tried to keep my face emotionless and my tone dry. It wouldn't do to let her see she was getting to me. If I wanted to succeed in finding Tolliver, I couldn't let go of the upper hand. Besides, if Lisa could control herself right now, with her fiancé's life on the line, so could I. "He died by his own hands. He rushed into your pack of sprites and fought them off, alone, to save me. That sounds like bravery to me. I wonder what your followers would think."

"They'll never know," she said, the madness causing her eyes to glow a brilliant gold color instead of their normal hazy green. "They'll believe whatever I tell them, and I'll tell them that you dragged him into a pit of imps and let them tear him limb from limb. There's only you to say otherwise, and who do you think they'll believe? A demon or me?"

"There's only one problem with that," Lisa said. "You're here and your poor, pathetic followers are not."

"You can't keep me trapped in an apartment in the mortal realm forever. People will begin to talk. The police will come. Then how will you explain what you've done to me?" Valerie tried to lean forward but the bonds held her in place.

"We have no intention of keeping you here. You're right—someone would notice. Besides, you're too much of a nuisance to keep next door." Lisa relaxed into the easy chair like they were having a discussion over where to have lunch and not about the fates of two men.

"Then what's the point of your threat? It's not like you can send me to Hell. There are other demons besides Borisiphan who are corruptible. I can raise an army," Valerie boasted. Her voice grated with triumph at the thought she had bested us somehow.

"Probably not." Lisa crossed her legs and let the right one swing back and forth like the pendulum of a clock. "Not for anything you've got to give away at least. No, we won't keep you in Hell because we don't like you and we don't want you there. Hell's too good for trash like you."

"Trash?" Valerie asked, her voice feral. "You, a demon, are calling me trash?"

"You're a crazy nephilim who hides inside a reality bubble because you're terrified of a bunch of mortals."

"People fear what they don't understand," she sniffed. "Once we've taken our rightful place everything will be revealed, and they'll come to understand our dominion over them."

"Um, no." I shook my head. "I don't know how we haven't gotten this through to you yet, but you're not going to have control over anyone. Ever again. The Angale are never going to control the Earth. You thought your son was a coward. But he was a realist, desperately trying to escape the insane fantasies you spun inside your cracked out mind. Like the fantasy where you kidnapped the Crown Prince of Hell and thought you'd get away with it."

"Okay." Lisa popped out of her seat, cracking her knuckles. "I think I've had enough of Crazy Time with Valerie. It's time to play a new game. Let's play Fifty Ways to Torture the Nephilim. I bet we'd be good at that game. What do you think, Faith?"

"Oh, I'm sure we can come up with something inspired." I glanced at Lisa, who'd started pacing, and then back at Valerie. If we were lucky, Valerie would start spilling and we wouldn't have to actually try hurting someone else. Because, no matter what Lisa might think, there was a difference between being soulless and committing torture, and I wasn't quite so eager to hop over that big, fat line. "We work in a children's hospital and people do seriously sick shit to their kids sometimes. Some of the stuff we've seen is bound to come in handy on occasion."

"Now." Lisa stepped closer to Valerie and pointed at her nose. "The rules are simple. I'm going to beat the Hell out of you for no reason whatsoever. For as long as I want. And when I get tired of it, Faith will take over."

"How is that going to get me to tell you where the demon is?" Valerie asked.

"It's not, but you said you had no intention of telling me that. So there's no point in trying." Lisa shrugged and gave Valerie a bone-chilling smile.

"Besides, we've already got a way into the Angale compound." I hoped she trusted me enough to go along with my lies.

"No, you don't," Valerie said, her upper lip curling into a sneer.

"Oh. But we do," I replied. "See, while we've been distracting you, the rest of my father's forces have been burning your compound to the ground and taking your followers prisoner."

"You have no way into the Angale compound. With my son dead, the only person who could take you there is me." She gave me a smug smile, her eyes twinkling with self-satisfied madness.

"Nope." I looked at Valerie, the smile still on my face, and wrinkled my nose at her like an annoyed teenage babysitter trying to keep her patience while dealing with a naughty two-year-old. "We've got your stepson, and let me tell you, he was more than willing to help us out. Especially with the deal my father agreed to."

"Deal? What deal would your father strike with Levi?"

"Well, you inspired it, actually," I said. "The Angale need a leader and you know what's better than a Plain Jane old messiah?

Or a martyr?"

"What?"

"Someone charismatic. Someone who's been *touched*."

"Touched?"

"By God," I explained. "Levi was a nephilim with no powers, the weakest among your group. To suddenly appear with all of your powers…"

Valerie swallowed, her eyes filled with doubt. "The Alpha wouldn't dare."

I faked an incredulous laugh. "He'll take all of your powers and more. He'll give them to Levi and let you take his place inside the Grey Lands. He wouldn't even hesitate. Now, I've told you everything, so let's quit talking and get back to the game. Lisa? If you'd like to do the honors?"

"Gladly," the demoness said. She curled her fingers inward, toward her palms, letting the nails transform into razor sharp talons. "Last chance to play nicely. Tell us where exactly to find my future husband."

"You don't scare me," Valerie said, her voice trembling, and the sour notes of fear mingled with the almond scent of her madness.

"She is a walking cliché, isn't she?" A cool, mocking voice came from the doorway. I spun and found my father's former consort standing there with her hands on her hips and a mocking smile on her face. Lilith was dressed in black linen drawstring pants with a red, kimono-style top wrapped around her curvy frame. Her black hair was tied in a messy bun at the top of her head.

She tucked a stray lock behind her left ear and sauntered into the room and turned to Lisa. "And you, my little dove, you've got to learn to control your temper. Otherwise, you'll kill my son by your second wedding anniversary. What have I told you before?

Clawing someone's face off is always your last resort in any situation."

"If I keep my temper much longer, I won't have a second wedding anniversary," Lisa pointed out, her voice brittle.

"True, but you haven't gotten anything out of her yet. Have you?"

"No." Lisa retracted her talons and shuffled over to the chair she'd been sitting in earlier, plopping down like a pissed off teenager.

"Well then why don't you let me try?" Lilith sat on the coffee table, in front of Valerie so that their knees touched. She reached for the silver crucifix Valerie had around her neck and lifted it with her finger, giving it the once over before dropping it. "Children. What can you do? So temperamental."

Valerie sneered at Lilith, her eyes glowing, and dampened power crackling around her in waves.

"Now," Lilith continued, "you and I are going to talk. Mother to mother."

"I have nothing to say to you." Valerie struggled against her bonds, trying to pull away from Lilith's touch.

"I think you do." Lilith leaned toward Valerie so that they were almost close enough to kiss. "Since you've taken my son."

"That sounds like your problem, Daughter of Lust, not mine." Valerie jerked her head back and her eyes were filled with fire.

"Oh good, you know who I am." Lilith crossed her arms and gave the other woman a vicious smile. "That will make things so much easier."

I glanced at Lisa. Lil had always been nice to me, but I couldn't claim to know her very well. Lilith had, obviously, kept her distance from me and Hope when we were kids. Not that I could blame her.

Watching the man you were totally devoted to constantly make up and break up with someone like Mom had to be sheer torture. Why in the name of Evil would you want to add insult to injury by getting close to the other woman's kids?

"Everyone knows who you are," Valerie said, her lips curling up in disgust. "From what I understand, most men know you quite well."

"None of that now," Lilith wagged her finger under the other woman's nose and kept her voice still upbeat. "We don't want to start this off by insulting each other. It will only make negotiations so much more difficult in the long run if we're both working from hurt feelings."

"What negotiations?" Valerie asked.

"You have taken my son," Lilith said. "I want him back."

"Right now, he's the only thing keeping me here and not in some type of banishment in Purgatory. Or worse." Valerie laughed. "What makes you think I'll give him to you?"

"You're going to give him to me because I have your children."

"You have my coward of a son. What good will that do? Keep him. He's served his purpose to me. I have no more need of the boy."

"You misunderstand me." Lilith shook her head. "I didn't say I had your son. I said I had your children. All of them."

"How?" Valerie asked, the scent of desperation rolling off her in waves of burnt cotton candy.

"It was easy. All I had to do was wait. While everyone else was out running around, looking over hill and dale for my son, acting like a bunch of novice succubi in a strip club, I've been waiting. I knew without you there to hold the Angale in with an iron fist, someone was going to take a chance at freedom." Lilith sat back and rested her weight on her palms. "You should have expected it really."

"They wouldn't."

"They did." Lilith shrugged.

Lisa's eyes were as wide as mine. Lilith had just waited in Biloxi for someone to appear out of thin air? They would have given off an energy signature, so she would have felt them the minute they stepped out of the reality bubble. She could've phased right to them and watched them go inside. Why the Hell hadn't we thought of that?

"If you had a way in, why send this one?" Valerie jerked her head at me. "Why send my son into an ambush for no reason?"

"That wasn't me," Lilith said. "That was all Tolliver's father. Men never listen. Not your son. Not his father. Not my son and most definitely not his father. Waiting is a concept that is beyond their ability to understand. Much better to rush in and see what happens. But you and I know better, don't we?"

"We are nothing alike," Valerie spat.

"No, we're not." Lilith shook her head. "But right now, we're in the same place. That's why I know you'll tell me what you won't tell them. They're just silly girls without children of their own who think a little physical pain is the worst you can take. I know better."

"What are you going to do?"

"It's not what I'm going to do. It's what I've done." Lilith rested her elbows on her knees. "I've taken your grandchildren. Every. Single. One. And once I had them, their parents came stumbling after. They aren't as willing as you are to sacrifice their young for your cause. Now, if you want them back, you're going to tell me where my son is."

"Never."

"Then I'm going to start by taking the souls of your grandchildren," Lilith said.

"I don't believe you," Valerie said, and I couldn't help but agree with her. Turning a group of nephilim children into demons? It had never been done. I didn't even know you could steal a child's soul.

"I expected you to say that." Lilith snapped her fingers and a young couple appeared, frozen in a bubble, next to the island in Matt's kitchen. The woman, who could have been Matt's sister, was holding a tiny infant in her arms. "So perhaps a little demonstration is in order?"

The girl inside the bubble let out a scream when the baby in her arms levitated and flew across the room to Lilith. The demoness cradled the baby against her chest and cooed. "Isn't she a lovely thing? Definitely worthy of joining my ranks in a few year's time, aren't you? Yes, you are. You'll make every man in a fifty mile radius fall to his knees."

"Lil," I said, my voice wavering.

"Now," she continued, focusing on the baby. "This is going to tickle. But I promise, you won't notice a thing afterward."

She nuzzled the baby's neck and put her finger to its lips. "Out you come." A tiny tendril of golden light flickered briefly and attached itself to Lilith's finger. She tugged gently, twining the thread around her finger as it pulled free.

"Lil," I persisted, my voice more urgent. She was actually going to remove an infant's soul. Against its free will. That was a very big no-no in Dad's book. We didn't steal souls. That was Rule One. Rule Two was that we did not take the souls of children. Rule Two Point One was probably that if we were going to break Rule One we never it broke it and Rule Two at the same time.

"Hush now." She waved her hand at me and the golden light

tangling around her finger wavered. "I need to concentrate."

"Mother," the woman inside the bubble wailed. "Tell her what she needs to know."

"She won't do it," Valerie said, her voice steady. "She wouldn't actually cut the cord and take your child. It's all a bluff."

"He's in my mother's house. Hidden in the basement," the girl screamed. "I'll take you to him. It's on the main road. The house at the end. The one next to the church."

"Wonderful." Lilith nodded, not bothering to look over at the girl, cooing at the baby instead. "Faith, go tell your father I'll be with him in a moment. Then we'll go get my son."

"What about my baby?" the girl inside the bubble wailed. "I told you what you wanted. Please give me my daughter back."

"Of course," Lilith replied and untwined the child's soul from her finger, feeding it back into the baby's mouth. "One second, though. We want to make sure it's all back in place."

"You fool," Valerie snapped. "She would have never hurt the child."

"She's right." Lilith watched the last tendril slip back inside the baby's mouth. The child giggled and clapped her hands. "We don't steal souls, and we never harm children. Unlike some people, we actually follow the rules."

"I told you!" Valerie yelled, struggling against her bonds.

"Faith," Lilith said, her voice calm. "Please go get your father. You don't want to have any part in what's coming next."

"But…"

"Now," she insisted, her eyes a matted obsidian.

"Are you sure?"

"Faith Anne, I said go now." Black power enveloped Lilith and she started to shift from the gorgeous succubi form she normally wore to that of an eight foot tall pissed off demon lord instead.

I swallowed once and decided that whatever was about to go down in here, Lilith was right. It was better if I didn't have any part of it. I did my best to keep my pace steady and not run like a demon child with my tail on fire. Unfortunately for my dignity, I barely managed a terrified scurry.

"What happened?" Hope asked. She stopped pacing and shook her head. "I wanted to go inside but Lilith told me I wouldn't be useful without my powers. I can't believe I missed a chance to work with the harbinger of Evil herself. Stupid, miserable, worthless curse."

"Lilith threatened to remove a baby's soul so the mother told us where Tolliver was." I looked at Dad. "She said to tell you she could take you to the Angale compound in just a moment. She has some business to finish first."

The wind picked up outside and the hallway turned icy. A flash of dark power flared from underneath the door, and the light above us exploded into a thousand tiny shards. What the hell had she just done?

"Temperamental woman." Dad pinched his nose. "I told her I'd handle things. But no, she just can't resist zapping people who piss her off into a zillion pieces. Let's hope she didn't set Matt's couch on fire in the process. That would be a pain in the ass to explain."

Chapter Twenty-Four

The door opened and Lilith, back in her regular *MILF from Hell* form, stared at Dad, her hands on her hips.

Dad rolled his eyes. "I take it our little problem has been taken care of?"

"Of course it has." Lilith smacked the back of his head. "I don't leave behind messes. You know that. Now let's go before your fiancée and my lover get annoyed at all the time we've been spending together. "

"Your lover? What lover?" Dad rubbed the back of his head and frowned at her. "No one told me you had a lover."

She crossed her arms over her ample chest and scowled. "I've spent long enough waiting around for you to come to your senses. You've chosen another mate and there's nothing to keep me from doing the same. Besides, eternity is a long time to sleep alone. Now, if you could redirect your not inconsiderable energies toward helping me retrieve our son, I would be grateful."

"We will be discussing this later," he said.

Lilith pushed past him and opened a phase portal in the

middle of my hallway. "Oh, we will not. Now are you coming or aren't you?"

"Fine." He stepped through the portal behind her. I turned to Hope and she shrugged. What could we say? It served Dad right that Lilith had gotten fed up with waiting for him and had taken a lover. I walked into the portal behind Dad, my sister and my best friend following behind me like the Holy Ghost was on their asses.

We stood behind a tiny, old-fashioned gas station. Steam simmered off the blacktop while waves of heat came off the green fields behind us. I took in a deep breath, and it felt like I was sucking air in through a wet washcloth. We weren't in Pittsburgh anymore. This place was much too green, and besides, it was hotter than Hell. I mean, Hell was warm, but this place was scorching.

"You want to go in there, just the five of us?" Hope asked. "I mean, not that I don't think we could take them. Hell, I could take them on my own if Dad hadn't robbed me of my powers. But don't you think a shock and awe tactic of a hundred howling, bloodthirsty demons would be more effective? Plus, way less damaging to my manicure. Which I just got done, by the way."

"We don't need an entire legion of demons to get your brother back," Dad said.

"Well at least give me my powers back so I can be useful." Hope crossed her arms and tapped her silver stiletto sandal-clad foot on the ground.

"You can be useful." Dad grabbed her hand, without bothering to even look at her bright pink nails, and pushed her behind him. "If someone sneaks up behind us, scream. Then kick them with those ugly ass shoes."

"Hey!" She looked down at her shoes. "What's your problem with my shoes?"

"Where do you want me to start?" Dad asked.

"Excuse me?" Lilith stuck one of her hands up and waved it. "Not that this discussion about your daughter's… What are those? Prada?"

"Stella McCartney," Hope corrected.

"Right." Lilith nodded. "Could we maybe focus a little more on finding Tolliver and a little less on Hope's choice of footwear?"

"Absolutely." Dad grimaced. "Where are they at?"

"Just around the side of the gas station." Lilith pointed to the scrubby looking field behind the ramshackle building. "They're pretty well hidden, but that's where they seem to be coming in and out of their bubble."

"Right." He nodded. "So how are we going to handle this?"

"We blast our way in and zap anyone who looks at us cross eyed." Lisa announced, her voice hard.

"Well it does seem straightforward enough," Dad said. "But who's going to start? I mean we don't just want to start blasting all at once, do we?"

"Would you like the honors, dear?" Lilith looked at Lisa. "It is your fiancé we're saving after all."

"Right," Lisa said. "They can hear me from inside there?"

"I'm sure they're listening right now," Lilith said.

"Good." Lisa stepped forward. "Hey, assholes! I just snuffed your queen, and I'm going to blast your little reality bubble straight to Hell if someone doesn't get their ass out here right now to negotiate."

"Well, that was a little more blunt than I usually go for," Dad said.

Hope snickered. "Well, you're not running things, are you?"

"And I'm not the one sitting here with no powers either, now am I?"

"Just wait until I get them—" Hope stopped as the field in front of us shimmered, and a man only a few inches taller than me stepped out. He looked like a weasel in his three-piece suit, his gray comb over barely covering his sunburnt scalp.

The weasel sniffed. "Who are you?"

"Who am I?" Lisa leveled a finger at him, zapping him in the chest with enough force to throw him backward. Instead of waiting for someone else to stick their head out, she followed him inside, my father and his former consort hurrying along behind, keeping Hope and I behind them.

We walked into the middle of a group of rundown houses, and my entire body went cold, like it had inside the sprites' encampment. Lisa sneered at the assembled mass of nephilim while my dad and Lilith flanked her, still keeping in front of my sister and I so that we weren't directly in the middle of the shit when it hit the fan.

"I told you who I was already," Lisa said. "I'm the demon who killed your idiot generalissimo wannabe and if someone doesn't get me my boyfriend in the next thirty seconds, I'm going to kill everyone else in here as well. Are we clear?"

"She's bluffing," one of the women called out. "Her Holiness would never be taken by a mere demon. Bassano wouldn't allow it."

"Bassano didn't even notice," Lisa said. "He's being entertained by a dread demon disguised as a supermodel and a game of naked Twister."

"Ugh." I was going to have to disinfect Malachi once this was over. Or give him some sort of reward. I couldn't imagine he would enjoy spending this much quality time with Bassano, but this was

Mal—there were some things it was just better not to contemplate.

"The Celestial One wouldn't have left us for a demon," the woman argued, clearly in denial when it came to certain angels.

"Um, yeah, I think he would for one if there was a naked Twister game involved," someone else in the crowd said.

I closed my eyes and tried not to laugh at the insanity of the situation. Matt was being put through an incredible amount of pain while my uncle and cousin fought to save his life and his own family was more concerned about whether or not his dad was a kinky bastard. If I wasn't careful this group was going to send me straight past hysterical and right into a total mental break.

"Time is tick, tick, ticking away," Lisa sang. She turned her attention back to the guy on the ground and shook her head at him. "You must not be the most popular guy around if they're willing to let you die while they argue about whether or not your boss is a perv."

"I'm the church accountant," he said, his voice squeaky. "I collect the tithes and the rents. I also manage all the businesses while Her Holiness and the Celestial One are busy with other things."

"Oh, you're the toady." Lisa gave him another quick zap. "No wonder they don't care if you live or die. But, regardless, someone better get me my man before I get too angry. Otherwise I might just kill the toady, kill the mortals, and then start in on all of you."

"Get the demon," the man on the ground whimpered.

"But Her Holiness—" one of the women countered.

"I told you." Lisa zapped into the crowd at random and Lilith stepped closer to me to give her future daughter-in-law room. "I killed her. Turned her into a little pile of ash and poured her down the garbage disposal. No more crazy homicidal leaders for any of you."

"You can't expect us to believe—"

Lisa pulled the silver crucifix Valerie had been wearing earlier out her skirt pocket. She held it up for everyone to see and then tossed it onto the ground next to the accountant. "Now, bring me my demon."

"But—"

"Tolliver. Now." Lisa raised her finger at them, and three of the women pointed toward the largest house in the compound.

"He's in there," the weasely accountant sputtered. "In the basement."

"Good." Lisa zapped him. "Go get him."

"But…"

"I said"—she pointed at him—"go get him. Now."

He flinched, and addressed some of the men behind him. "Dale, Leroy, Jethro, go get the demon. Bring him up here."

"Get him gently," Lisa said. "I might start getting itchy and Evil only knows who I might kill after Toady here."

The man sniffled. "Earl."

"What?" Lisa looked down at him and zapped the ground in disinterest.

"My name," he said, and I wrinkled my nose when I smelled the sickly sweet stench of urine. "It's Earl."

"Sure it is." She zapped at the other side of him, missing by a feather's breadth. "Now get your muscle boys in there to get my man before I change your name to Imp Food."

"Go, now," he whimpered and the three burly men in overalls hurried to do his bidding. While they were inside, Lisa kept her finger pointed toward Earl like a magic wand. My father and Lilith faced down the cowering group of Angale "warriors" who were trying to hide behind each other and stay out of sight.

Meanwhile, I tried to figure out how the hell someone like Matt had come from a place as backward as this. I mean I'd thought his mother's crazy little hidey-hole had been bad but this place was just *ugh*. No wonder he'd never wanted to talk about his life here. He'd wanted to be a normal guy, not some freak from a compound. He'd been successful at it, too. Or at least he had been before this afternoon. Who knew what he was going to be like when he finally woke up again?

"You," a younger woman said, her black hair pulled back in a messy braid and her blue eyes glittering at me. "You're the demoness my brother is in love with."

"No I'm not." I shook my head. The last thing I needed was for them to recognize me as his girlfriend. That'd be like putting a big "attack here to draw a demon out" sign right over his heart.

"Yes, you are," she insisted. Her eyes were wide and filled with tears. "Brenda showed me a picture of you she stole from Levi before she left the compound with Her Holiness. You're the woman he wanted to be with instead of her."

"I'm just his landlord," I insisted.

She grabbed my hand, clinging to it. "Please, tell me my brother is okay? Tell me he wasn't hurt when the other demon killed Her Holiness. Tell me you protected him."

"He's fine," I finally said. My heart clenched at the thought of Matt on my living room floor this afternoon. "He wasn't there when Valerie was executed."

"Will he come home now?" she asked. "Is he going to lead us now that Her Holiness is gone?"

How could I tell them what was happening to him while we were all standing here? How could I even begin to guess what he was going to want once this was all over? Maybe he would take his mother's place and lead his people. Maybe he'd want to give them a chance at a better life than the one they'd been living. Maybe let them see the world wasn't something to hide away from. If anybody could do that, it was Matt.

I swallowed past the lump in my throat. "I don't know."

At least he'd be safer here than he'd been with me. If he was with his own kind, no one would try to kill him. But then again, they were a bloodthirsty lot, so who knew what he'd be walking into?

"Tolliver," Lisa shrieked, and I pulled away from the woman and watched Lisa sprint across the clearing. My brother sauntered toward her, his hands in his pockets and an Angale on each side of him with another one bringing up the tail like some sort of imbecilic honor guard. Except for the blue jeans and John Deere T-shirt, which I knew were not his, he looked normal. The jackass.

Lisa launched herself into his arms and wrapped her legs around his waist. He caught her and pulled her close while she squealed in delight. She planted her lips against his in a furious kiss and tangled her fingers in his hair.

"Ah, young love," Lilith chuckled and zapped at Earl.

"More like lust," Hope snorted.

"That, too." Lilith smiled and zapped at the side of Earl's head again, enjoying her new game.

"Oh. My. God." Lisa yelped and hopped off of Tolliver, looking at him in horror. "What are you wearing?"

"It was this or a towel, dear." He looked down at his ensemble. "At the time this was the preferable choice, especially since the woman in charge of bathing me seemed a little too over-eager in her task."

"Which one?" Lisa spun around, toward the pack of nephilim cowering in front of my father and Lilith. "Which one was it?"

"It doesn't matter." He grabbed her around the middle and pulled her back up against his front, nuzzling her neck. "Let's go home so I can take a shower and burn these clothes."

"I'll wash your back." Lisa smiled up at him.

Hope and I turned to each other and gagged.

"It's good to know you're all right," I said when they reached us.

"I'm fine." He shrugged. "Except for being trapped with the Angale. Without cable television. Why? Were you worried?"

"You could say that." I opened a portal from their little hidey-hole to the hallway outside my living room so we could wait for news on Matt's condition.

"Listen up," my father called behind me. When I turned, I saw that he had his hands over his head, dark energy crackling between his fingertips as he addressed the Angale. "This compound is no more. Your army is no more. Disperse from this place and live in peace. If you do not, I will come for you, and when I do, there is nowhere you can hide, no one that will save you. Go now. While I'm feeling merciful."

There was a sharp *crack* as he released the energy he'd been holding. The walls shimmered and began to dissolve. "Your hiding place will be gone in a few hours. I suggest you find your way out of here before then. Otherwise there may be uncomfortable questions for all of you to answer."

Chapter Twenty-Five

I paced the length of Matt's living room. Twenty-three paces across. Turn. Twenty-three more paces. Rest your head against the door and try to hear something from across the hall. Twice a day I stopped and made myself a pot of coffee. I drank one cup and emptied the rest down the drain when I went back to make the next pot.

Tuesday night I tried to sleep. I curled up in Matt's bed and buried my face in his pillow, trying to smell sunshine and cookies. Two hours later blood-curdling screams across the hall in my apartment woke me.

No way could I sleep. I had to be closer to him. So I moved to pacing the hallway. Eleven steps from his door to mine. Eleven steps that could either destroy me or save me. I made that eleven-step trip one thousand times before giving up and going back to Matt's apartment to hide again.

My cell phone rang sometime on Wednesday, two days after we'd gotten Tolliver back from the Angale, and I reached for it numbly. Probably work. Lisa and I had taken emergency leave but someone from PICU always called each day to check on us and see if we needed anything.

I slapped my hand around on the empty granite counter and let my tail roam across the floor toward the ringing. I thought it was somewhere on Matt's island. I remembered throwing it there sometime after the screaming stopped and before the long silence began. When had that been? Yesterday? Last night? I wasn't sure.

"Hello?"

"Hello, Miss Bettincourt. It's Detective Kastellero, from the Pittsburgh Police."

"I paid my parking ticket," I mumbled. I buried my head back into Matt's pillow, breathing in the lingering trace of his scent.

"That's wonderful, Miss Bettincourt," he said, sounding amused. "But I'm not with the Parking Authority. I'm with the Police Department. We spoke last week? You made some unfortunate jokes that I would have happily arrested you for?"

"Right." I remembered now. "What do you want?"

"I wanted to let you know that we've closed the car bombing case. My superiors believe all the loose ends have been tied up and so the case is being closed."

"You don't sound so sure, Detective. Do you think I'm still in danger?" "

"It's too convenient," Kastellero said. "It's too convenient and way too damn elaborate, but my superiors believe that Dr. Cosgrove and his brother were responsible for the stolen morphine at Rogers Hospital. Dr. Winslow found out and confronted him and Dr. Cosgrove, in an act of desperation, killed the pediatrician to protect his secret. After that, Miss Bettincourt, we believe you and Miss DeMarcos were in the wrong place at the wrong time."

My heart rate picked up at the suspicious tone in his voice.

"What do you mean?"

"Dr. Cosgrove may have attacked you and Miss DeMarcos because he thought you could tie him to the missing drugs and the murder. He may have seen you outside Dr. Winslow's office or overheard one of you talking about meeting with him. He may have even been worried that you had seen him kill Dr. Winslow. No matter what the reason, he saw you as a threat and he decided to get rid of you."

"But you don't think that's what happened?" He was right. Lisa had tied the ends up too well. Everything was neat and tidy. No wonder Kastellero thought it was a setup.

"It doesn't matter what I think. The case has been closed," he said. "I wanted to call and notify you myself."

"Thank you," I said.

"Miss Bettincourt?" Detective Kastellero dropped his voice to a whisper.

"Yes?"

"I heard about your brother's disappearance. Mr. Cheswick mentioned it when I came by the hospital to speak with you."

"And?"

"And," he let out a long breath, "your family didn't notify the police that he was missing."

"The police weren't necessary. My brother simply got cold feet before his wedding," I said. "He got over it and came home."

"Miss Bettincourt." His voice was soft now. Friendly. Like he was concerned and not just trying to give me an extra ration of grief. "You don't have to lie to me about what your family does. I've looked into your past."

"You've what?" My stomach dropped. He'd been looking into us? He knew what we were? Or at least he thought he did. What did he think we were?

"It was part of the investigation related to the bombing," he explained. "I saw that your family moved quite a bit when you were younger. Several college transfers on your part. Strange notes in the local police department files right around the same time as the moves. But no follow-up on any of the complaints. Then someone tried to kill all of you? Your brother's come up missing only a few weeks later? It doesn't take a very smart man to figure out your father has involved all of you in something dangerous. I've seen the websites about you. About your father's cult."

"I—" He thought Dad was some sort of crazy cult leader? Well, that was definitely better than him finding out the truth.

"You don't have to tell me anything," he assured me. "I just wanted to let you know that if you ever need anything—absolutely anything—I can find a way to help you. No questions asked. No police involvement, even. I would rather save your scrawny butt than sit at your funeral while the world laments the loss of one of its greatest smart alecks."

"Thank you." I sniffled and tried not to cry at the mere thought of someone—especially him—being nice to me right now. "I appreciate that, Detective Kastellero."

"Have a good day, Miss Bettincourt." The phone clicked once and then nothing. He'd just hung up on me. Even with everything else going on that might be the weirdest thing I'd ever experienced—and that was saying something, considering what my day was normally like.

I set the phone down on the counter and caught a whiff of myself. Ugh. Demon funk mixed with *Eau de Angale*. With slight undertones of Mississippi related sweat. I stalked into the bathroom and threw myself into a hot shower. I had no intention of going any farther than Matt's coffee machine but that didn't mean I had to stink.

Besides, I was a demon. Pain was a part of my life and it was time I faced that. I was giving myself one more day to wallow in my own misery and then I was getting out of this apartment and getting on with my life.

Once the water was scalding hot, I scrubbed myself down. The sharp, tangy smell of Matt's soap made my eyes tear up, and I curled up on the floor, sobbing. So much for not wallowing.

What if he died? What if the resurrection didn't work? What if it did? What if he hated me? Even worse, a resurrection always involved some form of memory loss. For J it had just taken the two days leading up to his death. He remembered Pilate's sentence, but everything after was hazy. Lazarus though had lost almost three months. Dad had always claimed resurrections were like alcohol; they affect every person differently. Some people, like Lazarus, fell down drunk after one drink and lost months of memories. Others, like J, could drink his own weight in tequila and lose just a few days. What would happen with Matt? Would he only lose Tolliver's disappearance?

Or would he lose me entirely?

The water turned cold, and I huddled in the far corner, shivering as tears ran down my cheeks and snot ran out of my nose. Great, tearing sobs rattled my chest. I lay my head back against the shower wall and fought the urge to vomit.

"Oh, for Evil's sake," Lilith said from the doorway.

What was she doing here? This was a pity party for one. I hadn't invited any additional guests.

"Get up."

I scrubbed at my eyes with the palms of my hands. Lilith

grumbled under her breath, coming into the bathroom. She turned off the water and grabbed me by the arms, pulling me up and out of my glass box of grieving.

"Get a spine, would you?" she said. "You're a Royal Princess of Hell. Not some common woman. Stand up straight. Wipe your eyes. Look like you're meant to be your father's daughter."

I followed her commands on instinct, a lesser demon following the commands of her superior. I threw my shoulders back and wiped the tears on my cheeks. She was right. I was a Princess of Hell. Even if Matt hated me for what had happened, I couldn't hide forever. I had to get back out there and prove I wasn't beaten.

"Now," she said, turning her back to retrieve a pair of sweat pants and a T-shirt from Matt's closet. "Why are you sobbing in the shower like a lovesick teenager?"

"Where do I start?" I sniffed, trying to stop my nose from running.

"At the beginning, of course," she threw the clothes at my head and shook her head. "Where else would you start?"

"Well, my boyfriend...ex-boyfriend—I'm not sure what he is because we sort of made up but didn't come out and say that we were back together—he died for me. Died. Dead. Shuffled off his immortal coil. For me." I pulled on the sweatpants she'd handed me and rolled the waistband down so they'd fit. They were still too long but now at least they wouldn't fall when I walked.

"Yes, and your uncle resurrected him. So why are you crying?"

"Exactly," I said and bit my lower lip. "My uncle resurrected him; which, from this end of the hall at least, sounded painful. What if he can't forgive me for this?"

"Then you take back up with the mortal."

"Dan?" I shook my head and then pulled on a T-shirt. "He's

not the man for me. Even if Matt never speaks to me again I won't go back to Dan."

"The mortal isn't the man for you? The mortal you had once planned on marrying?"

"How did you know about him?" I asked, suspicious.

"Your father told me. Plus the mortal's been calling your apartment like an incubus on deadline for a soul extraction. I got sick of answering the phone and told him you couldn't come to the phone because you were sick due to the stress of your brother's disappearance. He offered to bring soup. Very charming."

"Oh no." I groaned and pulled my hair back into a ponytail.

"What?" she asked. "It was lovely soup. Very tasty. You could tell it wasn't out of a can, and he'd actually gone to a restaurant and ordered it for you."

"You ate it?"

"What was I supposed to do? Let it go to waste? It was good soup. Besides, you were busy here, sulking, while the man you're supposed to be with is resting in your guest room."

"He's…"

"Resting. A resurrection is draining for everyone involved. Especially the person on the receiving end," she said. "Your mother has been with him. She's a surprisingly good nurse. Very compassionate. It must be where you inherited it from. I don't think the crystals and the protective runes she's scattered about the room are helping, but for all her faults, she is quite a good mother, isn't she?"

"She's not bad." I shifted my weight from one foot to the other. It was always weird talking about my parents with Lilith. She'd always been nice about things but that didn't mean I wanted to rub salt in the wounds of my Dad leaving her—the world's most famous sex goddess—for Mom—otherwise known as the world's loopiest witch.

"She's better than that," Lilith answered. "Even the Alpha said that she's been instrumental to his recovery."

"Has he said anything about me? Matt, I mean."

"He worries about where you are, and why you're not with him." She pulled me out of the bedroom, half dressed, behind her. "He thinks you're angry at him. He wants to know you're safe."

"What does he remember?" I asked.

"He's a strong man," she said. "The strongest I've ever met in fact. He remembers everything. But his first question was to see if you were safe."

"Has someone told him what happened to Valerie?"

"We let the girl have a supervised visit with him when he woke and she told him. She claimed that we murdered his mother in cold blood and destroyed his home. I believe your ghost may have given him a kinder version of the story afterward. But it's not my place to snoop."

"Sure it's not." I snorted and finished getting dressed. "You, the demoness who invented the idea of pillow talk and espionage. You'd never dream of snooping."

"Don't be silly." She gave me a sad smile. "The feverish murmurs of a half dead nephilim aren't what I trade in. Besides, it's better if you figure it out for yourself. And your father wants your opinion on how to best deal with the female nephilim. She makes me nervous."

"I want to go over there." I started toward the door and then stopped. "But I can't."

"Why?"

My stomach clenched and I tried to slow my breathing so I

didn't hyperventilate. When that didn't work I covered my face with my hands and tried to collect my thoughts, doing my best to stay calm. What was I afraid of? That he'd be different somehow? Strange? Unnatural?

He was going to be different, but he would still be Matt. Who he was wouldn't change because of this. But it might change who we were together. We were no longer two paranormal beings pretending to be a normal couple. We couldn't do that anymore. Every time he saw me from now till the end of eternity he would think about this.

Tears pooled in my eyes. "Because I'm scared. I don't know what I'm getting myself into by walking in there, but I have this feeling that everything else in my life hinges on what happens in the next five minutes."

"Welcome to being alive." She opened the front door, motioning for me to go into the hallway. "But for the record? The things that change your life forever?"

"Yeah?"

"Those things happen when you least expect it. They're not the things you have time to prepare for. Now, quit trying to work up the nerve to be someone you're not and go in there." She pointed at my apartment door and then used her tail to give me a gentle prod on the butt.

"Oh thank Evil you're okay," Lisa cried. She jumped off the love seat she'd been lying on and rushed over to me, wrapped me in a tight hug, and buried her face in my neck.

"Did you think I wasn't?" I asked, confused.

"I wasn't sure." She shook her head against my shoulder and squeezed tighter. "After everything that's happened I've been worried about you."

"I'm fine." I patted her on the back for a second before disentangling her arms from around my neck.

"Faith," Harold said and tried to wrap his arms around me. He didn't manage it of course but the sentiment was still appreciated. "I've been worried about you. Did you hear about Dr. Cosgrove?"

"Yeah." I shifted away from him and tucked my hands underneath my armpits. "I'm sorry that they basically convicted the wrong guy for your murder and you'll never actually get justice. If you want to smite someone for it, I'm sure we can tie Tolliver down and let you mess with him a bit. Give him ghostly wet willies or something."

"I don't need justice. I forgave you and Lisa for my death weeks ago." Harold narrowed his eyes at my uncle. "But I still don't think using a good man's moment of weakness was the right way to go to fix things. We could have found another solution."

"Right, good, thank you for forgiving me. That really does mean a lot to me." I stepped away from him, avoiding everyone's gazes. "Now, if you'll all excuse me, I need to check on Matt."

The living room fell silent, and I made my way down the hall, knocking on the door that used to belong to Lisa.

"Yes?" Mom called out from the other side of the door.

I pushed the door open. Mom was sitting in my desk chair, reading aloud from what looked like an old school bodice ripper—complete with naked man chesticles and a fuchsia background, while he rested on my bed. "It's just me."

"Oh." Mom dog-eared her page—which would have killed Matt if he'd been feeling better—and smiled at me. "Faith, you're here to sit with Matt. That's wonderful. Super, in fact. I'll just go… well, I don't know what I'll do, but I'll come up with something."

Instead of waiting for either of us to answer she hurried out of the room, taking the kitchen chair with her, leaving Matt and me alone, and for the first time since we'd met completely at a loss for what to say.

Chapter Twenty-Six

I looked at the door and then at Matt. My heart clenched at the sight of him. He was bare-chested, my comforter drawn up to his waist, and he was rocking a serious case of bed head. If it weren't for the heavy bags under his eyes he would look sleep rumpled, charming, and absolutely drool-worthy. Considering the fact that he'd died and been brought back to life this week I'd say he still looked amazing.

"Hey," he said. His eyes widened, like he was surprised to see me, and then he gave me a shy smile as he tried to push himself upright, his arms trembling. "I've been so worried about you."

"I've been worried about you, too," I said, leaving out the part about how he wouldn't be in this situation if it weren't for me.

"So…" I smiled, my lips trembling and my stomach rolling with tension at the thought of being alone with him. I shoved my hands in my pockets and shuffled my feet against each other. Yeah, because that made me look cool and confident. Right.

"So…" He shrugged and plucked at the hem of the sheet.

"How are you?" I glanced around my bedroom, knowing

there was nowhere besides the bed to sit down, but not trusting myself to be so close to Matt. I sank further into my thirteen-year-old girl lameness.

"Tired." Matt patted the bed beside him. "Are you going to sit down?"

"I don't know if I should," I said, scooting closer to the wall. "I don't want to jostle the bed or make you uncomfortable. I…don't want to hurt you."

"I don't think you can hurt me. Not physically, at least." He held out his hand for me. His eyes were soft and I could see his vulnerability. "Whatever the Alpha and Jesus did to me it managed to heal everything. Even my tonsils grew back."

"Okay, that's interesting in an odd sort of way. I mean I know Dad always said that Resurrection is like the Celestial version of a system reboot for the body. But growing your tonsils back? That's just weird." I tugged at my ponytail.

"Will you please sit down?" He motioned toward the mattress next to his hip. "All the fidgeting you're doing is making me nervous."

"Sorry," I mumbled, moving to perch on the edge of the bed.

"I said sit," he said. When I didn't reply he shifted closer to me and dragged me into the bed beside him, then buried his head in the side of my neck, planting a tender kiss behind my ear. My skin tingled under his lips and little jolts of electricity shot through me. I breathed in with relief at the fact that I could touch him, that he would let me touch him and not shrink away in disgust for what we'd done to him. I breathed deeply against his neck, trying to capture the scent of cookies. But there was nothing. No sunshine smell in his hair. No cookie scent lingering on his skin. No natural, guy scent every man I knew had. Every man I knew except for three. And now Matt was the fourth.

My stomach sank. All that relief I'd been feeling a moment before fled, and the hole it left filled with dread.

I pulled away and settled beside him, leaning against the headboard. We sat silently, our fingers interlaced, trying to find the words to make this change between us okay. Trying to find a way to make us okay. What was I supposed to say? Thanks for saving my life? Sorry you died? Good thing we knew a couple of guys who could pull off a resurrection?

"So, how long are you on bed rest?"

Stimulating conversationalist I was not.

He shook his head and smiled. "You're trying to throw me out already? The Alpha said I should try to stay in bed, supervised, for as long as I could manage. But if having me here and not being able to ravish my broken body is too much for you, I'm sure your mother won't mind nursing me to health at my place."

I rested my head on his shoulder, trying to ignore the flight instinct inside me telling me to run like my tail was on fire, as I not so covertly reveled in the comfort his touch brought. "I'm getting concerned about all the time you're spending alone with my mother. Does Dad have anything to worry about?"

"Hardly." Matt chuckled. "She's only here because I can't do anything for myself yet without getting dizzy, and we all knew you were exhausted so I wouldn't let them wake you."

"So you're on bed rest until you get your strength back?" I ignored his comment about how even in the middle of a resurrection he'd been concerned about my welfare.

"And until we can get things finalized."

"Finalized?" I asked.

Matt pulled his arm off my shoulders, and hugged his stomach.

"Jesus called work for me this morning and claimed to be my doctor. He told them I was in a pretty serious car accident and had fallen into a coma. Now we don't have to worry about them expecting me back anytime soon."

"Oh." I hadn't even thought about how they were going to explain his absence from work. Hell, I hadn't even thought about his job this past week. None of us had. We'd just walked all over him while we tried to solve our own problems, not caring about how he was chipping away at his vacation time while we tortured him.

Matt shrugged and picked at the loose thread on my comforter, not meeting my eyes. "J told them I'd fallen asleep at the wheel coming home from work. He's going to call back next week and tell them I didn't survive."

"Why?" I took his hand and laced our fingers together. I brought it to my mouth and kissed the back of it, noticing that instead of being rough it had become smooth and unblemished.

"Look at me," he said, sighing. "I can't go back there like this. Not with what I am."

"The changes you've gone through are all so subtle that the human eye won't register them. Or if they do they'll see that something is different but they won't be able to figure out what."

"*I'll* register them," he said. "I'll know that I'm different and I can't explain why, but that matters to me. Besides, I think everyone knows that I've got bigger things to deal with than my law career. Your uncle didn't just bring me back because he's nice. He doesn't do that. Remember?"

I stilled and considered his words, the tension in my gut shifting instantly into a giant knot of dread. He was right. My uncle didn't do things to be a nice guy. "Then why did he do it?"

"The Angale can't live on their own," he said. He moved so that our foreheads were pressed together and our lips were only centimeters apart. "They can't be out in the normal world and interact with people. I'd love to tell you that they can, and that it would just take a little work on their part and they'd acclimate. But we all know they won't. They can't."

I froze, and the entire world turned to ice around me. The ball of dread in my stomach careened upward like a cannonball, smacking into my heart broadside and shattering it into a million tiny pieces. How could they decide such a thing? How could he agree to it?

"My uncle wants you to lead the Angale? He wants you to be the leader of a cult full of bloodthirsty nephilim? Or *you* want this?"

"They can change," he said. "They *will* change. I won't lead people like my mother did. But the most important part is if I'm in charge I can keep you safe."

"So you're going to lead an army of Celestial beings that want to kill me and it's for my own good?"

"Biloxi has been compromised. We've found a place near Greensburg where I can create another home for them. That way I can stay right here with you. Plus, your father and uncle will be able to help me manage them, and they'll help me try to integrate those who want to live out in the world."

"It won't work."

He held the sides of my face, forcing me to look up at him. His eyes swirled with passion and a type of haunting intensity I'd never seen before. "It has to. I refuse to let it *not* work. You could have died and I wasn't able to protect you. I won't let that happen again."

"No." My knees were trembling, and I had to fight the urge to run out of the room crying. He wasn't supposed to be so supportive. So caring. He was supposed to be angry and resentful. Instead, here he was acting like he needed to protect me. Why couldn't he be decent and act like an asshole? Just this once?

"Let me protect you. Let me keep you safe. I love you, Faith. Let me show you that by trusting me to take care of you."

"I can't." I looked down at the comforter, refusing to meet his eyes. "You died and then they wouldn't let me help save you. They made me go outside and you were here and I was so…so…"

"Scared?" he asked. I nodded, and he squeezed my hand. "I was scared, too. I have been so scared because there were times I thought everything I knew had never taken place. That you weren't real. But then, there would be these moments where my mind would clear, and it would all make sense again. I would make sense again. We would make sense again and I wasn't scared anymore."

I tried to think of something to say that would make this better. Some way to save what we had. For both of our sakes. The problem was, I loved Matt. I adored him. He was the key that made everything else in my life make sense. But he had died trying to save me. And now he was going to give up everything he'd fought for in some desperate attempt to keep me safe. How could I love him and let him do that?

"About your mom." I started in my usual, utterly tactless manner. I didn't want to bring it up, but at the same time I couldn't let Valerie's elephant-sized absence stifle us, either. Not with everything else we had to face.

"She tried to kill you. She kidnapped a demon. All of it was part of some grand plan on her part to set up my father as a false

God with herself as his prophet. The Alpha said my father is claiming he had no idea what she was doing, but there's a pretty heavy cloud of suspicion hanging over him. Two attempts by his followers at a Celestial power grab in less than two months makes him look incompetent."

"Well..." I bit my lower lip. He wasn't acknowledging she was dead. Okay, so he knew she was guilty of what could have become some pretty terrible things, but did he realize Lilith vaporized her on his couch? "I just wanted to say I was sorry about what happened to her."

"Why are you sorry?" he asked. "Lisa told me what happened. Mom managed to slip free of her bindings because of all the weird energy flowing through the building during the whole *Bringing Me Back to Life* thing, and she attacked you. If it would have been me there instead of Lilith, I would have killed her, too."

"What Lilith did wasn't a heat of the moment, kill or be—"

"Lilith killed her to protect you. My mother was determined to keep after you until one of you was dead. She got what she wanted, just not the way she wanted it. She's not the first person to have that particular outcome happen when they messed with your family."

Right, Levi. When the Alpha caught him trying to steal power from other immortals, starting with me, He'd put him in a pocket of Purgatory and granted him the powers of a pure Celestial Being. He was a god among men. Then, before Levi even got the chance to enjoy his new powers, the Alpha pushed them just beyond his reach and cut off his access to them for all time.

Now we had been forced to deal with a potential uprising by a group of psycho nephilim and Matt had almost died. No, scratch that—he had died.

"We can't see each other anymore." I blurted out.

"Excuse me?" Matt looked at me, his face stunned and his mouth hanging slightly open.

"You keep getting hurt because of me. I'm like a Celestial danger magnet for you. Your brother blew up your car. Your mom almost had you killed by garden sprites. The risk is just too high."

"*My* half-brother blew up *my* car," he said, pointing at his chest. "*My* mother sent *me* to die by garden sprites. *My* family members are the ones who keep trying to kill *me*."

I turned away from him and shoved my hands under my armpits so that I wouldn't lose my nerve and fall into his arms like some weak-willed girl having her first lover's tiff. "You're only in their sights because of me. If you lived anywhere else but next door to the Devil's youngest daughter, they wouldn't have had any idea where to find you. You'd be safe right now."

"I am safe right now," he said. "I'm here, you're here, your father has an entire legion of demons on call and waiting for the moment I'm not safe. Besides, all things considered, your uncle's little parlor trick has made sure that I'm invincible. So I can't imagine a world in which I'll ever not be safe again. I promise you Faith, I'm fine. We're fine. You just need to trust me."

"He's sending you to lead a group of crazy nephilim into a new life. Just because they can't kill you doesn't mean they can't find a way to hurt you."

"So what? We're through? Is that what you're telling me?" Matt threw back the sheets and stood. I tried to keep my eyes focused forward and not stare at his naked butt. They'd even managed to cure the scar on his back from the bike accident he'd had in college. The Alpha was thorough. "Right now, what you're doing to us is hurting me more than anything that I've been through in the past three days."

I squeezed my eyelids shut, trying to keep from getting distracted. "I think it would be safer for you."

"This isn't about me being safe," Matt said. I peeked at him through slitted eyelids. He was pacing at the foot of my bed, his wings extended and his hands tugging at his hair. "This is about you being scared."

"You're right. I'm terrified. What if something happens to you because of me?"

"I know," Matt grabbed my arms and hoisted me off the bed, "that nothing I've ever felt in my life compares to what it feels like when I'm with you. Nothing."

He laced his fingers through my hair and pressed his lips against mine. An electric spark shot between us and my knees went weak while the world spun around us. I grabbed at his shoulders, melting into his kiss, my knees wobbly. If I had to give him up, at least I'd have this last moment to cherish.

He pulled away from me and paced over to the window, resting his hands on the windowsill while I stood there stunned, my fingers over my mouth and tears welling up in my eyes.

"I love you," he said. "Can you even comprehend that? Or is that beyond you as a demon? I love you, Faith."

"It's not that I don't love you, it's—"

"Don't," he turned to stare at me, his eyes filled with anger and hurt. "Don't give me some tired old 'it's not you it's me' bit. I love you. And I'm going to go on loving you for the rest of eternity. I don't want anyone, or anything else in my life besides you. I don't need anything besides you."

"Matt." I pulled my hands free and turned away from him. "Please respect my decision and go."

"You want me to leave?" I could hear him rustling around behind me, pulling on his clothes. "Fine. I'll leave."

I kept my head down and tried to hold back my emotions.

He stood before me, and tilted my chin up so I could look him in the eyes. "You can declare that we're over, Faith Anne Bettincourt, but you can't keep me from loving you anyway.

"Because there's still an 'us.' Even if you won't accept it. No matter what, I'm still going to be right here and I'm going to keep standing here until you realize that we're meant to be together."

I didn't bother to answer, just jerked my chin from his grasp and looked at the floor. He let out a huff and stalked away, slamming the door to my bedroom loudly behind him.

I sat at the edge of the bed and clasped my shaking fingers together. Sure he was angry now, but soon he'd realize that he was wrong and that we most definitely didn't belong together. Then he could find a nice girl and settle down. A girl who wouldn't cause him pain. Someone who deserved a guy like Matt in their life.

"I'd go torture him for making you this miserable," Malachi said. I glanced up to see the dread demon hovering in the doorway. "But you've done this to yourself and managed to destroy him in the process. So, there's nothing left for me to do, but stand here and wonder exactly what those sprites knocked loose in your noggin."

"Shut up." I stomped into my bathroom and turned on the sink so I could splash some cold water on my face.

"You're making a mistake," he said. "I've never been a fan of the white light brigade but—"

"Don't." I held my hand up.

"But—"

"I said don't." I walked to my bed, curled up where Matt had been a moment earlier, and ignored him.

"Fine, lay there and sulk. Pretend to sleep if it helps. But when you wake up, nothing's going to have changed. You'll still be an idiot who made the biggest mistake of her life. Plus you forced me to agree with a member of the other team. Something I'll never forgive you for, by the way."

"Shut up."

"He's right. You are run—"

"Shut. Up." I flopped onto my side, pulling the blankets over my head, ignoring the angrily twitching dread demon, so I could wallow in my own misery instead.

Chapter Twenty-Seven

"Faith," my mother said through my closed door. She pounded on my door and I didn't bother answering. After four hours of me not answering I hoped she'd give up and go away for good. No, instead, she was coming back to knock every five minutes now. "Open this door or I will break it down. I'm not kidding this time. I will do it."

"Fine. It wasn't locked anyway." I stalked over to the door and pulled it open. Mom wore a pink bathrobe and her hair was rolled into bright purple foam rollers. The green mud mask on her face was starting to crack and I could see that she'd gotten some of it matted in her eyebrows. What in the name of the Alpha and the Omega was she doing dressed like that?

"You mean I've been standing here beating on your door all this time and it's been open?" She gaped at me, her mouth hanging open and her eyes wide.

"Yeah." I turned to go back to bed. What was these people's problem with letting a demoness be miserable? You'd think they could get the obvious signs that I wanted to wallow in self-pity alone.

"So why didn't you open the door four hours ago?"

"I didn't want to talk to you, obviously. If you didn't hear the latest news, Matt and I broke up."

"We all heard." Mom followed me over to the bed and started to rub my back. "I'm sorry, sweetheart. I'm sure you can find another nice boy. Maybe one of your father's legions?"

"Because that worked so well for Hope?"

"You could always get together with Malachi," she suggested.

What was she playing at? "Mom, Mal has been my bodyguard since the day I was born. Besides, he's three feet tall and wears a cloak."

"Only because it made you laugh the first time he showed up that way," she said.

What? Malachi was, well *Malachi*. A whole legion full of bad in one tiny, travel-sized package. Wasn't he?

"Mom, Malachi has always appeared that way in the mortal realm unless he chose to shapeshift into another body. Normally a *female body*."

"The girl body thing is just Mal's way of dealing with his own issues." Mom rolled her eyes. "But the reason he shows up in floaty form is because he doesn't want to freak you out."

"Why would he freak me out?"

"Look, when you were an infant, Malachi was an invisible presence. Karanthian lived with us as a nanny demon and the only time Mal physically manifested was if we called him. But when you were about two, Karanthian left and Malachi stepped in to be your bodyguard fulltime. The first day he showed up looking like a normal mortal man—tall, muscular, black hair, big chocolaty eyes. He was sexy in this sort of bad boy way, and when I say sexy

I mean he could literally stop traffic at the mall during the Black Friday sales. I always said if your father wasn't around—"

"Mom!" I grabbed her shoulders and gave her a quick shake. "Enough mooning over my bodyguard. Focus."

"Right, sorry." Mom shook her head like she was trying to clear out the memories of how hot Malachi used to be. "But I mean is it really any surprise that Matt's mom would have tried to seduce him? Really, Bassano can't compare."

"Valerie tried to seduce Malachi?" My eyes widened. "Was that the whole thing going on between them at the Church Brewworks?"

"Well obviously that was all anger and unresolved sexual tension between them." Mom rolled her eyes at me. "But anyway, Malachi showed up looking like a mortal man, but you were terrified of him and wouldn't let him near you. Which made guarding you and Hope almost impossible. So he tried turning himself into a dog. A black French poodle, if you can believe it. You peed yourself when he got near you."

"Great, thanks for that memory. My own bodyguard made me wet my pants." I couldn't believe this. Malachi was a man. I mean sure, he did the demonic equivalent of drag on occasion but he still identified himself as a male demon. But I'd never thought of Malachi as a *man*. Like a man *man*. "What I don't understand is how he went from being a man to being what he is now."

"There was this commercial on television. I don't even know what it was for. Something stupid. I think it might have been a used car lot talking about how the only person who could slash things better than them was the Angel of Death. Then they had this little cartoon of a reaper slashing prices on their cars, and it made you howl with laughter. So he shifted into that form and you kept laughing. You even let him float down to sit beside you and that was that. He's stayed that way ever since." Mom shrugged and gave me one of those *what-can-you-do?* smiles she seemed to have perfected over the years.

I shook my head and rubbed my eyes, trying to find some way for this to make sense. "I still don't think it's a good idea for us to date. No offense to Mal but I think I might give up on the whole enterprise if you don't mind. Maybe celibacy isn't such a bad idea."

"Well, your dad said I can't push you on anything but I want to say I think you're making a mistake. Life's difficult Faith, you shouldn't spend it alone." She patted my back. "But I think I have something that will perk you up."

I tried to muster some enthusiasm. Otherwise she'd come up with something truly horrible to torture me with. Like chick flick marathons. Or even worse, hours of watching Lifetime.

"Ooh! Has Dad decided to go destroy a city? Can we level Paris? I'd really like to level Paris right now."

"Why Paris?" Mom lifted one of her eyebrows and gave me an appraising stare. "What is there in Paris that you want to destroy?"

"Nothing." I tried not to think about my and Matt's first date, which happened to be in Paris. I'd rather not think about what my stupidity since then had cost us all. "I just thought Paris would be a good city to destroy."

"Your father isn't leveling a city. But you need to get up anyway. You know how Lisa and I had agreed to just have a double wedding since my wedding got canceled?"

"You and Lisa were planning a double wedding tomorrow? Does that mean I don't have to wear that fugly monstrosity that you bought us and I can just wear the nice black cocktail dress I had picked out for Lisa's wedding?"

"Oh right, you were MIA when Lisa offered to let us share their wedding. That doesn't matter. What matters is that your father doesn't feel right about making me share my special day with someone else. I'm going to be the Devil's consort. I should have my own day. Well, my own night, I guess you could say."

"Mom, not that this isn't terribly compelling," I said before pulling the pillow over my head. "But could you cut to the punch line? I'd like to go back to my pity party so I can get it all out of the way and be able to fake enthusiasm for my best friend's wedding tomorrow."

"Well, you're going to have to speed up that order of fake enthusiasm," she said, bouncing on the edge of my bed.

I lifted the pillow off my face and gave her my best bitch stare. "Why?"

"Your father and I are getting married tonight." She glanced at the clock and frowned. "In six hours."

"You're getting married at nine at night?" I asked, looking at the clock. "Why so late?"

"It was always supposed to be an evening wedding," Mom said. "They're very trendy. Besides, it will take your father's kitchen staff that long to get the food prepared and set up on this short notice. But your uncle is here. All of you children are here. Everyone is safe. We're having the wedding."

"Are you sure it's not so you can beat Lisa down the aisle?"

"Of course not." Mom huffed. "Now, up. I need you to start getting dressed. We have a full day's worth of pampering to do and not nearly long enough to get it done. Come on."

"Fine." I sighed. "I'll get up. I'll be happy that you and Dad are getting married. Does that mean I don't have to wear the dress?"

"You're wearing the dress." Mom pointed at me. "Get over it.

And don't worry, I've already found someone else to escort you up the aisle since I didn't think Matt would feel up to coming."

"Who?" I asked, wary about what sort of crazy, and most likely inappropriate, date my mother had found for me.

"It's a surprise. But your father wants to make sure you have ample protection so he'll be your date to Lisa's wedding tomorrow, too."

"I'll be fine with Malachi." I fought the urge to give her a solid jolt of dark power. The last thing I needed was some demon I barely knew hovering over me. Or even worse, thinking that I was in the market for a new man in my life.

"I never said that you wouldn't be fine with Malachi," Mom said. "Now get in the living room so we can start making you look like the Princess of Hell your father claims you are."

"I'd be more believable in the dress I picked out for Lisa's wedding." If my life had to fall apart around my ears, couldn't I at least meet my fate looking somewhat fashionable? It just seemed pathetic to meet a lifetime of loneliness in a dress that hideous.

"Tough." My mother stalked out of the room. "You have five minutes. Then I'm coming back in here."

"I'll be two minutes or less."

She left, slamming the door behind her, and I grabbed my phone, looking at the picture of me and Matt on the front of it. I opened my settings and my finger hovered over the Delete key. It didn't do me any good to keep it now. No matter what he said we weren't going to be able to work things out between us.

The phone buzzed and I glanced at the screen. Rogers Hospital. But it wasn't one of the lines from my contact list. That was weird. I answered it and hoped it wasn't Harold, trying to keep me up to date with the latest who's screwing who gossip. "Hello?"

"Faith?" Dan sounded nervous. "I just wanted to call and see how you were doing. You haven't answered your phone in the past couple of days. I don't want to be a pain in the ass but—"

"I'm fine," I said. Why could this guy not get the hint? We weren't meant to be together. I wasn't meant to be *together* with anyone. "We found my brother and things are fine."

"How are things with the boyfriend? I know the last time we talked you said it was complicated."

"Not too complicated really," I said. "Since he's not my boyfriend anymore."

"Oh." I heard him swallow and clear his throat. "I'm sorry. I know you were hoping that you could work it out. Is there anything I can do?"

"No," I said. "But is there anything else you needed?"

"I just wanted to check on you. And well…I guess there is this other thing."

"What?"

"I'm done with the MEDTECH software update," Dan explained. "My project at Rogers Hospital is done. I'm flying back to Chicago tomorrow morning."

"Oh, well thanks for telling me."

"I'm going to be back in a month, though," he said, his words coming out in a rush. "A longer project, too. All of the University Hospital System. Twelve weeks."

"That's great. I mean it's great that you're on such a big project."

"I was thinking," he continued, "if you want, maybe we can get together for dinner. Maybe just drinks even, as friends of course. Because right now, you sound like that's something you need."

"I don't think that's a good idea. You're a nice guy and all, but right now I just don't think I'm in the place for that. I'm sorry. Congratulations on your new project, though. You deserve it."

"Are you sure?" he asked.

"Yeah, I'm sure."

"Well, if you need to talk to someone, you know you can call me. Don't you?"

"I don't think that's such a good idea either. Good-bye, Dan." I felt a sharp ache inside my chest. I'd never gotten to say that before. It should've felt like closure of some sort, but no matter how many memories you wipe or how many things you manipulate, the past is always there, waiting below the surface like piranha, just waiting to rip your hand off and leave you bleeding to death while it munched on your flesh.

Six hours later I'd been primped, pampered, polished, and then crammed into the world's ugliest bridesmaid's dress and a pair of stilettos that could double as torture devices for questioning terrorists. Standing in the back of the mock church that the Alpha had made appear out of thin air, I was pretty sure my night couldn't get any worse. Then I remembered that Mom had set me up on a blind date for the next two days and realized that in this family it could always get worse.

"You know, you don't look too bad in that dress," Malachi announced from the top of a set of stairs that I thought might have led to the choir loft. I resisted the urge to laugh. Mom was right, if it weren't for the fact it was Mal I'd have agreed with her that he was probably one of the five hottest guys I'd ever seen. Hell, even though it was Mal, he was still in the top three and that was just all kinds of wrong. But at least I didn't have to worry about making small talk with a stranger tonight.

He tugged at the cuffs of his suit and gave me the once

over with his caramel colored eyes. He lifted the side of his lush lips upward in a crooked smile and quit fidgeting. "But I forgot how difficult it is to get dressed in this body. Everything is so constricting."

I could see how most men's clothes would be. He was tall enough that he could rest his chin on the top of my head, and he had enough muscles without being one of those weird, gross looking *super-body-builder-I-eat-small-children-for-breakfast* types, but I didn't need to ask who to put my money on in a bar fight, either. He'd neatly combed his black curls back and he was channeling the whole *Bad Boy Who Needs Love* thing like it was going out of style. I'd even noticed the shadow of a tattoo on his left bicep underneath his white dress shirt before he put on his jacket.

I smiled at him. "You're pretty good-looking yourself."

"Please. Mortals don't look this good." He gave me a wink. "This is…*me*."

"Well then, why don't you go this way all the time? If you don't like your other form, wear this one. Be who you really are for Evil's sake."

"But you're more comfortable with me in the other form. This one scares you."

"It scared me when I was two," I said. "I've grown up a bit since then."

"I keep trying to remind myself of that but it doesn't help." He smoothed his hands over his jacket and turned to face me. "You know, I talked to Matt this afternoon."

"Grownup, Mal," I patted his arm. "Time to let me make my own decisions."

"Well then, quit making all the wrong ones. It would make the job of protecting you so much easier if I only had to worry about bad guys. Right now, I feel like most of my workload is protecting you from you. And I have to tell you that's a job for two of me right now."

"Maybe it's time you let me go," I said. "Let me take care of myself. Hope doesn't have a bodyguard anymore. Why should I?"

"Hope doesn't have a bodyguard because no one will take her on. Besides, I'd get bored in Hell. There's nothing there for me but paperwork and meetings. It's much more fun topside with you. Or it was until you sailed off on the Good Ship Crackpot and ruined your one chance at happiness."

"I had to." I tried to keep my fake, bridesmaid smile on my face from slipping. "I'm not sure what would be worse—taking the chance and the Angale hurting Matt, or hurting someone else in this family or just some random stranger who happened to get in the way."

"You think that by breaking your own heart, and Matt's, you're going to somehow prevent the Angale from being crazy? You think that will prevent them from a war if they decide to wage it? They have been bred to destroy demons." Malachi tugged on my arm so that we were face to face again. "That is their only purpose in life and, if they choose to stay that way, nothing you and Matt do will change their minds."

"You don't think they're going to change, do you?" I asked as he took my arm, leading me toward the sanctuary. "Valerie's death just brought us closer to war."

"We've always been coming closer to war." Malachi stopped at the doors to the replica of Notre Dame my mother had asked the Alpha to provide her for the wedding. He dipped his fingers in the water and crossed himself. "Being stupid and breaking Angel Boy's heart won't pull us all back from the brink and it won't save innocent bystanders, either. If war comes, no matter what you do, people will get hurt."

I fought the urge to throw my arms around his neck and cry like I had when I was a kid. Back then Mal would turn himself into a pillow and let me sob myself to sleep on his chest. Not that it would do me any good now. "It won't pull us back from the brink, but if war comes it will prevent..."

"Don't count on it," Malachi said.

The music started and I wrapped my arm around his bicep. Lisa and Nahamia started up the aisle and I psyched myself up to walk down the aisle with Mal and not wobble in my shoes. Even though I'd lost all feeling in my toes.

"Can I give you a little bit of advice about war?" Malachi asked.

"What?" I watched Lisa hit the point that my mother had told me was my cue to start marching. Malachi straightened and started us up the aisle in time with the music.

"In war there are no sides," he whispered, keeping his face forward, not acknowledging the demons sitting in the pews. "Battles are nothing but a clusterfuck full of chaos and the only way you survive them is to grab onto the people who matter to you and try to keep each other safe. All that matters is keeping the people you love safe, even if you have to split the world apart and reign down hellfire on anyone who stands in your way."

He let go of me at the top of the aisle and I turned to him. He was right. If war came I would do whatever it took to keep Matt and everyone else I loved safe. But for right now, the best way for me to do that was to let Matt go. No matter how much it killed me.

Dad looked at me and then at Malachi, his eyebrows drawn together. Instead of answering, the dread demon just patted my father's shoulder and turned to the back of the church.

All my father's subjects except for Lilith were in the audience. Not that I could blame her. I doubted I was going to find myself at any of my ex's weddings in the future.

When Hope reached us, the music changed and everyone stood, facing the back of the church. Except for Dad. Always the proper gentleman, he kept his back turned while Mom walked down the aisle. My sister started to giggle, her shoulders shaking, and I craned my head around her to see what was so funny. Mom made it farther up the aisle and I stared, stunned, at the hot mess she'd managed to make of herself in the short time since we'd left her alone in the dressing room.

When would Mom learn she wasn't eighteen anymore? She was the mother of two grown daughters. Besides, was it really appropriate for the soon to be Consort of Satan to be walking down the aisle in a knock off of the Princess of Wales's wedding dress? Especially a version that was two sizes too small in the bodice. I was pretty sure that much cleavage was something they'd frown upon at Westminster. But, even if they didn't, a proper royal bride always knew it was better to leave your pageant tiara at home when you were in a church. Diadems were so much classier.

• • •

"The past couple of weeks have been hard on you," my uncle said and handed me a glass of champagne. I clinked it against His and turned back to watching the rest of the guests from the sidelines of my parents' wedding reception.

"You could say that," I said. We sipped our champagne, and I tried to ignore the fact that I was standing there drinking with the Creator of All Things while a group of demons did the

Electric Slide. What was I supposed to say to him? "Thanks for resurrecting my boyfriend but you know, I would have preferred him dead rather than in charge of the Angale." Yeah, even if that were true—which is wasn't—it might sound a tad ungrateful.

"Blech, I always have hated this stuff." He waved His hand over our glasses and I saw that He'd changed it from champagne into Guinness. Who said the Alpha didn't have good taste?

I laughed and took a large drink, savoring the change. "You realize Mom paid three hundred dollars a bottle for that champagne, right?"

"I think that makes it taste worse." He laughed. "Besides, it'll be our little secret. Your father has already turned his and about half the other guests' drinks to whisky anyway so it's his ass she'll go after first."

"That'll make an interesting honeymoon. I'd be prepared to control a demonic incident in Hawaii next week if I were you."

"I'll keep that in mind," He said, and we both stood there watching the silly demons in front of us for a few minutes, not bothering to talk.

"Hey, Faith?" He took my hand in His, His tone suddenly serious. I knew that the polite small talk had come to an end. "I just wanted to tell you I'm sorry for everything."

"Me too." I pulled my hand away before taking a long drink of my beer.

"If I had any other choice—"

"Please don't," I said.

"But—"

"You and him"—I pointed to my father with my glass of beer—"The two of you have nothing *but* choices. It's the rest of us who have to live with them. So don't tell me there was no other way. You made a choice and now I've got to live with it."

"Would you rather I let him die? Or perhaps I should have destroyed the Angale when they first started? Strangled them to death in their infancy? Then he'd have never existed and who knows what we'd be facing now? Because trust me, with or without Matt Andrews in the picture, this has been coming for a long time."

Instead of answering, I walked away. I loved my uncle but the last thing I needed right now was to listen to Him justifying why, for once, He couldn't just be fair.

Chapter Twenty-Eight

"I can't believe we're doing this," Lisa said the next morning. She tugged on the hem of her dress and followed me up the front steps of the funeral home. "I'm getting married in"—she looked at the gold watch on her wrist and glanced back at me—"less than four hours."

"This shouldn't take more than a half hour," I replied. "Besides, we owe it to Harold. He'd do the same thing if it was us."

"Of course I would," the spirit in question said, appearing next to me in a somber black suit. "I mean after all, I did plan on making it to your wedding, which happens to be on the day of my memorial service. If I can make it without a conflict, you should be fine."

"Point taken." Lisa nodded and gave Harold a warm smile. We stopped at the guest book, and I hastily scrawled both of our names before taking two of the donation envelopes and putting anonymous cashier's checks for $100,000 in each. In lieu of flowers Harold's family was asking that donations be given to Ronald McDonald House charities. Fitting, all things considered.

We stepped into the reception room and found ourselves face to face with a middle-aged woman wearing a black pantsuit that set off the gray in her short bob so that it looked like liquid silver. She gave us both a disgusted once over and the smell of rage and affronted dignity wafted off her like rotten eggs mixed with burnt tea.

"Hello, this is a private memorial. One meant for my father's friends and family."

Harold sucked in a breath beside me, and I could feel his presence wavering. Not that I blamed him. I was a demoness and his daughter was sort of scaring me right now with the vibes she was giving off.

"We were friends of your father," I said and gave her a sad smile. Lisa kept her head down and didn't say anything. "Well, work friends you could say. We're very sorry for your loss."

The woman's eyes were red rimmed and I could tell she was trying to keep herself under control so she didn't break down in front of the assembled crowd. "My mother is already upset, and she doesn't need any more of Dad's little flings showing up. Can't you people leave us in peace?"

"We weren't flings," I said, keeping my voice low, so I didn't embarrass anyone. Lisa's face flushed, and I hoped that Harold's daughter thought it was out of modesty and not because I was lying through my teeth to protect her. "We are nurses who worked with your father and respected him a great deal. We only wanted to come pay our respects."

"Oh," Anne said, her shoulders slumping and her eyes filling back up with a light sheen of tears. Gone was the Amazon prepared to go to war to defend her mother, and back was the woman who'd lost her father years ago and hadn't gotten the chance to make her peace with that yet.

I felt sorry that she and Harold couldn't fix their relationship now that he was gone. Although, given how persistent he was, I wouldn't be surprised if he came up with something.

"Thank goodness," she said. "We've had a parade of tarts coming through these doors acting like they owned the place. That bitch Mona has been a total nightmare, screaming about how she's going to contest the will and how she's owed something now that Dad is dead."

I took her hands in mine. "There are kids, well adults, too, if you think about it, that are alive today because of what an amazing doctor he was. We're all going to miss him and we won't do anything to ruin his memorial. Harold was as much a part of our family as he was yours."

"Thank you." She pulled me forward, toward the picture mosaic of Harold dominating the front of the room.

"I don't know if they told you he was a hero," Lisa broke in. "With what happened to him I mean."

Anne nodded. "The police told us. Mom said she wasn't surprised. She always claimed he had more guts than he did common sense."

"She did say that," Harold murmured. "Harriet always claimed I was her stupid knight in shining armor. 'Where fools rushed in,' she'd tell me, 'that's where I'll find you, Harold.'"

"He used to tell us that, too," I told Anne.

"He did?" another voice piped up beside us.

I looked over toward the voice and saw a slender woman with her gray hair tied back in a knot and a demure black sheath dress staring at us. Harold froze beside me, and I knew the woman in front of us had to be Harriet.

“Yes, Mrs. Winslow,” I said. “We worked at Rogers Hospital with your husband. Lisa was one of his surgical nurses, and I’m the night shift charge nurse on PICU. I’m Faith Bettin—”

“Faith Bettincourt,” she said and stuck her hand out.

“Yes.” I took her hand and shook it. “Your husband mentioned me?”

“Not while he was living.”

I glanced at Harold out of the corner of my eye. He shrugged and held his hands up like he had no clue what she was going on about.

“Mom.” Anne wrapped her arm around her mother’s shoulders. “The doctor told you those were just vivid dreams and that they were part of the mourning process.”

“That’s okay.” I sat in one of the chairs at the front of the room and Harriet took the one beside me. “I’m always fascinated in hearing other people’s dreams.”

“Right about the time they said my Harold died, I had this dream and a dark-haired young man with a ponytail came to me and told me Harold was gone and I’d never see him again. But that it was okay, because my Harold was going to help you save the world.”

“Well, I don’t know.” I detached my hand from hers. I was going to *kill* J when I saw him again. What the Hell was he thinking going out and interfering in people’s dreams? Way to keep a low profile. Not. “I am just a pediatric nurse after all.”

“You’re so much more,” Harriet said and patted my cheek. “Even I can see that.”

“Okay, Mom.” Anne smiled at me, her cheeks turning red, and shook her head. “I think it’s time we get you another sedative. The emotions of the day are starting to get to you.”

"I think you're just worried about your mother sounding crazy," Harriet said when her daughter led her away.

"That was weird," Harold muttered. "Harriet never was one for paranormal mumbo jumbo before now."

"And you were?" I asked.

"Not until I became a ghost."

"See? There's always time for personal growth," I said. "Now I take it the cluster of hideously dressed harpies in the corner are the Three Ex-wives of the Apocalypse?"

"That would be them." Harold nodded. "Mona, Kitty, and Jannelle."

"Right." I threw back my shoulders and stalked over to them. "Ladies?"

"Yes?" the dark-haired one in a spandex, leopard print mini dress asked.

"I have a message from the Great Beyond for the three of you. Courtesy of Harold."

"Uh-huh?" The blond ex-wife tugged at the top of her skintight black pantsuit, adjusting it so even more cleavage popped out. "What's that? The money is buried in the cellar?"

"No." I shook my head and gave her my sweetest smile. "Harold said to tell you that you're all money-grubbing, backstabbing bitches, and he's glad to know he'll never have to see your sorry faces again. Oh, and every single dime of his money is going to Harriet and Anne. If you even think about causing a ruckus, he's not only going to haunt your asses, he's going to send me and my friend Lisa here back around to talk to you again."

"What's that supposed to do? Scare us?" the blonde asked.

I glanced at Lisa, and she shrugged, letting her horns peek through. I let my own come out as well and turned to face the three of them, my eyes flashing red. "It would sure scare *me*, if I were you. Now, I suggest you leave and don't do anything that is going to make me come by for a little chat. You never know, I may forget to eat along the way."

The three of them just stood there, wide eyed, and the smell the fear wafted off of them. The blonde was starting to break out into hives and the brunette was trembling. Good.

"Okay," the auburn-haired one said and pushed her two partners in crime toward the doors of the funeral home. "We'll just be going now."

"I thought you might see things my way." I inspected my nails, buffing them against the hem of front of my white shirt. That wasn't too bad if I did say so myself. My horns retracted and Lisa was back to her normal, perky self as well.

"Thanks," Harold said and gave me a warm smile. "For that and for what you said about being family a few minutes ago. It means a lot to me. Really. Now you two get out of here. You've got to meet my man Tolliver at the top of an aisle in a few hours."

"Are you coming with us?" I asked.

"I'll meet you there." Harold looked at where his former wife and his daughter were sitting, talking with the other mourners. "I think I need to stick around here for a while yet."

"Don't be late," Lisa warned him.

"Not even my own memorial could keep me away." Harold floated away.

I shook my head and the two of us slipped out the exit and into the parking lot before anyone else noticed. "Well," I said and looked over at her when we reached my Civic. "That went better than I expected."

"It was nice to do something good for a change."

"I was talking about the whole *Scaring the Crap Out of the Ex-Wives* thing," I said.

"So was I. Now, let's go shackle me to your brother for the rest of eternity. What do you say?"

"I'd say you're a damn fool and we need to run off to Mexico until you see sense." I turned my car on and pulled out of the parking lot, making my way toward the church the Alpha had glamoured into existence for her wedding. "But you're not listening to me are you?"

Chapter Twenty-Nine

"I can't do this." Lisa scurried into the tiny bathroom the Alpha had so kindly remembered to put in the bride's staging area. "I'm going to be sick."

"No, you're not." I stared at my reflection in the mirror and applied more concealer to hide the dark rings underneath my eyes. I was not going to ruin this wedding by looking like some sort of wretch.

"I'm going to vomit," Lisa muttered.

"No, you're not." I stood, smoothing the black satin of my dress so it didn't bulge at my hips. "Demonesses don't vomit. Take a deep breath and try to relax. Just think, it'll all be over in less than an hour, and you'll officially be the Princess Consort to the Heir Apparent of Hell. If Dad ever decides to retire, you'll even be queen. Then you'll outrank me."

"I will?" Lisa's head popped out of the bathroom door, and she stared at me with wide eyes, sweat glimmering on her forehead. She actually was a little green. That was strange. I didn't think demons could get sick.

"No." I grabbed her hands, pulled her out of the bathroom, and led her to the makeup table. "Dad's already said he's going to make us rule by committee if he ever decides to retire. That means you get the same title as Hope and I do, but no voting rights. Sorry to burst your bubble."

"No feathers off my wings," Lisa said. I picked up a tissue and blotted at the sweat beading on her face. A quick pat of her hair, and she was stunning. Absolutely the most beautiful bride I'd ever seen in my life. "I was just curious about who got the crown your mother had commissioned for herself. I couldn't believe she managed to keep it on her head through the reception. That thing had to weigh forty pounds."

"Consider it yours, a wedding present from me and Hope, and since we're on the subject of your wings…"

"The olive oil worked." She made a face. "But you were right. It was disgusting."

"Just think, once you're married—"

There was a sharp knock on the door and we froze. Lisa had gone from pale mint green to a sort of ashy gray color. She took another deep breath while I went to open the door and ushered her father into the room.

"Ready, sweetheart?" he asked, tears welling up in his eyes at the sight of her. "'Cause if you're not, I can sneak us out the back and we can be on a plane for Jamaica before that boy you're marrying even knows we skipped town."

"That might not be such a bad idea," I said before grabbing both of our bouquets. "I mean, he's my brother and all, but you could do better and I've always heard Jamaica is nice this time of year."

"No. I want to marry Tolliver. He's the perfect man for me."

She kissed her father on the cheek before taking his arm.

"Trust me." I gave her a quick hug and opened the dressing room door. "You could do so much better."

"Yeah, I probably could. But I don't want to."

"Well," Mr. DeMarcos said. "Let's get you married then. But I have to say, Faith, your family's church is amazing. I'd never even heard of St. Bruno's before Lisa told us the wedding was being held here. Absolutely stunning."

"Yes, it is." I glanced up at the soaring white marble arches, meeting in high domes where beautiful angels frolicked about us in scenes of heartbreaking simplicity. The large side windows were plain glass, designed to fill the church with light, and as I stepped to the end of the aisle, I couldn't help gasping at the beauty of the stained glass window over the altar. A hidden choir of children sang from the loft, filling the sanctuary with a melody older than time itself.

Tolliver stood, wringing his hands at the front of the church, refusing to turn around to peek at his bride. J stood with his hand on Tolliver's shoulder, and winked when I reached my place. My brother looked like shit. His face was pale and his hands were trembling worse than the bride had just a moment before. Which was insane. How could both of them be so worried about what was about to happen? Anyone could see they were madly in love with each other. Why, I had no idea. But then again, most of Lisa's decisions didn't make a lot of sense as far as I was concerned.

The music rose to a crescendo when she reached the top of the aisle and kissed her father on the cheek before taking hold of Tolliver's hand. The Alpha smiled at the two of them, golden light reflecting around His head.

The Alpha began the wedding mass, and I let myself tune out, refusing to think about how complicated my own love life had become. Right now, I was here to be supportive to my brother and my best friend.

I felt a tingle of static and turned to see Harold slip in through one of the open windows and float into the pew the rest of my family was sitting in, still dressed in his suit from the memorial service. Malachi sat next to him in his human form, and both the dread demon and the ghost radiated happiness in all their burnt toffee-smelling glory. Hope sat next to the two of them, her eyes focused on the ceiling and a tissue clutched in her fists. She hadn't lost it yet, but I could see she was trying to keep her cool. Hope, crying at a wedding. That wasn't something I'd ever thought to see. She hadn't even been misty-eyed last night.

Mom, as usual, had a sour look on her face, and I saw her tiara sitting in her lap. Apparently someone had told her it wasn't appropriate to outshine the bride on her wedding day. As for Dad, he looked pretty comfortable, for a guy sitting between his ex-wife and his current one. Lil smiled at me from her place at the end of the pew, and I couldn't help smiling back.

A faint scratching sounded behind me, near the altar, and swung my head around to glower at the sprite peeking out from underneath the altar cloth. My eyes flashed red, and he froze, staring at the den of demons looking back at him.

Instead of continuing with whatever mischief he had planned, the sprite popped out of sight instead, leaving behind the musty smell of wet dirt and a few wayward green sparkles. He was a fast learner. Or he had better self-preservation instincts than the rest of his kind. Either way, for his sake, he'd better hope I didn't catch him alone somewhere. I wasn't a vindictive demoness, but it was best not to take any chances where those little monsters were concerned.

"Tolliver and Lisa have requested to use their own vows," the Alpha said, bringing me back to the wedding taking place in front of me. "Tolliver, you may go first."

My brother swallowed, his hands shaking while he held onto Lisa's. "I just utterly adore you," he said. "I've been in love with you from the first moment I saw you. Like the very first second. Not even that long. The very first split second. It was like being hit by lightning and I knew, from that moment on, there was no me without you."

Hope sniffled and my own eyes grew hot with fresh tears. I sniffed and wiped my eyes before I could make a mess of myself, keeping my eyes upturned and focused on the picture of Gabriel and Michael playing chess painted on the ceiling.

"I want to spend every single moment of forever with you," Tolliver continued. "I want to do all those big things with you, like having babies and buying a house, and the little things like arguing about whose turn it is to take out the trash. I want to finish each other's crossword puzzles and interrupt each other to say the punch lines of jokes we've told each other a thousand times before. I want to be with you. For as long as you'll let me."

"Okay," Lisa said her voice watery.

I heard a few more sniffles from the audience and a tear trickled down my cheek. What the Hell? I was wearing waterproof mascara at least.

"Okay?" Tolliver repeated.

"Okay," Lisa said, her own voice sounding watery. "Tolliver, I want to be your wife for the rest of eternity. I love you. And I want all that other stuff you said, but for the most part I just want to be with you. More than anything else I've ever wanted in the world."

"Okay." Tolliver nodded and looked at the Alpha, whose mouth was hanging open. My brother raised his eyebrows and the Alpha shook His head, trying to right Himself and get back into His role.

"So," the Alpha said, still looking a bit stunned at the vows they'd made to each other. "If there are any objections to this wedding they should be spoken now or all present should forever hold their peace. Eternally. For all time. No speaking up, ever again."

Nobody moved a muscle and the Alpha's shoulders relaxed.

"Okay, then." He licked his lips. "By the authority invested in me by our mutual faith, and by the State of Pennsylvania, I now pronounce you man and wife. You may kiss the bride."

"My pleasure," Tolliver said and caressed Lisa's face before leaning in to kiss her. The choir started up again, and I peeked into the loft to see that it was empty. I should have known. It wasn't like St. Bruno's was going to have a very active choir group. It wasn't like they needed one. Unless Jesus was planning on getting married sometime soon?

• • •

I limped back into my apartment building early the next morning and slipped my shoes off in the main floor entryway. I'll say one thing for the DeMarcos clan—they sure knew how to throw a party. It was almost dawn, and I'd been one of the first to leave. Malachi had left me at the front door of my building and had changed back into his grim reaper form. He said something about doing guard duty outside and then floated off before I could ask any more questions.

I stumbled up the stairs and cursed myself for not having

pushed Dad to buy me a building with an elevator. Or not commandeering a first floor apartment. I slouched up the stairs, dragging myself up the final flight with my hands brushing across the steps as I went. When I reached the landing between mine and Matt's apartments, I set my shoes on the ground and pointed at the door lock, zapping it.

The door behind me creaked open and I froze. Awareness of Matt washed over me, some primal knowledge that he was there even if I couldn't see him or smell him or even hear him, and I fought the urge to turn around and stare. I'd been avoiding him like a plague of missionaries, and I wasn't sure I wanted to stop now. Couldn't we give it a little more time? Six months? A year? Two might be nice.

"Just getting back from Lisa and Tolliver's wedding?" Matt asked, his voice rough with sleep.

"Yeah." I turned around to face him. He was dressed in a pair of shorts and a gray T-shirt. His iPhone was strapped to his arm and he was fidgeting with the earphones.

"How was it?" He wouldn't meet my gaze.

"It was nice." I gave him a brief smile. "Very sweet. Everyone missed you."

"I thought, all things considered, maybe it would be better if I gave it a pass. No use in making a scene, your Dad deciding to punch me in the face again or something," Matt said, still not looking at me. "Tell them I said congratulations?"

"I will." I pointed to my door. "I guess I'll see you around, huh?"

"Sure." He looked up at me and put his hands on his hips. Instead of waiting around for the situation between us to become tenser, I walked into my apartment.

"Hey, Faith?" he called out before I could shut the door.

"What?" I turned my head to look at him and my heart broke. He was adorable. Everything I'd never known I wanted in a man. But now he was off limits and I couldn't help wishing that I'd savored having him more when I had the chance.

He stepped across the hallway and pulled me into his arms, pressing his lips against my forehead. "You look amazing."

I closed my eyes, biting my lower lip.

"And I meant what I promised you yesterday. I'm not giving up on us. Not without a fight."

"I know you won't. That doesn't mean it's a good idea, though," I said. "You have to know this will all end in tears one day."

"I don't care about the end," Matt said. "What I care about is right here and right now. With you."

"I love you, Matt, and whatever comes next, nothing will change that." I slipped out of his arms and stepped into my apartment, closing the door behind me. I sank onto the floor and let my head rest against the door, trying to pretend I couldn't feel his warmth radiating through it.

I sighed and gave up trying to keep my tears in check, letting them run down my cheeks.

"I'm never going to stop fighting for you," he said, and then he was gone, taking all that heat with him.

And even though I knew it was wrong, I couldn't help clinging to the fact that Matt was the type of guy who didn't back down from a fight. No matter how much the odds were stacked against him.

Acknowledgments

No one writes a book alone. Absolutely no one. Meanwhile someone as scattered as me can barely get dressed on their own so the fact that this book is now out in the world is most likely a miracle cobbled together by my own personal team of angels.

I could have never finished this book without the loving support of my family, who have always been my biggest cheerleaders, or my friends, who have willingly listened as I cried about how the plot just wasn't working. There are too many of you to name who have held my hand and I don't want to forget anyone so let's just go with you know who you are and how much I owe you and leave it at that.

I'd also like to thank the team at Entangled Publishing who helped make this book more than a random pile of scribbles: Libby Murphy and Danielle Poiesz, two of the most amazing editors I've ever had the pleasure to work with; Heather Riccio, Debbie Suzuki, and Jaime Arnold, the world's most fabulous promotions team; and Liz Pelletier, the person who saved Faith Bettincourt from a life hidden under my bed as the heroine of a novel that was never submitted. This book literally would not exist without all of you.

To all my other Entangled Sisters and the rest of the Goddesses at the Naked Hero, thank you for being the most amazing writer's therapy group that anyone could ask for.

To the readers and the bloggers and the people who send me emails telling me how much they enjoyed my books. I can't believe you guys don't have anything better to do than read my stuff. But I'll always be eternally grateful that you don't.

About the Author

Patricia Eimer is a small town girl who was blessed with a large tree in the backyard that was a perfect spot for reading on summer days. Mixed with too much imagination it made her a bratty child but fated her to become a storyteller. After a stint of "thinking practically" in her twenties she earned degrees in Business and Economics and worked for a software firm in southwestern Germany, but her passion has always been a good book. She currently lives in eastern Pennsylvania with her two wonderful kids and a husband that learned the gourmet art of frozen pizzas to give her more time to write. When she's not writing she can be found fencing, training for triathlons, and arguing with her dogs about plot points. Most days the Beagle wins but the Dalmatian is in close second. She's in a distant third.

Keep reading for a sneak preview of

BEFORE THE DEVIL KNOWS YOU'RE DEAD

by Patricia Eimer

Coming soon from Entangled Select...

Chapter One

A split second before the alarm in Room 527 started to blare I found myself staring at the world's most annoying, know-it-all archangel as he made his way slowly up the long corridor toward me, trailing the tips of his huge white wings along the walls. He gave me a smug glare and grinned before slipping inside her room, stepping through the closed door instead of opening it. Instead of screaming for help I took off at a dead run down the hall of the ICU, cussing under my breath about stupid celestial beings and my own aversion to cardio exercise.

Two other nurses bolted out of the rooms they were working in and came running from the other end of the hall while the attending physician on duty sprinted out of her office in front of me. I side-stepped around her and hunched my shoulders to keep from running into her back as we all raced toward the horrible shrieking wail of the alarm.

I snapped my fingers and time stopped around me. I needed a bit more time if I was going to keep six-year-old Madeline Stavlinski—otherwise known as the transplant patient in Room

527—out of the clutches of the archangel. So rather than explain to my attending that I had to fend off the angel of death and her life-saving skills weren't necessary at this time, I swung around her and rushed to Madeline's room.

Dr. Malan had both feet off the ground, stopped in mid-run. Her knees were going to hurt like a succubi's after a busy night of soul collecting by the time she got off shift tomorrow morning. Long-term levitation was killer on the joints but that was so very much not my problem right now. I'd offer her a couple Tylenol for it later and then call it a wash.

"Step away from the ankle biter, Mike." I pointed my right hand like it was a handgun and I was some sort of strung out gangbanger trying to hold up a liquor store after too many rounds of first person shooter games.

"Faith." The Archangel stopped, his hand outstretched toward the girl. Icy blue eyes sparkled and golden energy crackled in a halo around the blond hair curling around his face, caressing his chin. "What are you doing here?"

"I work here, moron. I'm a pediatric nurse, this is a children's hospital. The two sort of go together like fish and freshly baked bread."

I pointed at the heart monitor still blaring away next to the bed. I zapped the machine with a jolt of demonic power and it reset itself. The little girl in the bed jerked and the machine began to beep in a nice, steady—*quiet*—rhythm.

"You're supposed to be off tonight," Michael said, his voice high and whiny like a little girl who'd been told for the third time that she couldn't have a puppy. "Two of the other reapers swore to me that you were off tonight. You don't work Thursdays."

"I'm covering for another nurse. She called in sick. Now, what in the name of Dad are you doing in my hospital?"

"Faith, there's no need to get touchy. You and I both know that this is a normal part of life. It's nothing for you to get upset about."

"Why are you on my ICU unit?" I asked, my voice steady, ignoring his "*death is a normal part of life*" shtick. "She doesn't have a folder. A reaper would have come by to warn me if she had a folder."

"She's on the potentials list." Michael held up a light beige file folder and waved it at me. Madeline's name was on it with her picture attached to the front for easy identification.

"That means she might die," I said, "but that folder is beige, not red. So, I repeat, more forcefully this time, why are you on my ICU?"

"Look." Michael stepped toward me, trying to angle himself between me and Madeline's bed, and my finger shook as dark power raced down my arm. "I lost a soul tonight. I'm one shy, and trust me when I tell you that the AOD is not a tolerant guy when it comes to not meeting your quota. I need someone to make up the difference."

"What happened?" I asked, stunned that he had somehow managed to lose a soul. For all the television movies and books that talk about people being snatched from Death's cold and greedy claws at the last moment, it rarely happened. The reapers were good at their jobs and it was a rare soul that slipped through.

"Your sister-in-law pulled out a miracle on a pinch hit. Full cardiac arrest and she gives him a zap while the mortals are busy, and the little bugger perks right up. My folder goes from blood red to white like she'd dunked it into a vat of industrial strength bleach.

"Heaven protect me from cranky ex-succubi," he said. "She's worse since she's gotten knocked up. You know that, right? She's become completely irrational about things."

"So?"

"So?" Michael's eyes bugged out and his face went purple. "I looked inside the folder to see when I could recoup my loss. I figured your girl Lisa's temper tantrum wouldn't matter in the end because I'd be back to get the kid in a few months. I could tell the boss we'd put the kid on the back burner and it would be no big deal. Right?"

"No?" My smile grew wider at his obvious distress.

"No. Turns out the rug rat is going to live a full and happy life—a writer of children's books if you can believe that. He's going to go teach kindergarten and write books that will be praised for their lush and realistic artwork. I can't come back to collect him for another ninety-seven years."

He paced in a tight circle, tugging at his hair as he stomped. He stopped, stared down at Madeline, and his hands dropped onto the metal bed rail, gripping it so tightly his knuckles were white. "There's no way I can pass that off as a minor technical glitch. The soul is lost and I'm up for my quarter century performance review."

"So?"

"So? It's bad enough that your Uncle demoted me to running the angelic contingent of the Reaper Squads. If this review goes badly Valentin could promote Daniel into my position and knock me down to running the Hospitaller subteam. I'd be middle management, Faith, the equivalent of a human shift manager at McDonalds."

"Oh gee." I laughed, making sure enough evil leaked out to

let him know that I was amused more by his suffering and less by the living kid's choice of career field. "I'd feel bad for you but it seems to me that the world needs more writers of kids' books with realistic artwork."

"Faith..." He dropped his hands to his sides, clenching his fists.

"Besides, what does your miserable career progression have to do with my transplant patient? She's six—she can't tutor you on how to ask if someone would like fries with their mortal coil shuffle."

"Ha, ha, very funny. Now let's be serious. She's high on the potentials list. She's got what? A day. Maybe two? Why make her suffer? You can turn your back and I'll take her soul and everyone will be happy. I've met my quota, save my performance evaluation, and she's in a better place. It's a win-win situation. Right?"

"Not a chance." I pointed at his folder and gave it a solid jolt of demonic power.

The folder burst into blue-black flames and then crumpled into a neat pile of ash. "Oh look! No folder. You know what that means? No paperwork means no soul. Now go away, before I decide to keep zapping."

"That was pointless, Faith." He crossed his arms over his slender, well-sculpted chest, and glared. "I'll go back and get another copy of her file and then I'll be back. If not today then the day her status turns red. You can't stop the inevitable so why not give me the soul and save yourself the hassle?"

"No."

"No? What do you mean no?" Michael asked. "I need that soul."

"Too bad." I leaned forward, lifting up on my toes so that we were nose to nose and then snaked my arms around his sides to grip the rails of her bed, penning him in between my arms. "You can't have her."

"Look, I know you're protective of your *patients*." He put his hands up, knocking my arms away from his sides, and air quoted around the word patients. "Look at this from my perspective. I need to take that soul and meet my quota. If our positions were switched I'd help you out."

"No you wouldn't, and there's no way in Hell's fiery lake that I'll ever need your help. I do my best not to associate with parasites."

"Parasite? I provide an essential service."

"Yeah? So do dung beetles."

"You know what?" Michael spat, his eyes filled with disgust. "Keep the brat if she means so much to you. I'll come back and get her once the folder turns red and I'll make sure to do it on a day where you have to watch. Once she's formally on my list there's nothing you can do but stand there and watch as I harvest the little twerp."

"Really?" I stepped forward and jammed my finger into his chest. "It seems to me Lisa managed to stop you. I could do the same."

"Her time has come. Let the child go, Faith. Let her find peace."

"It's not her time." I pictured the most remote, desolate island on Earth, a small spit of land near Antarctica, covered in snow and surrounded by icy water, and did my best to make it seem real in my mind. A window in reality slid open behind Michael, opening on the coldest part of that very remote bit of nowhere.

"What's one day? Twenty-four measly hours? What does it mean in the end?"

"It's everything." I lifted my hand to his chest and gave him a solid jolt of dark power straight to the sternum.

The archangel burst into flames and he let out a tortured scream. Dark power licked along his chiseled jaw and his hair caught fire. He swung his hands up and started to beat at the flames around his halo, screaming at me in Latin the entire time. My ancient religious languages were pretty rusty but I was pretty sure that the words he was shrieking weren't part of the Holy Catechism.

I gave him another push and then stepped away, watching Michael topple backward through the portal. There was a splash and then another, sharper scream as he hit the icy water. He pushed himself up, head first out of the water, and I let the portal shrink.

"Hey, Michael," I said once the portal had shrunk to the size of a bowling ball. "Stay out of my ICU. Or else."

"You demonic slut," Michael screeched before a wave crested over his head and dunked him under the freezing waves. His head broke the surface and he started to splutter, coughing up water as he tried to keep himself afloat. "You wait. I'm going to call your uncle and I'm going to—"

"Oh please." I snapped my fingers and the portal slammed close with a sharp *crack*, trapping him on the other side.

"You should have trapped him under an iceberg," Harold said.

I turned to see my favorite poltergeist pediatrician leaning over Madeline, checking her over.

"Or with a particularly horny narwhale. Those are the ones with the sharp swords on their snouts, right?"

"I think so." I came over to stand beside him. "How is she?"

"Fine. Vitals are stable. She seems to be responding to treatment. No signs of infection that I can see. My gut feeling is that she's going to make it—potentials list or no potentials list."

"Good. That will be something to tell her father when the poor man finally gets here."

"What happened?" Harold asked.

"The Army had a delay and he didn't make it for the surgery. What with her being bumped up the list so quick because of the compatibility match. It's good to know he's not going to come all this way for bad news."

"She's not going anywhere." Harold was the best pediatrician I knew—alive or dead. If he said she was going to make it then I was going to believe him. "I can't believe you set the Archangel Michael on fire. Not that he didn't deserve to suffer a bit, but you know how long it takes an angel to recover from hellfire burns."

"Yeah, blame the human part of me for that little show of demonic temper. I refuse to give up the belief that life is sacred. Besides, she wasn't on the dead list. I don't care if I have to set an entire legion of angels on fire. I refuse to hand over one of these kids until I don't have any other choice."

"Stubborn to a fault Nurse Bettincourt." Harold floated close enough that I could feel his shadow brushing against my shoulder as we stood staring down at the little girl in the bed.

"Stubbornness is an integral part of being a demon. I mean, did you hear what he said about Lisa? Zapping a patient during surgery to keep them alive isn't just stubborn—it's downright ballsy. "

"Yeah. Which means both of you girls did well tonight. I'm proud of you."

"Thanks." A warm rush of pride flooded through my chest. I mean I knew I was a good nurse but it sure didn't hurt to hear someone else say it on occasion.

"I've only got one complaint. The next time you girls decide to go all superhero could you please warn me ahead of time? Do you know how much I would have loved to get that on video?"

"Really?"

"The other doctors on the ghost golf circuit would have paid good money to watch you set the Archangel Michael on fire—especially when you toppled him into the water afterward. Where was that? Alaska?"

"Fifty miles east of Antarctica."

"Nice." He wrapped an arm around my shoulder, his fingers sliding through my skin and making me shiver.

"Now what are you going to do about Dr. Freckles and her two sidekicks?" He nodded toward the door and I turned, suddenly remembering everyone else outside of the room.

"Play dumb?"

"That's only going to work a few times on that one," he said, pointing to Dr. Malan. "She's young but she's pretty clever. She's got that 'sense' if you know what I mean."

"You don't think she's been warned by Dr. Lee, do you?" I thought about the tiny pediatric oncologist who frequently gave me sideways glances.

"Nah. Bai has agreed to keep her mouth shut about us. I think Dr. Malan is a bit more tuned in than she realizes. Throw a confusion spell on her and you should be fine, though. Her sight isn't nearly as strong as Bai's. We can keep her clueless for a while longer yet."

"Right. Good." I snapped my fingers and felt time begin again. Dr. Malan rushed into the room, the nurses hot on her heels.

She slid to a stop and looked first at the now quiet monitor and then at the patient. She looked over at me, then through Harold to look at the monitor, and then back at the patient, her jaw working the whole time.

"Is something wrong, Doc?" I raised an eyebrow while I wiggled the fingers on my hand to cast a quick cloud of confusion across all of them so they wouldn't decide to start trying to figure out how I'd gotten here before them.

"What happened to the alarm?" Dr. Malan asked. "I heard the alarm and came running."

"The alarm?" I asked, trying to keep my voice even. "The alarm for this room?"

"Didn't it go off?" Confusion and doubt filled her eyes.

"No. The alarm in here didn't go off. Everything in here is fine. I've been in here for a few minutes, doing treatments. I was working toward Leslie and Kim so that I could tell them to go on break. Why? Did you hear an alarm?"

"I could have sworn..." Dr. Malan looked from me to the alarms again, her mouth hanging open. She shifted her weight from one foot to the other and then flinched as she tried to move her weight off back off her right knee. She turned to look at Leslie and Kim standing behind her. "Tell me you two heard the alarm?"

"No, Doc," Leslie said her voice full of conviction. "We saw you running and followed."

"I don't know what to say." Dr. Malan ran a hand up over her face. "I know the alarm was going off."

"It's late, it's quiet, and you probably dozed off for a second and dreamed you heard one." I gave her my most reassuring smile.

"You think?" she asked, sounding skeptical.

"I do it all the time on my days off," I said, and both Kim and Leslie nodded in agreement. "I'm sound asleep and then all of a sudden I dream that I can hear an alarm or a call light. Next thing

I know I'm wide awake and half out of bed before I realize that I'm home in my jammies and not here on the ward. It's part of the job. You'll get used to it over time."

She shifted again and then winced. "I guess, but man do I feel stupid right now. Running after phantom alarms and scaring all three of you."

"Don't worry about it." My shoulders relaxed. She was going to let this go easier than I expected. "Hey, Doc, are you feeling okay? You keep grimacing."

"I think I banged my knee against my desk when I decided to go on a mad dash down the hall. I'll probably have one heck of a bruise by the time we go off shift."

"Ouch." I wrinkled my nose at her and pretended to be sympathetic instead of relieved at how easily she was letting this all go. "Why don't you take a minute and take a breather? Go grab a bottle of water or some coffee. We'll be fine up here."

"You're sure?" she asked.

"Go, take Kim and Leslie with you. All of you could use a few minutes of peace. Bring me back a Mountain Dew. I've got some money stashed in the nurses' station."

"Don't worry about it." Dr. Malan shoved her hands in her lab coat pockets. "I think after all this excitement I can buy everyone some caffeine."

I watched the three of them make their way to the stairwell and sighed in relief as they left the hall. The last thing I needed was someone catching on to the fact that patients tended to die less when I was on shift than they did otherwise. Medical people were always a superstitious lot and the last thing I wanted to bring attention to was the fact that Satan's youngest daughter was a charge nurse on the pediatric intensive care unit. People tended to get touchy about those sorts of things.

"You know we wouldn't have this much excitement if you'd have gone to secretarial school," a deeper voice said behind me.

I turned to see my bodyguard turned personal Greek chorus floating next to me in his three-foot grim reaper costume, the black cowl pulled low over his skull and two large, black eyes staring back at me from the shadows. "Come on, Mal, I thought you liked all this excitement?"

"Yeah, well, I knew typing wasn't your strong suit. Now, how long until you're off shift and we can go get some decent coffee?" he asked, his deep voice rumbling around in the empty black cloak where his body should have been.

"About four hours."

"Four hours? Christ on a cracker that's a long time. I'm going to go find late night porn on the visitor's lounge television and try to stay awake."

"Hey!" I put my hands on my hips and glared at him. "We've got kids in here."

"It's the middle of the night," Malachi retorted as he turned and began to float off. "They should all be asleep, genius. That's why they put porn on late night TV."

"Hey, Mal?"

My personal demon stopped then slowly turned to face me. "That thing with Michael tonight…"

"What about it?" he asked.

"You don't think it's weird that he tried to show up and poach someone who wasn't on the list do, you?"

"Faith, he's a reaper. Everything they do is weird. Don't let him get to you."

"Do you—"

"They all get a little crazier than normal around review time." Malachi shrugged his tiny shoulders toward where his ears should have been. "Don't worry about it. I mean, it's Michael being his usual idiotic self."

"You think?"

"I know. Trust me, if you'd ever met his boss you'd think Michael was the angelic version of a knight in shining armor." Mal hovered there for a second. "Then again, there's a good chance that if you two ever met, the Angel of Death would try to draft you into service."

"Ugh." I shivered. "No thank you. Death is definitely not my thing."